Prin
Cast

OLIVIA GATES

Published in Great Britain 2013
by Mills & Boon, an imprint of Harlequin (UK) Limited,
Eton House, 18-24 Paradise Road, Richmond, Surrey TW9 1SR

PRINCES OF CASTALDINI © by Harlequin Enterprises II B.V./S.à.r.l 2013

The Once and Future Prince, The Prodigal Prince's Seduction and *The Illegitimate King* were first published in Great Britain by Harlequin (UK) Limited.

The Once and Future Prince © Olivia Gates 2009
The Prodigal Prince's Seduction © Olivia Gates 2009
The Illegitimate King © Olivia Gates 2009

ISBN: 978 0 263 91034 6
ebook ISBN: 978 1 472 01614 0

05-0813

Harlequin (UK) policy is to use papers that are natural, renewable and recyclable products and made from wood grown in sustainable forests. The logging and manufacturing processes conform to the legal environmental regulations of the country of origin.

Printed and bound in Spain
by Blackprint CPI, Barcelona

Olivia Gates has always pursued creative passions—painting, singing and many handicrafts. She still does, but only one of her passions grew gratifying enough, consuming enough, to become an ongoing career: writing.

She is most fulfilled when she is creating worlds and conflicts for her characters, then exploring and untangling them bit by bit, sharing her protagonists' every heart-wrenching heartache and hope, their every heart-pounding doubt and trial, until she leads them to an indisputably earned and gloriously satisfying happy ending.

When she's not writing, she is a doctor, a wife to her own alpha male and a mother to one brilliant girl and one demanding Angora cat. Visit Olivia at www.oliviagates.com.

THE ONCE AND FUTURE PRINCE

BY
OLIVIA GATES

To Melissa Jeglinski.
Thank you for the wonderful new path. I wish you happiness and success in everything you endeavor, MJ.

To Natashya Wilson, my incredible editor.

Can't be happier that we're a team, Tashya.

Eight hundred years ago, Antonio D'Agostino founded the Mediterranean kingdom of Castaldini. With a culture mixing Italian and Moorish influences, the kingdom was unique. But what set it apart from the world's monarchies was the succession law Antonio D'Agostino created. He knew none of his sons was fit to wear a crown after him, so he decreed that the succession would not be by blood but by merit. Anyone from the extensive D'Agostino clan, all now considered the royal family, could prove himself worthy of being the next king. He set stringent rules that had to be satisfied before someone could be a candidate for the crown, including that the selection of the next king had to be with the unanimous approval of the royal council of the reigning king.

And the other rules? That the future king be of impeccable reputation, of sturdy health and no vices, of solid lineage from both sides, a leader people followed due to the power of his character and charisma, and above all, a self-made success of the highest order.

So it had always been—D'Agostino men vying for the crown, striving to deserve it. Throughout history, one D'Agostino man always won over all competitors and claimed the crown. He chose his council from the royal family and during his reign selected the next king to be his crown prince, so that the transition of power occurred smoothly in case anything befell him.

And the kingdom's motto was *Lasci l'uomo migliore vincere*. Let the best man win.

Prologue

Eight years ago

"Come closer, Phoebe. I won't bite. Not too hard."

Leandro's rumble reverberated in Phoebe's bones.

She choked on the surge of response, on the breath that was trapped inside her lungs. The breath she'd been holding waiting for him to contact her. The one she always held until he did.

She still couldn't breathe. He stood as if carved from rock, staring out of his penthouse's floor-to-ceiling windows at the Manhattan skyline, which glittered like clusters of stars set in arcane patterns. Her starved senses registered only him.

The power of his physique, the silken layers crowning his head, dimmed spotlights overhead caressing copper overtones from the hairs' deepest mahogany. Her hands stung with the memory of convulsing in that hair as he'd exposed her to the mercilessness of his pleasuring.

His scent invaded her with a maleness and a potency that were only his, an aphrodisiac even from the distance he bade her to eliminate. He'd already gotten her to travel four thousand miles to "come closer."

Eight hours ago, she'd received a message from Ernesto—Leandro's right-hand man, and their secret go-between—during Julia's daily physiotherapy session. She'd thought he was inviting her to yet another clandestine rendezvous, one even more secret because Leandro's situation in Castaldini was more delicate than ever after his resignation from his ambassador post. But she hadn't found Leandro. Just his jet. There'd been no word from him all through the seven-hour flight to New York.

There hadn't been one in four months. She'd feared silence had been his way of informing her it was over. But it wasn't....

"I turned thirty, two months ago."

She lurched at his rasp, a twist of longing in her gut. She'd known that. On October 26th. The urge to call him that day had frayed what had remained intact of her nerves. But his rules had been clear. *He* contacted her. It had seemed he wouldn't anymore.

"Happy birthday." She winced as the lame response left her lips.

His huff abraded her. "Indeed. The happiest birthday ever."

He turned to her then. She would have staggered if she hadn't been incapable of moving a muscle, even involuntarily.

"Nothing more to say, *bella malaki?*" My beautiful angel. The endearment shuddered through her, that mix of Italian and Moorish only he used. He prowled toward her, his shirt phosphorescent in the dimness, unbuttoned to his waist, revealing chiseled power that bunched and gleamed with every step. "Shall I make it easier? Give you a lead?" He stopped half a breath away, his emerald eyes flaring and subsiding like pulsars. "Miss me?"

She'd thought so. She'd been wrong. She'd *starved* for him.

He reached out to her, warm, large hands singeing her, steadying her body, shaking everything else. "Shall I find out?"

Yes, her every cell shrieked.

But he did nothing, stilled. She started to shake.

The moment her tremors hit him, his pupils obliterated his irises, black holes that sucked coherence from her mind, wrenched hunger from her depths. She pitched forward, a helpless satellite yanked to an inexorable planet, hurtled into his containment.

It was like a dam had burst. Violent. Deluging. Their mouths collided, merged, flooding her with what she'd never thought to find until him. Oneness. Need that sliced her open.

Her world churned, with the delight of reconnection, with his savagery and what it betrayed of a hunger as searing as hers as his power bore them deeper into passion.

"Next time, *bellezza helwa*…next time I'll take hours… *days* to worship you…but this time…this time…"

He threw her down, and she could only moan as she sank into the luxury of silk sheets and his scent, anticipation becoming agony as their clothes disappeared under the force of his impatience. Her arms shook, begged for his possession. He obeyed, impacted her with the force she was gasping for, thrust inside her, no preliminaries, no way to withstand any, fierce and full and beyond her endurance, razing her with pleasure, ripping an orgasm from the core that clenched around his invasion. He snatched her scream of release into his ravaging mouth, roared his own, jetting into her depths to the rhythm of her convulsions until she lay beneath him, boneless. Devoured. Replete. *Leandro.* Her lion man. Back in her life. No longer in secret…?

He drove deeper inside her, ending questions. She arched beneath him, taking, offering all. He growled into her neck, the darkness of it shaking through her with the reverberation of satiation, the accumulation of renewed need.

Until the words it carried lodged in her brain.

"I will never return to Castaldini."

Everything stilled. She knew the situation had been tense for him in Castaldini. But not to return there, ever? Nothing could be that bad. That final. Could it?

She squirmed beneath his suddenly crushing weight. "What d-do you mean you w-won't return? You have to…"

He pulled back, stared down at her for a long, incredulous moment, before he made an explosive sound deep in his gut, then jerked away, separated from her body, left it aching. Bereft.

"You don't *know?*"

She winced at his rage. "Know what?"

"*Dio,* could it be? They've kept their decree a secret in Castaldini? This is much worse than I thought. They're not only culturally and economically isolating Castaldini, they're keeping it behind their own brand of iron curtain."

"Please, Leandro…I don't understand."

"You want to know what spread like wildfire through the world news before the media found something else to exploit? The trivial news that I, Prince Leandro D'Agostino, whom the world was certain would be named Castaldini's crown prince and next king, through merit and lifelong achievement—the moment I defied the current king and his men, I was declared a renegade and stripped of all my titles."

"Oh, no…"

He barked a harsh laugh. "Don't 'oh, no' yet. There's more. I was stripped of my Castaldinian nationality, too."

She went still, as if under the weight of a collapsing wall. She struggled for breath. "That c-can't be true."

"Oh, it can. I've been offered American citizenship and I've accepted it. I'm never setting foot on Castaldini again." Suddenly he hauled her to him, stabbed his fingers into the tumble of her locks, plundered her lips in a kiss that branded her. His urgency chased everything away, had her clinging until he rasped against her lips, "And you're never going back, either."

The fierceness of his declaration jolted through her, had her wrenching her lips away. "I have to."

His eyes became slits of hypnosis as he spread her, loomed over her, the embodiment of her desires. "No, you don't. This is your country, as it now is mine. You'll stay with me."

She wrestled the rest out. "I have to go back to Julia."

His hand stilled its caresses on her aching-from-pleasure breast. "Oh, yes, your poor dependent sister. The princess with a whole kingdom at her disposal and her service."

"You know it's not like that. She needs me."

"*I* need you."

The agonized confession lurched through her heart, each syllable a stab. Of shock.

Out of paralysis, hope started to quiver, only to be stilled in the cold grip of…suspicion.

He *needed* her? How? And why now? He hadn't needed her before, apart from the obvious. Leandro didn't know the meaning of need. His one and only need had been to become king of Castaldini, and nothing else had mattered in his quest for the crown. Least of all her. He'd proved that over and over.

He'd kept her a secret, had escorted other women—especially his second cousin Stella—to formal functions, passing Phoebe with that malignant woman on his arm and nodding to her as if she were nothing more than his cousin Paolo's sister-in-law.

He'd said he'd done it to divert suspicion from their intimate liaison, which would have damaged both his chance at the crown and her reputation. At first she'd thought his claim that his measures were "to protect them both in these sensitive times" meant that he'd been planning for a future together and was being discreet to protect her reputation in the highly conservative kingdom.

But he certainly hadn't said or done anything overt to support this belief. And that had been before Stella—who went around swatting away fawning females from Leandro as she would flies—had told her what Phoebe realized she'd been the last to know. A fact that was widely accepted. That in order to take the crown, Leandro would have to marry an "acceptable" woman. And Phoebe was certainly far less acceptable than the royal-blooded Stella D'Agostino. In fact, Stella herself was second best, and it was just as widely known that she'd get him only if his perfect match and ideal running companion for the crown turned him down. That woman was someone who'd become Phoebe's friend—Clarissa D'Agostino, the king's daughter.

Now, finally, she let herself face it. The truth. He'd feared exposure not for the sake of their future together, but for his as king. That Clarissa, or even Stella, boosted his chances and she didn't—she'd never even been in the running for his future bride. That she'd been cowardly, fearing that if she brought up any of her grievances or suspicions, he would have ended their affair. That she'd been so weak, so in love, she'd forced herself not even to think about it, had buried her head in the sand so that she could take what she could get.

But self-deception hadn't done a thing to stop her anguish from mounting. Hadn't she become more distraught the closer he'd gotten to the crown? Hadn't she subconsciously wished he wouldn't get it, so that he could settle on her? Hadn't she feared that if he did take it—and Clarissa or Stella with it—and still wanted her, that she wouldn't be able say no? She'd started to understand how some women ended up being the "other woman."

And she'd gotten the wish she'd hidden even from herself. He was not in the running for the crown anymore. And he wanted her. Had said what she'd never thought he'd say. That he *needed* her.

Yeah. Right. After treating her like a dirty secret for more than a year, then cutting her off for four months without a word?

All her anguish burst out of her. "What do you need me for, Leandro? As your on-demand lover, like before? Or perhaps something a bit more permanent, now that you've run out of better options? What would I be in your life at this point? The ever-present outlet for your frustrations? The convenient body when you need sexual relief? Would I even be the only one to provide that? *Have* I been the only one?"

He gaped at her, as if she'd metamorphosed into an alien being right in front of him. The cold rage that crept into his eyes almost made her cringe and cry out a retraction.

Almost. She stood her ground. She had to. She *needed* to. It felt as if she'd been slowly poisoned by humiliation.

He tore his hands off her, stood and glared daggers at her enervated body. "*You're* accusing *me,* after all I've done, all you've cost me? Why don't you be up-front about what's really happening here, what I suspected during those four months that you didn't even bother to pick up the phone to inquire if I was alive or dead? I was worth your while when I was lined up to be the next king. Minutes ago you melted in my arms when you still didn't know there was no longer any chance of that. Now I'm suddenly patently resistible."

His aggression and the unjust accusations felt like a one-two combo. But the sting only strengthened her resolve, ignited her anger, sent it raging.

She struggled up. "You can think what you like."

He swooped down on her, dragged her into his arms. "You're not turning your back on me, too."

She looked up and started to push at him and…stopped. Slumped into his hold. His eyes. What she saw there hit her harder than a KO would have. Pain. Such Pain.

And it all slotted in her mind. The loss that must be gnawing at him, corroding his spirit as the realization that he'd ceased to be everything that defined him congealed into reality. Need to absorb his pain, need for *him* hammered at her. And he'd said he needed her….

No. He didn't need her. He'd never needed her. He just needed to assert his thwarted will, to placate his wounded pride.

All the pain that she'd been fooling herself she hadn't been accumulating for the past year and a half ripped through her as she tore out of his arms and jerked on her clothes.

"I hope you'll be very happy in your new country with your miserable view of others and your self-absorption. They sure are winning you many allies."

He approached her, his fury causing her to freeze. "So first you throw this out-of-the-blue accusation at me, and when I throw back something relevant, instead of showing me I'm wrong, you use it as the excuse to do what you'd do anyway. Desert me. And I'm supposed to take part in this act? Speak the lines where we pretend I'm the callous offender and you're the noble accused?"

Indignation thawed her. She yanked up her zipper. "It's I who've been reading the lines you dictated. And I'm through."

"I dictated that you tell me you only felt fully alive when I touched you, took you? That was an act? That's why it's so easy to walk away now? To leave me?"

His harshness no longer shook her, only stirred all the pent-up hurt and humiliation she'd hidden from herself. "Leave you? When was I ever *with* you? All I ever was to you was the adoring fool who stroked your ego when you could spare me the odd hour. You sure liked hearing me say those things, didn't you? That colossal ego of yours is wounded, and you need a constant supply of worship." She stopped, panting. Then another wave of bitterness gushed out. "You don't need me, Leandro—you just need to know that I need you. But contrary to what I may have let you believe, my life doesn't revolve around you. I have responsibilities and aspirations— I'm not a toy you can drag out whenever you feel the urge."

"Yet when I felt that urge you begged for more." He caught her against his body, his rough breathing a furnace blast against her neck as he nuzzled her, his hands dipping below her clothes, one cupping her breast, the other her core, each knowing probe and caress a jolt of stimulation. "Your body is mine, has just writhed in need beneath me, convulsed in pleasure around me, is still begging for me now even as you say otherwise."

The cruelty of his manipulation of her emotions and responses even as he exposed his true opinion of her smeared her self-worth in the truth. A truth she'd *still* been hoping she was wrong about.

He cared nothing for her. She'd merely served a purpose to him. Now that she was refusing to serve it anymore, he'd torn off the mask he'd worn around her. Just like he had with his king and country.

She wrenched out of his arms, ran out of his penthouse.

She didn't stop until she'd put half a world between them.

Where she prayed she'd never hear of or from him again.

One

"Castaldini's future depends on you."

The slightly slurred words hit Phoebe Alexander like a sledgehammer.

She gaped at the man who'd spoken them before she'd even cleared the towering doors to his state room. He was approaching her like a slow-motion, head-on collision.

She watched King Benedetto limp across the gigantic Castaldini crest that bulls-eyed the carpet sprawling over acres of mosaic hardwood floor. Each shuffle transmitted its struggle to her muscles. His cane thumped the ground to the rhythm of her haywire heartbeats.

If she hoped she'd misheard what he'd said, he said it again as if to underline the acuteness of her hearing.

"It all depends on you, *figlia mia*."

Every word from his mouth tugged on a rawness inside her.

She'd come to love him like the father she'd never had, her own having walked out when she was two and her mother was pregnant with her sister, Julia. But she still couldn't handle him calling her *daughter*. She sure didn't belong in the same place in his heart where his grandchildren and their mother—her sister—reigned supreme. She never knew what to do with the reflected affection, but tried to be of as much use as she could to feel entitled to it. She still wasn't close to feeling that.

How could Castaldini's future depend on her when it was facing dangers only a king could divert?

She searched his steel-blue eyes for a qualification. They had that look she'd seen during too many crises. It always meant his mind was made up, his decree final. And in her experience, he had yet to be proven wrong.

King Benedetto hadn't become the longest-reigning and most beloved king since King Antonio for nothing. In her opinion, he was the shrewdest, most effective ruler of the twentieth century. He was also the most controversial, as his politics had practically segregated Castaldini from the rest of the world during his forty-year reign. But his policies *had* protected the kingdom from the upheavals that had swept the world during those decades. What's more, this detachment from the global political scene had boosted Castaldini's allure, translating into a booming tourist industry.

That had lasted until the end of the twentieth century. The twenty-first century hadn't proven to be his domain so far, and everything seemed to be falling apart. To compound problems, he also held another record. He had ruled the longest without choosing a crown prince.

He'd been a gracefully aging Olympian who everyone believed would live and rule for forty more years, would turn things around in time. Until he'd been struck down by a stroke four months ago. And the lack of a crown prince was now taking on potentially catastrophic meaning.

King Benedetto stopped a dozen steps from her and leaned on his cane, the asymmetry of his injury exaggerating the spasm of suffering and agitation on his face. "I will never recover enough to continue to rule Castaldini."

She couldn't even blurt out reassurances. His stroke had sheared his life force in half. It hurt her to see him now, his face emaciated, his ornate regal uniform flapping emptily around a once formidable physique. But she could say one thing and mean it. "Your Majesty, you *are* improving."

"No, *figlia mia.*" He cut across her attempt at qualification. "I'm barely walking, my left side is all but useless and the least illness leaves me bedridden, barely able to breathe."

"But it's not like you need to be in peak physical fitness."

Half of his face softened, appreciating her efforts, pointing out their foolishness. "Yes, I do. You know it's the Castaldinian law. And it goes beyond that. My mental faculties…"

This she could contest. Vehemently. "Are as sharp as ever!"

His sigh carried such finality she felt her heart plummet. "That's not true, no matter how much I or you or my council want to believe it. I forget. I…drift. But even if a miracle happens and I'm back in peak health one day, Castaldini can't afford to wait in hope anymore. The circling vultures are becoming more daring with each passing day, and finding a successor has become an emergency. I cannot afford to dawdle anymore. I'm guilty of doing that for far too long."

She couldn't listen to him piling guilt on top of desperation and regret that way. "You did no such thing. According to the law, you couldn't have picked any of the candidates."

He shook his head as he limped to the nearest sitting area and slumped into a gilded Aubusson armchair. "But I could have. At least a decade ago. There's always been not one worthy candidate, but three. Each can take Castaldini forward into this century, which is proving to be even more turbulent than the last, to keep it safe against the dangers hammering down its doors. Yet they are the only three men who will not come forward to be recognized for their eligibility for the crown."

So there were three D'Agostino men around who had what

it took to be the next king? That was news to her. Another bombshell. One that had her mind veering off on a tangent…

No. Not the one man who'd once answered all the criteria. He *had* once come forward to be recognized for his eligibility. So the king couldn't be counting him among those three men. Could he?

Her feet started moving again under the influence of curiosity…and foreboding. "So, what's their problem?"

The king let out an uneven exhalation as she came to stand beside him. "Each has one. Each fulfills all criteria but one. A different one in each man's case, something that makes him unsuitable for the position by Castaldinian law."

"Then it isn't your fault you didn't settle on any of them."

"Oh, I tried to tell myself that for as long as I could afford to. Now I no longer can. Neither can Castaldini. I brought matters to a head with the Council. They argued that defying the laws Castaldini was built around for any reason would lead to the very loss of identity we guard against. I argued that overlooking the ancient laws this once has become a matter of survival, lest the monarchy crumble and Castaldini be absorbed by one of the neighboring nations vying to assimilate our history and resources into their boundaries. Then, yesterday, I had a ten-minute mental blackout during a council session."

She gasped. He reached for her hand, squeezed it. *He* was soothing *her?* His next words proved that he was. "I couldn't have asked for a better thing to happen. It seems the reality of my condition was jarring enough that when I regained my senses, my council were singing a different tune. They now unanimously concede that the only way to protect Castaldini is to choose one of the only three men capable of maintaining our sovereignty."

She pulled her hand back. She didn't want him to feel it shake. "Whoa, that's huge. For them to agree to waive the laws. That's problem solved, isn't it?"

He grimaced with what looked like self-deprecation. Loathing, even. "Not at all. Each of those men has reason enough to turn his back on me and on Castaldini. They'd be fully justified to leave both to our fate without their intervention."

"But you're their king. I know there hasn't been a precedent for it, but you can draft them into service."

His eyes widened as if she'd told him he could pole-vault. Then he barked a gravelly laugh, his face growing more asymmetric with the contortion of mirth. "You have no idea how outside my or anyone's jurisdiction they are. I not only can't draft them, I can't afford to antagonize them any more than I already have, or we'll lose any chance of having a deserving monarch wear the crown, and with it any hope of saving Castaldini."

"A man who has that much power and doesn't want to use it to save his kingdom—for *whatever* reason—isn't worthy of any crown, let alone Castaldini's. Whatever happened to the merit part?"

The king's face settled back into its grimness. "Oh, make no mistake, they all merit it. More than I ever did."

"I refuse to believe that."

"Thank you for your faith, *figlia mia,* but I had forty years to build the history you're judging me by, thankfully doing more right than wrong. But I did do a lot of wrong. Those three, what disqualified them, how I compounded everything when I alienated them, are among my major mistakes. Another sentimental mistake I've been guilty of was that I couldn't choose between them, leading to this point, where Castaldini is effectively leaderless. But my blessed blackout finally forced the council to choose for me. They recommended going after the one they consider the least of the three evils."

Though it made no sense, she *knew* the name he'd say.

She wanted to turn and run out, to outrace her suspicion and the moment he'd turn it into fact. Then it was too late.

"You know him well. My late cousin Osvaldo's son. Prince…*ex*-Prince Leandro D'Agostino."

Her nails dug in her palms. She thought she'd braced herself. Had been bracing herself for eight years. Spending her waking hours doing anything that demanded total focus so she wouldn't hear that name reverberating through her mind. Going to bed depleted in hope of not having it ignite her unconscious aches and struggles. She'd succeeded. When she hadn't had relapses and sought mention of his name like an addict would a drug.

Leandro. The man she'd loved beyond reason's dictates, and those of pride and self-preservation. The man to whom she'd been nothing but a convenience. As she was sure so many others had been. He went through life like a one-man invasion, leveling everything in his path so he could erect his own version of perfection.

And he was the *least* of the three evils? What were the other two? Demons?

The one thing ameliorating her upheaval at hearing his name again was confusion. At hearing it on the lips of the man who'd banished him from Castaldini, laced with such regret and…affection?

When King Benedetto spoke again, no doubt remained in her mind. It had been both. And more. Far more. The pining and pride of a father speaking of his estranged son. "There was nothing that boy couldn't do. A true jack-of-all-trades. He built a financial empire and was the best ambassador to the States Castaldini ever had by the time he was just twenty-eight."

She knew that. That had been when she'd met him, almost ten years ago. A month after she'd set foot on Castaldini, in the fairytale setting of her sister's wedding.

"You must remember how he walked out on the ambassador's position over irreconcilable differences in policies, how he escalated his antagonism until I could no longer defend him to the Council, was forced by his actions and their unanimity to declare him renegade and strip him of his Castaldinian nationality."

Oh, how she remembered that. And what it had led to.

"He is now a tycoon of global power, dividing his time between business and humanitarian endeavors."

She didn't want to hear this. But short of walking away, or yelling at the king to quit shoving Leandro's achievements down her throat, there was nothing she could do but stand there and listen to how he'd moved on, and so spectacularly, with his life.

Focused on his purpose, the king went on. "We approached him to come back, to be given full pardon and become crown prince and regent. He scoffed at our messengers and our offers."

"Surely that was anger talking." She started at the croaked protest. It had issued from her. It seemed nothing could silence the negotiator inside her. "Nothing some determined cajoling and ego-boosting concessions won't alleviate."

"Oh, yes, that's what the Council thought, too. I told them they knew nothing about Leandro. But they were confident they could negotiate with him. He told us what we could... do...with our attempts at pride-salving and our middle grounds."

Phoebe felt every word pushing her to the edge of an abyss. She couldn't bear to look down, tried again to inch away. "If he so adamantly refuses, why not turn to the other choices?"

"Because the objection against the second is weightier, and he hates me even more. As for the third, the objection against him is the weightiest of all. And I suspect he hates both me *and* Castaldini. Leandro, as impossible as it seems, is actually the least problematic of all, the one I project will be easiest to reach. And that is where you come in."

Her heart launched against her ribs. She rocked on her feet with the force of the collision. *Don't say it. Don't...*

He said it. "I'm sending you, the one person I believe can reach Leandro, can convince him to negotiate, or to at least hold down the fort until a more permanent solution is found, if he remains adamant about not accepting the succession."

Phoebe's mind emptied. Her tongue fired blanks. "I—I'm not..."

"You're Castaldini's most potent negotiator. You've bailed us out of situations where my old guard and I were ineffectual, detrimental even. And this is our darkest hour. I am counting on your ability, your infallible diplomatic techniques and your own charms, to lure Leandro back when all else has failed."

Her own...*charms?* Now wait a minute here...

Before she could choke out her alarm, the king hurled another declaration at her.

"You're my—and Castaldini's—last card."

"We're landing, *Signorina* Alexander."

Phoebe mirrored the flight attendant's smile, patted her fastened seatbelt. She waited until the radiant brunette had removed her untouched dinner and hurried away before she let her head thunk against her window. The bonfire of lights that was New York City at night was zooming up at her, an organized maze of the gothic and the postmodern that seemed to be unfurling to engulf Castaldini's equivalent of Air Force One.

She closed her eyes over the sand that seemed to fill her lids.

She hated flying. She'd come to equate it with upheaval.

The journey that started it all had been ten years ago. Her little sister, Julia, had accepted Paolo's marriage proposal only to discover he was the King of Castaldini's son.

Phoebe couldn't let her eighteen-year-old, special-needs sister go alone to a foreign country and an unknown future. She'd dropped out of law school to accompany Julia. She'd boarded that jet to Castaldini with anxieties and regrets preying on her. The first over the unimaginable future she and her sister were heading to, the second over the life she'd relinquished.

Not that she'd had second thoughts since then. Although she was only two and a half years older than Julia, she'd been more of a mother than a sister to her since their single mother had died just days after Phoebe's thirteenth birthday. When Julia had become afflicted with Hereditary Spastic Paraplegia—a rare form of partial paralysis—Phoebe's protectiveness had mushroomed. At fourteen, Julia had started suffering from weakness, stiffness and partial loss of sensation in her lower limbs. By the time she was seventeen, she'd been in a wheelchair. Then she'd met Paolo.

Undaunted by her condition, he'd swept her into a whirl-wind romance. It wasn't long before he'd proposed. And though Julia had accepted after nearly a year of cajoling and insistence that her physical condition made no difference to him, Julia's psychological state had been fragile and her dependence on Phoebe had deepened with the anticipation of all the upheaval that becoming a princess overnight would bring.

Phoebe had wondered too many times if she would have done things differently if she'd known her own life would change forever, too. And not just as spillover from the changes in Julia's.

What if the first time she'd set eyes on Leandro, she'd had the sense to feel alarmed at her volatile reaction, especially when she'd always been steady and cerebral? To realize that something so out of control would lead to a crash? That a man so voracious in both ambition and passion would end up consuming her while giving nothing of himself in return? What if she hadn't let him sweep her into that first kiss an hour after meeting, hadn't thrown herself into his bed a week later?

She'd always come to the same conclusion. Any alternative scenario wouldn't have derailed her life, and she wouldn't have spent years afterward trying to get back on track. She would have been whole, living a full life, with a family of her own.

And the king thought her the one best equipped to talk Leandro into coming back. The man she hadn't had one rational discussion with in the fourteen months she'd been his lover.

But she had to be fair here. Their past affair was unknown, thanks to the lengths to which Leandro had gone to keep it a secret. The king was asking her to do her job as Castaldini's diplomatic troubleshooter, who had negotiated many precarious deals and smoothed potentially treacherous situations on the kingdom's behalf. If she took personal history and emotions out of it, this, while a one-of-a-kind situation, was still within her job parameters.

Not that she hadn't tried to excuse herself from the chore, extricate herself from this impending mess. But without admitting why she couldn't face Leandro, she'd had no ground on which to squirm out of that trap. She thought even a confession would have backfired. The king's reliance on her "charms" would have only taken on new relevance. As a man, and a desperate monarch to boot, he would have believed a former lover who just happened to be the kingdom's best negotiator would be a double-barreled weapon that was sure to win the battle.

She had one more reason she couldn't have used. The consequences of this turn of events.

Leandro must be punishing the king and his Council, forcing them to grovel for his return after they'd banished him. But she had no doubt that when his pride was appeased and his conditions were made and met, he'd become part of the D'Agostino family again, would become its crown prince and future king.

And her time on Castaldini would come to an end.

The moment he came back to stay, she'd leave.

She was an hour away from meeting the man who'd made it impossible for her to love or even want another. From negotiating the deal that she had to succeed in negotiating at any price.

The deal that would end life as she knew it.

Leandro D'Agostino fought the urge building inside him until he felt as if his head were expanding under its pressure, heard the bones in his hand crackle under its force.

He stared down at that hand before he realized it was his cell phone issuing that sound. The cell phone he was crushing.

He swore, threw it away. It clanged on the gleaming wood of his desk, skidded and clattered to the mirror-like hardwood floor. He gritted his teeth as silence filled the racket's wake.

Dammit. How many phones had he damaged in the past eight years so that he wouldn't use them to call her? Even though that had been for the exact opposite purpose for which he wanted to call her now?

Well, he was *not* calling Phoebe Alexander. He was *not* canceling his meeting with her.

She wanted an interview with him? She was getting one. For all the good it would do her.

She'd picked a bad day to break an eight-year silence. A bad month. A bad lifetime.

And she was about to find out how a tiger felt when those who'd ripped a claw from his paw came to poke at the festering wound.

They *dared* call him back. They *now* offered the mantle of power and responsibility. After they'd slandered him and cast him out, stripped him of his identity before his people, before the world. After he'd spent his life in service of his kingdom and its people, after he'd been certain he'd be named crown prince as the one D'Agostino male who met all the ancient criteria.

The closer he'd come to the crown, the more the Council had panicked. They wanted to remain the ruling body for life, had feared—and correctly—that his first action as king would be to replace them. So they beat him to it while they still could. They'd turned on him, removing him as a threat. After all, they'd still had the power. And King Benedetto's ear.

King Benedetto. His kin and king. His hero. The king hadn't just stood aside and let the dogs shred him, he'd delivered the decree that had torn Leandro's guts out himself.

But being unable to call himself of the royal house of D'Agostino, ceasing to be a Castaldinian, hadn't been the worst injury he'd sustained. That had been *her* betrayal. Her desertion.

And she was on her way here. To negotiate on his former king's behalf. Or was it on her own?

It could be the latter, disguised as the first.

As if he'd fall for her again.

Whatever she was coming here for, he wasn't letting her have it, or any influence on him again. Not in this life. Or the next.

Si, let her come. He was in the mood to be provoked. Her memory had been the source of heartache for far too long. Let her flesh-and-blood presence inflict something less pathetic. Something hot and harsh. Something he could sink his teeth into. And rip.

It was time to tear out anything soft or stupid from his depths, the remnants of the spell he hadn't been able to break. It was time to exorcise her…

All his hairs stood on end as if he'd been doused in a field of static electricity. A presence. Unmistakable even after all these years. Here. She was here.

Phoebe.

Ernesto must have met her downstairs, let her up here. Let her walk alone into his den. Like eight years ago.

Caution told him not to move, to make her initiate the confrontation. Every instinct screamed for him to turn, to catch her first uncensored reaction to seeing him after that lifetime.

It was the hot, sharp sound that spilled from lips he knew to be rose-soft and cherry-tinted, that had once wrung all coherence from him with soul-wrenching kisses and moans, that shattered the stalemate. He swung around.

Déjà vu engulfed him.

Time rewound to the moment he'd first laid eyes on her. To the last time he had. And like both times, like every time in between, everything about her bombarded him all at once.

Different droned in his mind. Raven-haired when she'd been caramel blond before, creamy pale when she'd been deeply tanned, curvaceous when she'd been willowy. The woman who stood two dozen feet away had little in common with the younger one who occupied his memory, who'd never relinquished her hold over his senses.

He took in the enhancements in one glance, knew he'd need hours, days, more…far more, to sort through them.

But he didn't have to catalog them to suffer their effects, to relive that incendiary—and to his rage and resignation, unrepeatable—attraction.

For a stretch that existed outside time, it was as if the only thing that could happen was that he would surge toward her, that she would rush to meet him halfway.

She stood as transfixed as he. As shocked.

That conviction jogged him from the surreal timelessness

he'd plunged into, the version where nothing had gone wrong between them. He crash-landed into the distasteful present.

Of *course* she wasn't shocked. She was here with full premeditation…

No. She *was* shocked. This was no act, not any more than his own dive into that time warp had been. So what did it mean?

He exhaled the breath trapped in his lungs, admitted he'd probably never know what anything meant where she was concerned, that he had no more grasp on this situation than he had on anything else that had happened in the past.

But he intended to take control of it. Or at least try to. He'd start by taking control of himself.

He turned fully to her, bracing for the change that would come over her expression as *she* regained control.

The last of the shock he'd detected in her drained. He caught a stinging lip in his teeth, counted down the seconds before her gaze heated, her posture relaxed, beckoned…

"For the record, I told King Benedetto what I think of a man who refuses to do his duty out of petty pride."

Leandro blinked. What the…?

"But it's my job to negotiate on the king's behalf. Even for a prize I don't think worth winning."

Two

Leandro consulted his hearing. And his memory.

Had she really said what he'd heard her say?

A prize I don't think worth winning.

And that would be…him?

He stared at the woman Phoebe Alexander had become. She strode into his den as if it were her own sanctuary and he the intruder, each stride loud with the bearing of someone who knew her worth, her effect, exuded it to perfection with each breath.

Confusion mounted as his gaze clung to the new lushness encased in the formal attire of her profession, the severity of which only accentuated each long limb and ripe curve. His eyes followed each undulation of feminine assurance and fluid grace, pored over the areas her suit left exposed. That smooth neck with the modest expanse of flesh just below, those molded legs. He could almost taste her new creaminess. Would it taste the same as her honeyed tan once had…?

Abbastanza, you fool. Focus on her face. Fathom her tactic.

He did, only to wish he hadn't. Lingering on features that

had been sculpted to their full potential by a connoisseur god of taste and elegance only intensified the rush of hormones through his system, had every nerve ending rioting like a wheat field in a storm. *And* there was nothing in her expression to guide him.

She reached the oak coffee table in front of his Chesterfield couch arrangement, bent to place her gray briefcase down with a concise click. Her thick braid fell forward, drawing his gaze to the femininity encased snugly in a jacket that reflected her silver eyes. Fantasies washed over him, of dragging her by the braid, undoing it with fingers made rough by haste to the cadence of her encouraging moans, releasing the twining locks into a cascade of glossy raven waves. Another kick of blood rushed to his loins.

Then she straightened, looked straight at him as if she were looking through spotless glass. She laced her fingers loosely in the pose of a saleswoman waiting on the whims of an ambivalent client, and all he could think was that those supple hands had once been all over him, stroking him to a frenzy, pumping him to oblivion, digging into him in ecstasies of release, that they were now linked right in front of…

Dio. What was wrong with him? He couldn't finish one thought without taking it to a carnal conclusion? Without imagining her abandoned in his arms as he did everything with her, to her?

He shouldn't have abstained. Even if he hadn't felt any urge for female company, for physical gratification, he should have sought both. Just like he sought sustenance. He shouldn't have convinced himself he didn't need the release, needed all his drive intact for his endeavors. Now it seemed he was starving.

Ma, maledizione…he *hadn't* been. Not until she'd walked in.

"Shall we begin the negotiation?"

He winced. Her voice was the same, velvety and rich like chocolate and red wine. But even when she'd spat her last words at him before walking out of his life, she hadn't sounded so—arctic. And that frostiness was nothing compared to how those eyes swept over him as if examining an icky lifeform.

She dropped his gaze like a hot potato, swept hers around as if seeking something worthy of her focus. "You do want to get this over with so you can get on with the rest of your day, don't you?"

The answer that almost escaped was *What I want is for you to tell me who you are and what you did with the Phoebe I knew.*

Did the change in her extend so deeply beyond the physical? Had the woman who'd inundated him with hunger and appreciation and exuded passion from every pore disappeared? Was this what had replaced her? A woman who was finally true to her namesake?

The name of a goddess of the moon had been such a misnomer for the sunny entity she'd been. But now the name and the myths woven around it seemed to have been invented for her. Where once her skin and hair and figure and vibe had glowed with the sun's heat and energy, they were now permeated by the moon's light, by its night and fullness. By its coldness.

But then the changes were probably only superficial. Her old spontaneity and warmth must have been an act. One he'd fallen for.

So why had she dropped the facade now, when she was here to insinuate herself into his favor?

A scoff almost burst from his lips. Favor? *That* she now hoped to win by telling him how worthless she thought him?

Which was a strange declaration. As one of the most powerful men in the world, he epitomized worth. She herself must have plotted to ensnare him the moment she'd recognized his potential.

She'd read him, played him like a virtuoso. The endlessly loving sister, the innocent who'd gone up in flames at his first touch, the one presence in his life that had been undemanding and soothing during conflicted times. She'd projected everything that had captivated him with unerring consistency.

She'd moved on after he'd been wiped out of the picture, looking for a replacement prince. And she'd found one—and lost him. To this day, Leandro had been unable to find out the true circumstances of her broken engagement to one of his second cousins, Prince Armando D'Agostino.

But she'd had a contingency plan. She'd become the indispensable presence that connected the über-traditional monarchy to the modern world. The one the kingdom relied on in its hours of need. The one they'd sent to him.

And she wanted to "start the negotiations." Wanted to get it over with so he could "get on with the rest of his day."

Not the words or attitude of someone who cared one way or the other if those negotiations bore fruit.

So what was she up to now?

She must have a plan. A new act. She must have decided to walk in here, pretend antagonism, condescension, and before he interpreted any level of emotional involvement in either, she would switch to indifference. Keep him guessing. Keep him off-balance and enmeshed in the game, trying to anticipate her next move and how to counteract it.

Masterful. A resounding success.

And why not? He'd let her perform this new scenario. Watching her execute it should be therapeutic.

He advanced on her with steps that he hoped looked measured. His resolve to purge her *wasn't* lessening her impact. He stopped two steps away, and it hit him two hundred times harder.

He made another split-second decision, to give in to it rather than fight it and lose more to its sway. He let her aura flood over him, took another step closer.

"And hello to you, too, Phoebe."

Her eyes swung up to his. Blood grew thicker, demanding harder contractions from his heart to push it through his arteries.

She took half a step back. Slow. Smooth. Dancing with him already? They'd once danced so…exquisitely together.

"There's no need to pretend we owe each other hellos."

The matter-of-factness of her tone was like an intravenous

stimulant, riding his circulation's rapids to his fingertips, his toes, his scalp, his erection. He made up for the half step she'd gained. "Don't we? You keep saying the most interesting things."

"I'm stating facts. Now, if we can move on?"

"So, me not being a prize worth winning, and us not owing each other hellos are 'facts.' Because you say so, of course."

Her gaze shifted downward. He felt it scrape down his body, as inflammatory as her nails had once been.

But what was the stirring he saw in her eyes? Irritation? At him? Or at herself? Because she hadn't intended to look? To notice? To become as inflamed?

Before he could make sure, her gaze moved back up to his, smothering whatever it had been in blandness. "Prince D'Agostino…"

The title—what he hadn't heard in eight years and the formality that had never before passed her lips were like a swipe of claws across raw tissue.

"Leandro." He couldn't temper his anger and affront, stop them from making his growl a predator's. "You remember my name, don't you, Phoebe? *Yalla,* say it. You once moaned it, sobbed it, screamed it. I'm sure you can now pay me the courtesy of using it."

Those eyes wavered before they hardened, those lips twitched before they thinned. "I see no reason to. 'Prince D'Agostino' is what's proper in this situation. And I demand *you* pay me the courtesy of not bringing up our past liaison again."

He gave a rough huff. "You'd better realize and fast that I don't respond well to demands, Phoebe. I'm also notorious for being impossible to steer. So quit wasting your breath trying to maneuver this 'negotiation' according to your preset plans."

To her credit, she didn't try to contest that he'd pegged her strategy right. Now she'd no doubt swerve into new territory.

But she said nothing. Stood silent. Still. Waiting for him to launch into more unchecked responses, to compromise himself more?

He quirked an eyebrow at her. "No more admonishments? Shall I wait until you think of something concise and annihilating? Something to devolve me from worthless to nonexistent?"

Her gaze remained steady. Vacant. It filled him with urgency. He took a step, farther into her aura, struggled not to breathe deeply of her freshness. He stopped before he touched, gathered, crushed. Her stillness and silence sent his senses haywire. He'd had enough unresponsiveness from her to fill ten lifetimes. He'd take no more.

He opened his mouth, not knowing what he'd say. Only she had ever been able to strip him of coherence.

What came out was, "Nothing more to say?"

Memory flooded him of when he'd said those very words to her before, in this very room. Of what had followed them. And... *Dio.*

He watched as a jolt emptied her lungs and vulnerability flooded her eyes. Had the memory hit her as hard as it had him? Why would it, if that encounter hadn't meant much to her, if her emotions had never truly been involved? Could it be there had always been another explanation, one he'd hoped for all these years?

Temptation became an ache, to demand she put him out of his misery once and for all, to reenact the rest.

Exhaling, hoping to purge the irrationality her nearness always afflicted him with, he gestured toward the sitting arrangement behind them.

She didn't move. After seconds of her ignoring his unspoken invitation, he exhaled again, walked around her. With all he had, he refrained from brushing against her. He still felt as if her essence followed him, enveloped him, its crisp sweetness filling his lungs, the charge of attraction sparking over his skin. Setting his teeth, he snatched a remote off the coffee table, pushed a button as he descended heavily onto the two-seater.

Ernesto appeared at the door in seconds.

The older man's shrewd gaze took in the situation before turning disapproving eyes on...*him?* What the...?

Tamping down the ridiculous urge to protest that this tense scene was her fault—past *and* present—furious that the man who'd practically raised him, who'd seen him at his worst after her desertion should have the temerity to have any doubt of that, he glared back. "See what Phoebe would like, Ernesto. She might talk to you. She seems to be on a speech strike with me."

Ernesto's hawklike face grew harsher with displeasure and disappointment, throwing daggers at Leandro's confused outrage, before softening into fondness and indulgence as he turned to Phoebe. "What would you like, *cara mia?*"

Cara mia? His dear? Since when? What was going on here?

Before more questions could form, Leandro's mouth dropped open wider as Phoebe turned a face transformed by affection into the heart-melting one he remembered, and gave Ernesto a tremulous smile that would shake the foundations of a metropolis. "*Grazie,* Ernesto. Anything. You always know what I like better than I do."

After the two people who had—*had* had, in Phoebe's case—the most emotional influence on his life exchanged one more glance that left Leandro feeling like an outcast, Ernesto walked out.

As soon as the door closed, Leandro's gaze swung to Phoebe, eager to see softness still possessing her face. But her features had settled back into that mask of impassiveness.

Disappointment roared through him. "Very touching. The affection feels very established *and* ongoing, too. Are you going to tell me what's been happening behind my back? Or should I take it up with Ernesto?"

He'd bet lesser men had shriveled up under the brunt of such a look as the one she gave him in answer.

He leaned forward, the better for his resentment to collide with her disdain. "Come here, Phoebe."

He counted three booming heartbeats, during which she remained unmoving before he ground out, "If you insist on testing the limits of my patience, do remain standing there. And if you insist on playing the prim and proper emissary, do call me *ex*-Prince D'Agostino. I've earned the title the hard way, after all."

"And you want to earn the removal of the *ex* part in an even harder way?"

"Ah, *there* you are. I knew you had plenty more to say."

He'd thought she'd clam up again when she murmured, "Not if you don't start behaving in a civilized and professional manner."

His mouth twisted with a jumble of irritation and stimulation. "There's another thing I have to warn you about. My severe allergic reaction to conditions and ultimatums."

Just when he thought she might turn on her heel and walk out, she moved. Forward. Nearer. One prowling stride after the other.

By the time she was standing about two steps away, his mind had hurtled into wish fulfillment, dreaming of bringing her down to straddle him, grinding her heat against his hardness…

Before he dragged her down himself, he bit out, "Sit *down*, Phoebe."

She finally did, in one downward sweep of grace and self-possession. On the far side of the couch, on its very edge. As if preparing to spring up and away at his least movement.

"Sit back, Phoebe, relax. Anyone would think you're afraid I'll pounce on you. Which is strange when you come to think of it, since you once wanted nothing more than for me to do so."

She turned on him, and… *Dio*. A tigress baring her fangs before slashing a tormentor's head off wouldn't have been more magnificent, more stunning. More effective.

He didn't know how he *didn't* pounce on her.

"Okay," she hissed. "Let's get it all out in the open and out of the way and be done with these juvenile, infringing, lascivious allusions. We had a sexual liaison a lifetime ago. It ended. We moved on. Eight years later, we're different people, and not only doesn't today have anything to do with the past, this has nothing to do with us as individuals. I'm not Phoebe to your Leandro here. I'm Ms. Alexander, international law consultant and diplomatic troubleshooter for the Kingdom of Castaldini, present in my professional capacity to negotiate the acceptance of crown-prince status with *ex*-Prince D'Agostino."

He stared at her. He'd wanted hot and harsh? He should have prayed he didn't get what he wished for. He was so engorged now, his jeans might be causing him permanent damage.

Act or no act, the verdict was in. Whatever he remembered of her effect on him had been diluted by time. Or she'd grown a hundred times more potent with maturity. He'd bet on the latter.

Which was weird. He'd thought the malleable, even-tempered Phoebe his ideal woman. So why was he finding the guns-blazing, machete-tongued Phoebe far more attractive? He'd never found anything to tolerate in cold, cutting women, let alone something to arouse him to the point of pain. So why did he find her sub-zero bluntness the epitome of overpowering femininity? Especially when she'd just finished confirming everything he'd tormented himself with since she'd walked out on him: That he'd been no more than a sexual liaison to her? That she'd moved on, no problem?

And she wasn't even finished yet.

He watched as she drew in a breath, the exquisiteness of her face preparing for the next salvo.

He couldn't wait to be blasted to pieces.

Phoebe felt her heart stumbling in her chest like a panicked horse trying to gallop on slippery ice.

And the source of the turmoil, that huge, criminally majestic and beautiful…*rat,* was looking at her as she tore into him as if she were showering him with compliments.

This was far worse than she'd expected. And she'd expected the absolute worst ever since she'd arrived at the same building where she'd last seen Leandro. Then Ernesto had ushered her into the same *room.* Déjà vu had suffocated her by the time she'd seen Leandro with his back to her. And then he'd *turned….*

She'd seen many high-resolution photos and hours of footage of him throughout the years. She'd had film-quality memories. She'd thought graphic effects had touched up his assets, that memories had been exaggerated by the distortion of passion and inexperience.

They'd been misleading, all right. And mercifully so.

The brunt of the reality of him had shut down her mind, possessed her instincts. *Mate,* they'd whimpered. She'd seen herself flying to him, seen him storming to her, felt him snatching her in mid-flight, crushing her in his assuagement.

She'd stumbled out of that alternate reality, reeling. She remembered, vaguely, what had hurtled out of her mouth. Survival. Like someone lashing out with flailing arms at a black hole.

Then he'd stalked to her, and with each step, she'd withdrawn into herself to ward off his incursion. But damn him, he'd kept coming, invading her senses, snatching her responses from her self-control's white-knuckled grip. Then he'd spoken. Teased. Taunted. Pushed and pulled. Until the last anchor of her restraint snapped like an overextended string. She could swear she'd heard that final *twang* echo throughout her body. And she'd let him have it.

It was as if she'd let him have exactly what he'd been wishing for. The pleasure flashing across his face singed her, the tension roiling through his body resounded inside hers, spiking when every verbal slash hit home. It was as if she were chafing the exact spot he needed scratched, the very nerve cluster he wanted stimulated.

Who knew he was into S-M. The verbal kind. Maybe the physical, too. No wonder her "yes, Leandro" persona had been so…peripheral to him.

She thought she'd expended all her angst in that tirade. But with Leandro all but licking his lips for an encore, another was coming on.

"Now, to elaborate on what I said as I first came in…" She stopped. Her voice sounded as it once had at the end of the stamina-testing ecstasy sessions he'd exposed her to. She gulped. "Even if you redeem yourself in some huge way, I think it'll remain inexcusable that you're playing games when your kingdom's future is at stake…"

"*Former* kingdom."

His indolent words thrilled behind her breastbone. "What?"

He leaned closer. Sucked whatever air was left from the universe. "I'm an American now."

She grimaced. "Oh, please."

Mockery intensified the emerald of his eyes. "Want to see my passport?"

She waved. "You'll always be Castaldinian."

The wings of his dense, perfectly formed eyebrows rose in mock interest. "Really? A whole kingdom disagreed for eight years. I don't have one official tie to the place."

"Like it or not, you *are* one."

He turned his lip down in a perfect parody of a petulant little boy. Yeah. Sure. As if. "I have no say?"

She shook her head. "None."

"I wonder how you have worked this out."

"You don't have a say in your genes, do you? Same thing."

"Oh, but we do rise above our programming."

"And you transcended your Castaldinian origins?"

"I was actually culled out of the Castaldinian pool. But I've adapted well to life as another species, thank you for caring."

"Oh, *please.*"

He leaned back, the seat dipping under his shifting weight, exacerbating her imbalance. He spread his daunting body in a pretense of relaxation, giving her a more complete demonstration of his upgrades. And her effect on him. "You know, the way you keep saying 'please'…anyone would think you're inviting more 'juvenile, infringing, lascivious allusions.'"

His words had the effect of quick-drying concrete. "Okay. It seems we won't get anything of any value said or done before we indulge your need to harp about the past and drag out the sordid details. Fine. Go ahead. Get it out of your system."

His gaze seemed to scald her body, to scrape it naked.

"There are…things I can't get out of my system. Certainly not by…talking. As for other baggage from that phase in my life, don't worry about it. I channeled any lingering resentment into my work. Whatever remains, I take care of with extreme sports. And punching bags."

"*And* turning your back on your kingdom when it needs you."

A laugh cracked out of his depths, loaded with astonishment and amusement. And virility. "That would be a great outlet. *If* I were into an eye for an eye."

"Only it would be a limb—or a life, or even a nation's worth of either—for an eye, in this situation."

A chuckle rumbled in his chest, revving up the itchy feeling in hers to an ache. "You think I'm that vital? Very inconsistent of you, when you already said how inconsequential I am."

"That was a personal opinion," she mumbled, furious with herself, with him, at the responses he kept yanking from her.

His gaze grew more baiting as he rubbed a languid hand over his chest, drawing her stare to the beauty and power of the first, the breadth and hardness of the second. "Off the record, eh?"

She did her level best to present him with her neutral look. "Do make it on. Your head must be swollen from all the buttkissing you get. Consider my opinion a deflating agent."

His laughter boomed again. Her heart ricocheted in her rib cage. "Ah, Phoebe, I'm having my head measured first thing in the morning." He sobered a bit, his grin becoming an X-rated health hazard. "So why try to convince such an irredeemable egomaniac to take the reins of a kingdom?"

She swallowed. "I'm an emissary, as you said. I'm not here to put forward my convictions but rather my employer's case."

"Even if you suspect he's senile and is turning the kingdom over to the one person who'll drive it into the sea?"

"King Benedetto isn't senile by a long shot."

"How else do you explain his change of heart?"

"I am sure he has his reasons."

"So he hasn't shared them with you? You're the little foot solider with need-to-know info you'll never need to know?"

"One thing I do know is that his heart has always been with you. I believe having to cut you off nearly cut it out."

He threw his awesome head back with a hoot of delight. "I didn't see *that* coming."

Her throat constricted as the rain-straight silk of his hair cascaded back to frame his head to maximum effect. "What?"

"Appealing to the insecure little boy inside me who craves his hero's approval, his validation."

God help her, she actually snorted. "The day I believe there's an insecure little boy inside you is the day I believe I'll sprout wings if I cluck hard enough."

His laughter was louder this time, lasted longer. Spread more damage. "Ah, Phoebe, you know me too well. How about the vindictive little boy inside me, then? Who wants to see the object of his hero worship groveling, admitting how much he's wronged him, and how the guilt of his transgressions has never given him a moment's peace?"

She stilled. His eyes lost the crinkle of amusement as he stared back at her. And she saw it.

A groan escaped her. "I don't believe I'm saying this, but I don't think there's a vindictive little boy inside you, either. Whatever you have in there, I think it's still just…just…"

"Angry? Affronted?" he offered, mock helpfully.

"Stunned."

He went totally still. His stare lengthened. Until she was sure he'd burned a hole between her eyes.

Suddenly he was surrounding her. All her nerves gave way at once. She melted back into the couch. He followed her, still not touching her. She felt as if he'd licked her all over, with fire. When he was inches away from her lips, he rumbled, "Didn't you notice that you haven't done any negotiating so far?"

Each word jolted through her, coating her lungs with his scent, his potency. "If—if I've learned anything as a negotiator," she gasped, "it's how to know for certain when my… opponent has no intention whatsoever…under any persuasion…to negotiate."

Another inch disappeared. "I'm your opponent now?"

"You're worse. An opponent I can handle. You're... you're..."

"I'm...what?" He obliterated half of the last inch.

Her hand went up. To keep him away? All she knew was that her hand met the convergence of silk and steel and searing heat and stuck there like a pin to a magnet.

"Phoebe..."

Her ears rang with her name, the very sound of wonder, of hunger, with the racket of doors slamming shut in her mind. All existence was his lips. Almost there. On hers. At last. *Please.*

She couldn't breathe, so she breathed him. He smelled so much better than air. Felt so much more vital. Necessary...

No. *No.* He *wasn't.* She'd let him be that once, and... *No.*

She twisted away, feeling as if she'd wrenched back from a precipice. Her heart hammered inside her; her lungs burned. Somewhere an auxiliary power source kicked in, yanked her up to her feet.

Her gaze slammed around. *Where is the damn door?*

"Signorina?"

She swung around blindly, seeking the voice. So welcome. As always. Ernesto. Her ally. Her solace. Her secret-keeper.

He was standing at the door, holding a laden silver tray.

She took a step toward him. The second was harder. The third was too hard to finish, as if Leandro's influence was pulling her back. Ernesto looked past her, at his master, no doubt, and gave a grudging nod. To her he gave a bolstering look. Then he retreated.

She opened her mouth to cry for him to come back, and Leandro's drawl lodged between her shoulder blades.

"Forgetting something, Phoebe? Your mission?"

Without turning to him, she gritted words out through her teeth. "You let me come here just to settle a score, to show me it was never anything but a wild goose chase. Just as well. You're not salvation material. In fact, you would probably be the worst thing that could happen to Castaldini right now."

She suddenly felt as if he'd let her go. She surged forward. As it had that last time she'd been here, the door seemed to recede…

"Phoebe."

His murmur hit her with the force of a gunshot.

"Tomorrow night. It's still up to you."

She felt as if she were drowning in the bass reaches of his croon. "Wh—what are you talking about now?"

Silence. Until she started to shake. Then she almost fell to her knees when he whispered, "It's still up to you to convince me. Why I should give…anyone…a second chance."

Three

Phoebe's gaze swept over the extravagance surrounding her.

To her right, sunshine soaked in vibrant color filtered through a ten-foot-wide stained-glass window, transferring its tinted image to the pristine white marble floor. All around it clear, eight-foot-tall windows nestled among silk-covered walls, framing glimpses of Central Park and staining the open-plan space with sunset's copper. Among the opulence of the French-chateaux style of décor and furniture, the hand-painted piano caught her eye, its French countryside scenery depiction a poetry of precision. Out of sight, in the bowels of the suite occupying nearly the entire eighteenth floor of the hotel, lay five bedrooms, five and a half bathrooms, two living rooms, a dining room, a powder room and a sauna. The attractions included three marble fireplaces, a terrace and a two-thousand-bottle wine cellar. Amenities included the services of a secretary/butler and the hotel's chefs.

In a nutshell, all the excess that fifteen grand a night could buy.

This was the upgrade Leandro had insisted she stay in, substituting the suite Castaldini had reserved for her for the Presidential Suite, which was evidently at his disposal year-round.

She'd failed to get him to let her stay in an accommodation made for a normal human being. The kind who had one body, necessitating one bed and one bathroom.

But that wasn't her biggest problem. Not when she, Phoebe Alexander, negotiator extraordinaire, had walked into a situation that had all the potential of diverting the course of a whole kingdom's history and had handled it with all the finesse of a bull in a china shop full of red dishes.

In another nutshell, she'd messed up. And she hadn't even realized it. Not during the process of messing up, anyway.

She'd walked away from that disaster of a meeting thinking she'd held up under Leandro's power, that although it had been a premeditated, mouse-torturing session run by a master feline, she hadn't let him get away with it without landing a few blows of her own.

She must owe that delusion to overexposure to him. He'd always nullified her insight, neutralized her logic. But with his evolution from one-of-a-kind male into force of nature, he'd metamorphosed her into her mirror image, the reverse of her hard-earned, calm and cool persona. Blunt, rash, reckless. Inflammatory.

Instead of delivering levelheaded arguments, she'd let herself be provoked and antagonized. Her verbal missiles had only turned him into the opposite of the younger man who'd taken life and himself too seriously, who'd been too consumed by the drive to reach greater success to have—or at least to make use of—a sense of humor.

The new Leandro had reveled in being crossed and criticized, had turned everything—starting with himself—into fodder for repartee. He'd also been blatant about the resurrection of his attraction. Everything he'd said and done had loosened her self-restraint even more.

Not that that excused what she'd done. The depth of un-professionalism she'd sunk to was appalling. Not only had she not tried to fulfill her mission, she'd done her best to sabotage it. Even his reminder that she hadn't done any negotiating hadn't jogged sense into her malfunctioning brain. One minute later, she'd run out, essentially saying *what's the point* and *good riddance*.

But he'd had the final word.

It's still up to you to convince me. Why I should give… anyone a second chance.

Two sentences that delivered volumes. She'd botched her shot at appealing to him. She'd walked away without garnering a new crown prince for Castaldini, or at least a regent and savior. In his benevolence, he was offering her a replay. Or was it a retrial?

Whichever it was, his charity, should she play her cards right this time, might even extend to her. *Awesome.*

The arena for this second and final parley was no neutral ground, of course. She'd never had a say in the timing or venue of their encounters, and he wasn't letting her start now. An official beggar wasn't any higher up the ranks than an unofficial paramour.

His decree? Dinner. Tonight. At another trap of his choice.

She got to jump through his hoops one more time. Yay her.

Ernesto had come to her hotel this morning bearing advice. And dresses.

His advice she'd accepted without a murmur. He recommended that she keep on doing what she'd done so far. She had no problem with that. She probably could do nothing else. Seeing Leandro again had damaged something inside her, the equivalent of brakes in a car.

What she had a problem with was the dresses. And his second piece of advice, dress to the nines.

"I'm sure as hell not giving Leandro license to get more personal than he already has, Ernesto," she'd protested. "And that's what I'd be giving him if I wear any of these— these…" She'd flung a hand in the direction of the haute couture creations crowding a wheeled clothes rack. "He'd take one look at me and think *I'm* getting personal, shoving feminine wiles into the equation when I've failed to do my job any other way."

"I am the world's leading expert on Leandro," Ernesto had said patiently. "I project a very favorable reaction."

"Favorable in what way?" she'd groaned. "I want his 'favor' in only one way, and that isn't obtained by dressing up like a Mata Hari. In case he *is* giving my diplomatic mission a real second chance, I may end up insulting him by implying a dress can sway him in such a matter. And even if it could, you're barking up the wrong tree. A swanky getup does not make a femme fatale. If you think feminine wiles will come to my rescue under fire, think again. I came off the cosmic assembly line without them."

"You don't need wiles," Ernesto had insisted. "You need only yourself. The dress is to suit the setting where he is holding this next session of…negotiations. Trust me *now, cara mia.*"

That had silenced her. He'd meant she'd never trusted him before, with the reason she'd ended things with Leandro. To him, it must have looked like she'd walked out on Leandro in his darkest hour. And she'd never been able to defend herself. The only way to do that was attack Leandro, the man Ernesto regarded so highly and loved like a son. She wouldn't risk tainting that regard, that love. Not when he was a far bigger part of Leandro's life, and losing Ernesto's esteem would be a far graver injury to Leandro than to her.

Not that she'd lost it. Even without the truth, Ernesto had remained kind and caring. He'd contacted her regularly, always tried to visit her when her job had taken her back to the States. He'd even come to congratulate her on her engagement to Armando, which had been announced on a day that he'd been in Castaldini.

At her continued silence, Ernesto had sighed. "*Va bene,* Phoebe. I don't presume to have an opinion on what went wrong between you and Leandro. And since neither of you chose to confide in me or seek my counsel, I haven't been able to do more than remain neutral, as his right-hand and as your friend.

"But as a friend, I have to point out a few things. No matter what you think of your initial encounter with Leandro, you got much farther than anyone before you. You obtained something other than outright refusal. You *did* luck out, and it *was* because of who you are, and what you and Leandro once shared. No matter what you think of him, or feel toward him, he is powerful beyond your dreams. And Castaldini does need him, one way or another. King Benedetto was right to send you, even if he has no idea how right or why. So whether or not you approve of the situation, or of Leandro's intentions and methods, you are the only one who has a chance to turn his position around."

And with that, he'd left her. To her fate, it seemed.

He believed she had a chance to turn Leandro's position around? What she had was the feeling that she was sinking in quicksand, and any move would make her sink faster.

And you know what? What the hell.

Stressing wouldn't reverse the swiftness of the plunge. The sooner she was submerged and done with it, the better.

She got up, crossed the three-thousand-square-foot reception area to the bedroom she'd selected at random. She walked through to the bathroom full of marble and gold fixtures and showered as if her life depended on it, scrubbing till her skin felt raw. She dried off and plopped down on the *capitonné* dressing stool across the room, staring at the designer collection laid out on the frilly king-size bed.

After battling the need to hop into the most austere outfit she had with her, she decided to bow to Ernesto's judgment. And when something wild and wanton seethed inside her, demanding that she go all out and wear one of the most outrageous and shameless creations, she restrained it, kicking and hissing, and chose the most understated dress she could find. She was not going to Leandro's torment session in blaring red or gold, declaring without words that she was indeed sizzling for far more than juvenile, infringing, lascivious allusions.

After dragging on her chosen dress, she inspected the result. Hmm. Probably dressed only to the fours or fives. They'd all have to live with that.

Half an hour later, she was waiting for Ernesto to escort her to his master, trying to ignore the buzz that was escalating inside her at the thought of seeing said master again. To give herself something to do, she reexamined her reflection in the gilded full-length mirror in the suite's foyer.

With the heels and freshly styled hair, probably sixes or sevens.

Appropriate. She was at them, too. And she had herself to thank for that. Instead of having one confrontation be the end of it, here she was, through her own idiocy forced to see him again, to hopefully get the result she should have gotten the first time. Or not. He might be…hell, he *was* stringing her along, to fulfill an objective that probably had nothing to do with Castaldini and everything to do with that still overwhelming attraction that had seared away her resolutions and intentions. She could only let him steer her and everything wherever he pleased. She'd deal with it when she found out where that was.

And if that new, reckless entity that had been awakened inside her told her that she couldn't wait to go wherever he led, she smacked it silent. Been there, done that.

Never wanted to be there, or do that, again.

Leandro glowered at his watch.

Late. Three…*four* minutes. And he had a feeling those minutes would soon be accompanied by many more.

Was it her doing, or Ernesto's? Which of them wanted to keep him human by denying the gratification of his every whim?

Both, probably. And both, damn them, pegged him right. Knew they were the only two people alive he'd let cross him.

A huff exploded from him. Cross him? How about walk all over him? Ernesto knew he could get away with anything. And Phoebe…

Oh, yes. She knew, too.

She knew what she'd been doing last night. She'd parried and attacked until he was at critical mass. Then she'd hit him with what he would have never seen coming. One word. One insight. One verdict. *Stunned*.

She'd known, when he hadn't known himself. Not until she'd uttered her analysis.

He was still stunned. And it wasn't because his king, his people, had gone so far as to exile him, but that it had gone so wrong between him and Phoebe.

He'd once been so certain of her, had plans. Goals. To be named the most worthy, the next king. Then to offer it all to her, his name and future and the controlling shares of his heart.

Be my queen had hovered on his tongue from that first night he'd claimed her, been claimed by her, burning for the moment he could utter the demand.

Ernesto, the one man he trusted, the man who'd raised him after his parents' deaths, had urged him not to let her occupy his focus as he campaigned for the crown. But he hadn't been capable of listening, had writhed in impatience until he could rush back to her, join with her, melt in her.

And it had cost him. His enemies had capitalized on his distraction, had hit where he hadn't anticipated, forced him into retaliations that had grown more uncalculated. They hadn't guessed to what they'd owed their growing advantage, but they'd used his dwindling finesse against him. And he'd been in the throes of all-consuming hunger for the first time, hadn't even noticed the damage until it was too late.

It had ended in an injury he couldn't have anticipated, a dishonor and a deprivation that had felt worse than a death sentence. Fury and frustration had almost finished him those first days. Only one thing had made him hang on to his sanity, had stopped the spiral of retaliation he'd embarked on. Phoebe. He wouldn't care that his country had disgraced and shunned him, or even if the whole world deserted him. He had her.

He'd waited for her to contact him, to pledge that he *did* have her, but she didn't. And each day of silence became a tentacle of suspicion spreading through his thoughts and memories.

He'd been eager to make her his princess, to claim her, but he'd done everything to keep their relationship secret. It hadn't been official, but it had been made clear to him that the crown came with the woman all those in power wanted as queen attached: Clarissa, the king's daughter. That was why he hadn't proposed to Phoebe. If he had, worthy or not, the council would have found a way to deny him the crown. He'd intended to take it, *then* enforce her as his queen. But they'd denied him the crown anyway.

And her continued silence had started to wear another guise. Self-interest. Could she have been so amenable to secrecy not because she realized the risks of exposure, but because she'd been hedging her bets in case their relationship didn't lead where she'd hoped? Wallowing in their clandestine affair while keeping her virginal image? Did her silence mean she'd thought it time to drop him now that he'd never be king of Castaldini, wasn't even a prince anymore? She didn't even think him worth a phone call? Not even one of consolation, for old times' sake?

Driven over the edge by the malignancy of doubt, he'd succumbed, reached out to her. But he'd been so damaged by her lack of communication, he'd later wondered if he hadn't steered their reunion to that mutilating end. He'd spent the next five years tortured by the memory of their last time together, dissecting her every word and expression until he almost went mad. He'd found himself constantly dialing half her number before hurling the phone away.

The only thing that had saved his sanity was launching himself into his work as if possessed, catapulting himself from the roster of prosperous businessmen to the top of the food chain of world-shapers.

And every step of the way he felt sundered down the middle, as if he were missing his other half. He told himself over and over she wasn't that. But he never succeeded in convincing his heart.

He sought news of her like he did sustenance. He found out the results of her every law-school exam, each report of her sister's improvement before she did. He made a deal with himself. In case she'd rejected him because he'd asked her to give up "responsibilities and aspirations" he had no right to, when she'd fulfilled those things, he would again demand that she join him in exile. She'd have no reason to say no then, if what they'd shared had been real.

When her sister's health and marriage had stabilized and she'd obtained her law degree and was about to begin a new phase in her life, he'd sent Ernesto to her again, with a note. All he could bring himself to write. *I do need you. Still.*

The five words felt like an exposure of his soul with no guarantee that he wasn't jeopardizing what was left of it.

He dreaded her response. He shouldn't have worried.

There had been none. In lieu of a response, she'd announced her betrothal to his cousin Armando. That very day. And he'd had to face it once and for all.

She *had* been after a royal title, like her sister. He'd been her best ticket once. Armando was her new one.

The obliteration of hope, of belief in her, in what they'd shared, had extinguished his humanity for a while, he supposed.

But he'd lived on, risen higher. And the days passed. Then she broke it off with Armando. Almost a year ago. And all his convictions had dissipated again. He went back to feeling like he was constantly holding his breath. He refused to ponder what for.

Then she'd walked back into his life last night.

And he'd admitted it. *She* was what for. Whatever she was, whatever she felt, her hold on him was unbroken. Maybe even unbreakable.

Just as he'd succumbed, reached for her, and she'd seemed on the verge of surrender, she'd pulled back. She'd left him doubled over from frustration and walked away. Again. This time telling him, in so many eloquent words, *good riddance.*

It *had* to be a ploy. What else could it be when she'd run

away without gaining any response concerning her mission, proving it wasn't her objective after all? What other explanation could there be for dangling herself in front of him only to snatch herself away? What else could she want, except for him to give chase?

As she'd walked out, it had come to him. The reason that had been missing from his life. And his plan had formed…

"A spendthrift as well as a man who muddies professional situations with personal vendettas. I'm scratching my head here wondering how you became a mogul and a billionaire."

Phoebe.

Announcing her arrival with another lash of provocation.

He closed his eyes, suffering his body's reaction in resignation now.

A groan still escaped as he turned to face her. She was framed in the entrance of the restaurant/nightclub, swathed in the stark light he'd had trained there. Wrapped in an invention designed to blow all his valves, a creation of gray-silver that seemed to have been spun from the luminous seas of her eyes, with the flawlessness of her neck and shoulders shown to distressing advantage by an off-shoulder neckline and a chunky, relaxed wave of raven gossamer brushing just above a hint of a cleavage, she could have stepped out of a black-and-white silver screen classic. With the only splash of color spread across the elegance of her cheekbones and the dewiness of her lips, she seemed like…like…

He didn't know. The feeling crowded inside him, yet couldn't be translated into words.

But what did he need words for, when he had actions?

He moved just as she did. As if by agreement, they kept a dozen feet between them, moving parallel to each other, mirroring each other's steps, seeming to fall into the choreography of a memorized dance. They'd always moved to the same internal beat, as if aware of every impulse powering the other's body. Blood pressure inched upward into that danger zone he was discovering he relished, was getting addicted to.

She glided up the walkway's curve to the table he'd had set for them, overlooking the dance floor on one side and the blazing Manhattan skyline on the other.

He reached the table the same moment she did, placed his hands palms down on the wine-red silk tablecloth, leaned toward her. "What have I done now to deserve a demotion from simply worthless to seriously wasteful and wretchedly unprofessional?"

She placed a tiny tasseled bag on the table, titled her face at him. "What *haven't* you done? First that fifteen-grand-a-night suite, and now this, an exclusive New York night spot where becoming a member carries a hundred-grand price tag and a single visit costs a few grand per person. I won't even guess what you had to pay for an exclusive night for two. It would probably amount to a developing country's monthly budget, and I might get sick."

He cocked his head at her, exhilaration thrumming through his nerve endings. "I'm impressed. Your knowledge of the particulars and costs of high-end living around here is pretty comprehensive."

"Glad you're impressed. I'm not. Depressed is more like it."

He could believe that. In the past, her thorough disinterest in material things had been another quality he'd admired about her. And she'd walked out on him when he'd been almost a billionaire.

But then, it could have been easy to seem disinterested when she already had material excess through her sister. And she could have been holding out for a billionaire with royal status.

There was probably no way to know what the truth was.

He huffed. "Don't be so eager to feel sick and depressed. And I believe the suite comes with a *twenty*-grand-a-night tag."

Her eyes widened, reflecting the indirect lights that made her look otherworldly. "It's *more* expensive, and that's supposed to slow my plunge into depression? I feel I should be arrested for criminal waste. After you are, of course."

He came around the table, holding his breath until he

brushed against her. Air rushed out at the contact, at the tremor passing from her body to his where his thigh seemed to stick to the side of her hip, his hand to the small of her back.

She broke the circuit, descended—to his satisfaction—very unsteadily into the chair his other hand had pulled back for her.

He waited until he'd taken his seat then drawled, "Strange to hear you talking of waste and extravagance. You live in a palace where most articles cost thousands or are literally priceless."

Her eyes held his as her fingers sought a silver fork, ran up and down its length. He imagined them doing the same to *his* length.

"You talk as if I furnished the place when I'm just a long-term guest. Even Julia has no say in being surrounded by stuff that belongs in a museum. And you won't see either of us spending thousands on anything that isn't needed or at least useful."

"Very commendable. Of both of you. But since you seem to know such a lot, you must have an idea about the size of my fortune?"

"Sure. A few hundred grand is pocket change to you. But a few here and a few there, and soon we're talking real money, even by your standards. And then it's the principle I'm talking about. Do you usually indulge this kind of extravagance, or are you out to make a statement? I hope that wasn't your goal as it sure backfired. Unless the statement is that you're an obnoxious show-off."

His chuckle overpowered him. If she'd always harbored this confrontational vixen inside her and had been able to project the restful and acquiescent angel he'd known on demand, she was an actress of a scope he couldn't imagine. "I'm so relieved I wasn't trying to impress you, then. My intentions were along the lines of…pampering you. I failed to do that, too?"

Her head inclined, sending his heart tripping as her hair cascaded to the same side. "I wonder what gave you the impression that I'd appreciate this."

"Everyone appreciates luxury."

"Luxury beyond reason is…"

"Criminal. You've already informed me. I can do no right in your eyes, can I? Strange. I remember when you once gave me the impression I could do no wrong." He gave a sigh of mock regret. "Oh well. I can now shower you with excesses knowing in advance I'll be reviled for it." Before she whacked him with another comeback, he went on, "But to settle your mind about my wasting the equivalent of a struggling nation's income, let me solve the riddle you hurled at me as you came in. I didn't become who I am by spending money, but by making it. And I make it everywhere you can imagine, and in places you can't. And no, there is nothing criminal in my pursuits. Everything you've seen since you set foot in New York makes me money. From the building I own to the hotel where you're staying to a dozen others, to this place. Having Presidential suites to offer my guests and exclusive entertainment with no notice are among the many perks of being the major shareholder."

She glared at him. He managed not to lunge across the table and drag her into his arms. He grinned mockingly at her. "Disappointed I didn't fork out an obscene amount of money to impress or misguidedly pamper you?"

Her lips twisted. "I was disappointed to think you had."

"So no perverse disappointment now that you know I didn't?"

"Now you're not a spendthrift, but a chauvinist? Harping on the age-old implication that a woman says no when she really means yes?"

"I don't think it's female, but human for your logic and morals to clash with your need to feel valued. Criminally extravagant gestures might be abhorrent to one's ethics, but they sure tickle one's ego."

And she smiled. *Maledizione,* she *smiled.*

As he tried to deal with a bout of arrhythmia, a giggle escaped her flushed lips. "You became who you are by being an expert on human nature, too, it seems. Okay, I apologize."

He pressed a hand to his chest. This woman was out to do him some serious damage.

"I jumped to conclusions, ignored obvious explanations because I resented the hell out of you and wanted to believe the worst. And all you did was offer me the benefit of the perks you worked so hard to obtain, when you didn't have to. When I gave you every reason not to care if I spent the night in a flea-infested motel. Your brand of hospitality may be hard to enjoy without severe pangs of conscience, but I appreciate the thought."

He pretended to melt back in his chair in relief. He did need the support of something solid with his senses swimming as they were. "Phew. So that's the obnoxious show-off charge taken care of. What about the unprofessional-wretch accusation?"

Her solitary dimple winked at him. "Yes, what about it?"

He guffawed at her volley, shook his head. The words came to him now, what she felt like; like the sum total of his desires.

And those were indeed fierce. More. They were all-consuming.

Which brought him back to his plan.

He would claim the crown that had once been ripped from him. *If* he could be convinced once more it was his destiny to wear it.

There were no ifs when it came to her. He *would* claim her.

If he claimed the crown, it would be on his terms. No negotiations. But in her case...this was were his plot thickened.

He'd pursued her the first time around, always coming back to her as if starved. This time, he would make her do the running. Then he'd claim her.

And when he judged the time right, he would walk away.

He signaled the staff to begin the night's service, leaned across the table and captured the hand that kept frying his imagination with its restless movements.

"*Va bene,* Phoebe. Let's get the myth of my un-professionalism debunked, too. Let's get down to business. You have the whole night to work...on me."

Four

The moment Leandro took her hand, Phoebe felt as if he'd taken her will away, infused his own inside her. She wrestled with his hypnotic gaze before snatching her hand away as if from a hot grill, pretended interest in her surroundings.

They sure warranted it, and then some. As he'd said, damn his insight, all this was one colossal ego tickle. He might have easy access to it, but that he'd put this much thought and planning into setting the scene was at once disconcerting and exciting as hell. And there was no doubt what kind of scene it was.

A seduction scene.

Oh, she'd tried to rationalize that this was the done thing, that businessmen flaunted their status and power by conducting negotiations over extravagant meals among backdrops of affluence and exclusivity, that as a businessman in a class of his own, he'd naturally gone beyond what others would.

Those rationalizations lasted for the three seconds it took her to get a load of the place.

With the eyes of experience, she could see this place as it

might be on a normal business night, when its three-level interior would provide space to those who craved it, and privacy to those who preferred it. There would be partitions separating the top-level dining area from the mid-level bar and the lower-level lounge. Each would be bustling with its own clientele, feature its own menu, table and bottle service and resident DJ. Tonight the place seemed to have been designed to provide a single couple with expansive, atmospheric surroundings for an unforgettable encounter.

The décor was at once dignified and decadent, bridging borders with a dip into Latin heat in its daring, in the originality of bold yet harmonizing colors and designs. All in all this place had the ambiance of a dimension a few realities removed from the one she belonged to, one that swirled with ultra-modernism, Machiavellian suggestions and a touch of the arcane. The realm of a fallen angel where mortals suffered sensual enslavement and carnal excess. Very appropriate.

And she'd walked willingly into the Prince of Dark Temptation's web. She'd stood at its threshold, caught in a spotlight, feeling like the subject of an experiment in human response conducted by some higher being.

Said being was sitting there, watching her, overshadowing their surroundings in a suit and shirt, sans tie, that had been sculpted around his magnificence, their darkness and textures deepening the spell that hung around him.

And he'd just invited her to get to work. On him.

The moment the parade of beautiful people dressed in red and black satin finished spreading their table with ingeniously prepared and arranged appetizers and filled their crystal glasses before leaving the bottle of Moët & Chandon in ice, Leandro leaned back in his chair, making his appraisal even more invasive.

"So, have you decided yet what you'll do with your second shot at convincing me, Phoebe?"

She took a sip from her glass. And inhaled most of it.

After she redirected the fluid down her throat, she managed a strangled, "I'll start with holding my tongue. How's that?"

He mirrored her actions, bypassing the coughing-his-lungs-out bit, lids heavy as he licked the taste from his lips, making her feel as if he'd tasted hers. "Is that within your range of abilities?"

She took another sip, bent on proving that she could still manage basic stuff like swallowing. "It used to be. I was renowned for it."

"*Quella è la verità*—isn't that the truth. You had such rare reticence. Only when it came to talking, *grazie a Dio*. It was a trait I valued beyond measure."

"Yeah, a woman who's unrestrained in bed and keeps her mouth shut out of it must be every man's dream."

His eyes flickered. Surprised? That she'd put his innuendo into plain English? "I'm not every man, Phoebe. It wasn't because I was interested only in bedding you that I valued your quietness."

She plopped one of the hollandaise-covered, crab-stuffed mushrooms on her plate, cut into it. "No? Could've fooled me."

He narrowed his eyes. "You're implying you were quiet because my attitude discouraged you from talking?"

She took a bite. Tasted nothing. "Not really. There was nothing to say. But with all you had going on then, I did get the feeling that you wouldn't have appreciated it if there was."

"Nothing to say, eh? Strange how there can be two entirely different perspectives on the same situation. I thought you didn't talk much because you had this innate…understanding of me and of our situation that transcended the need for verbal expression. I thought we didn't use words because we were on the same wavelength without them. Seems that's another thing I was wrong about."

She concentrated. Hard. Swallowing now could end in a real emergency. The implication of what he was saying…

Could be anything really. From the poignant and profound to the meaningless and superficial.

She'd take something toward the end of the spectrum of the second interpretation. This was the man who'd let her walk out of his life and hadn't even tried to call her again in eight years. She doubted he'd had one poignant or profound thought where she was concerned.

It seemed he was waiting for her to respond. When she didn't, he sighed. "So you can still call on your tongue-holding talents. I really hope you won't hold out for long. I find myself valuing your new intensity and contentiousness far more than I ever did your tranquility and acquiescence."

"That must be maturity. The 'me against the world until I take it over and no one better oppose-me' young man has become a 'the world is mine and I'm dying for a new challenge' man."

He threw his head back and let out another of those intoxicating peals of unadulterated maleness. "Ah, Phoebe, *siete una sincera, genuina, autentica shaitana rajeema* and I *sperare ardentemente* that you don't hold your tongue ever again."

Resigned that she'd live with constant arrhythmia with him around, she picked up what turned out to be a maple-bourbon-glazed chicken wing and nibbled on it. "So although you've outgrown some traits, you still make a salad of Italian, English and Moorish."

His chuckles intensified as he watched her, and she imagined him nibbling on her lips, her neck, lower... "Only when one language doesn't provide accurate enough words."

"You couldn't say I'm an honest-to-goodness wicked devil in English?"

"You understood!" His eyes sparked with wonder and approval. She felt like a child fluttering at her hero's praise. Stupid. "And no, I couldn't. The English words—and your translation is as perfect as can be—don't have the exact nuances I wanted. *Sperare ardentmente* is more accurate than 'I pray to God,' too. Your idiomatic Italian is impressive. Most people who learn it as adults never learn its subtleties. But what made you learn Moorish? Almost no one in the Castaldinian cities uses it anymore."

Phoebe reached for her glass. The lump in her throat suddenly felt much larger.

Should she tell him she'd wanted to understand what he'd crooned to her at the heights of ecstasy? What, in her reluctance to make any demands of him, she'd let go unexplained?

After she'd resumed breathing again, she decided to tell him part of the truth. "I was intrigued every time you used it. It sounded so…primal and passionate, so different from Italian and any other language I've ever heard. And though it's not prevalent anymore, it—and the people who still speak it—is an integral part of the cultures that weave Castaldini. I felt I should know as much as I can of it. I'm not good by a long shot, but I get the general picture. My pronunciation stinks, though."

He seemed to weigh her answer. Then he picked up her hand, encased its sweaty coldness in the warmth and torment of his long, beautiful fingers. "Say something…"

"*Shai'*," she blurted out.

Another boom of virile amusement rocked her. "And I was going to say don't take me literally and say *shai'*."

"How about I say nothing? *La shai'*?"

He laughed again as he gave her hand a squeeze that could have left burn marks on her flesh before rocking back in his chair and throwing his hands in the air. "I take it back. Say anything."

"*Ai shai'*."

He leaned across the table, two fingers sealing her lips, his eyes radiating amusement…and arousal. "*Ai shai'* out of those lips should be banned as a lethal weapon. But in Moorish it becomes one of mass destruction. Your accent doesn't stink, it scorches."

"I basically said one word," she mumbled against his fingers, wondering what it would do to the course of the evening—and of her life—if she sucked them into her watering mouth.

Good thing he saved her from finding out. He brushed her lips with the backs of his fingers for one heart-bursting moment before withdrawing the temptation. "It was enough to tell me that I need some serious preparation before I hear a full sentence."

She plopped back in her chair, hopefully out of reach of more will-destroying touches. "So now we know why I speak Moorish. Why do you? None of the younger generation D'Agostinos I know do."

"Alas, I'm no longer one of the 'younger generation.' Everyone from my generation was required to learn it at school."

"But no one speaks it, apart from smatterings that have made their way into mainstream Castaldinian Italian."

"There *is* a section of the population who cling to it as Castaldini's original language. To the rest it rusted from misuse like any second language learned in school. I had more incentive to learn it. My maternal grandmother was a full-blooded Moor."

"So that's where the overriding raider in you comes from!"

He put his glass down, stood, took two steps to her side, and without warning, bent and pulled her up and against him, breast to chest. "This seating arrangement was my worst idea yet."

Before she could blink, he urged her over to an ensconced corner of the upper level. He half carried her down onto a red leather couch, missing coming on top of her by an inch.

She almost reached out and made him obliterate that inch. This train *was* hitting her. Why not get it over with?

The knowledge that the impact wouldn't be the end of the devastation made her freeze as the staff zoomed around them, spreading the square quartz table in front of the couch with hot plates simmering over gentle flames.

As soon as they disappeared, Leandro picked up a shrimp, bit off a piece and leaned over to put the rest to her lips. She again wondered about the damage potential of nibbling on those fingers along with the offered morsel.

Holding his eyes, she bit, hard. Into the shrimp. A harsh intake of breath accompanied the blaze in his eyes. He fed her until only his finger remained, probing her moistness with a to-and-fro motion that kept reversing the polarity of the current zapping through her core until she whimpered, glared at him. She was *not* licking it. Even if her heart might burst from holding back.

He at last withdrew his hand, slumped back with a shuddering exhalation, threw his head against the couch's headrest and squeezed his eyes shut. At least she wasn't the only one having a sensual meltdown. The weapon he was using on her was double-edged.

He opened his eyes, turned his head to her. She realized she was slumped in the same position. Their breathing synchronized as they pored over each other's faces as if studying for a drawing-from-memory test. Suddenly he feathered one fingertip over the features he'd examined so thoroughly. "You and Ernesto seem to belong to a secret mutual-admiration society."

Her lips twitched with mirth and heartache. "You didn't take it up with him? Feared a rap on your knuckles, huh? And you're now trying to get details out of the easier-to-interrogate party?"

His lips spread to a new level of seduction. "Ernesto does pack one mean knuckle-rap. But where is that party who's easier to interrogate? You? I'm braving a scratched-out eye here."

"So you'd rather lose an eye than get a bruised knuckle. What kind of a businessman are you, anyway?"

He bit his lip. "What can I say? The…harder it is, the more I like it. Risky confrontations are the only things worth my while."

She tsked, ignoring the escalating pounding between her legs. "Not the mentality of a man suitable for any kind of office, let alone that of king. Certainly not ruler of a kingdom that has avoided risks and confrontations throughout its history. The way you make it sound, you'd provoke a war to revel in the ensuing conflict."

He ran his finger along her jaw. "Oh, I wouldn't go that far. But I'd give my enemies—and my allies—a few scares here, a few sleepless nights there. Keeps them on their toes, makes them more interesting to have in either status."

She sighed as she melted further into the couch. And into his power. "And you wonder why you were at such explosive cross-purposes with King Benedetto and the Council? They want everything to be steady, to avoid upheaval at all costs."

One eyebrow quirked in challenge. "And 'all costs' include freedom of speech and a few human rights here and there, right?"

She tsked again. "You make it sound like a dictatorship instead of a peaceful kingdom."

"Where everyone lives happily ever after? Are you sure you're not talking about a kingdom from one of the bedtime stories you read to your five- and seven-year-old nieces?"

She vaguely wondered that he knew their ages. "Oh, I'm sure, since I read Alba and Gemma stories about girls who save the day and ride into the sunset in search of the next quest."

"No knight in shining armor or Prince Charming?"

He pretended shock so well she had to snicker. "Not even if he was Knight of Burning Ardor or Prince Overwhelming."

The expansion of his pupils, the flare of his nostrils hit her before she realized what she'd said. She struggled up, reached for a plate and started piling it haphazardly with food as she felt him move, felt each pull of muscle, each flicker of desire to take her back into that cocoon of intimacy. Then he exhaled.

"Tell me what the king and the Council really want with me."

She put the plate down before she spilled it into her lap. "Don't tell me you refused an offer you didn't fully hear!"

"Oh, I heard it, all right. Go back, receive a full pardon and reinstatement of my titles and add a couple more while we're at it—crown prince and regent were thrown into the package. Future king was dangled, too, provided I live longer than King B."

"King B...!" A laugh burst out of her. "Oh, God...*King B.* I wonder what he'd do if you called him that to his face."

His grin widened. "I'll make sure you're around when I do, and you can have a front-row seat to his reaction."

She resisted the urge to explore those dimples with everything she had. "You've really loosened up, haven't you?"

He gave a pout of such mock hurt that she started hurting in earnest. "You mean I was a tight-assed bore before, don't you?"

She remembered the view she'd gotten last night of that certain part of his anatomy, and the comment that he was even more tight-assed now almost escaped.

When she opened her mouth, what came out was, "I don't know. I was too much of an awestruck idiot to notice."

Not much better. Judging by the heated look on his face, not better at all.

Before she could beg him to just…do anything, he seemed to make a decision to leave her hanging. "So—they're still not offering an apology, but a 'pardon,' right?" She nodded, not liking where this was going. "They can't bring themselves to admit even partial responsibility, want us all to pretend I'm the supplicant here. *Ajab*…incredible. And in return for their clemency what are they offering? Beside something I don't want anymore?"

"Wanting it or not isn't an issue here. You are *needed*."

"Am I? And am I needed beyond what my massive wealth and power can provide? Are my views—which got me exiled in the first place—suddenly necessary? Or should I leave those behind?"

"I am sure we can achieve a satisfying middle ground."

"If that's all they authorized you to offer me, let me tell you what 'middle ground' translates to with them: 'Our way, or the highway.' They keep saying 'make a commitment and we'll work it out.' But what they really want is for me to uphold the very policies I disagreed with so strongly that I paid the highest price for the chance of changing them. I thought ceasing to be a Castaldinian would be worth it if my punishment started a movement to support my views, instigated a climate to incubate change. But they made sure my side of the matter was never heard. And they want me to be king of this stuck-in-time land? Who do they think they're kidding?"

She exhaled. "I really think the time for kidding is past."

"*No* kidding, pun oh so intended. Say—I gather King B didn't tell you that his need of me isn't as desperate as he makes it out to be. He forgot to mention that tiny matter of two more men who are equally capable of taking on the role as I am, didn't he?"

The way he said *King B…!* Her lips twitched. "In fact, he did mention them."

His eyebrows rose, genuine surprise tingeing his expression. "He told you about Durante and Ferruccio?"

"He didn't mention names. Just that there have always been three candidates for the crown, with you topping the list."

His face settled back into that knowing expression. "Did he tell you *why* I topped the list?"

"Just that you, as impossible as it sounds, are less problematic, that you hate him and Castaldini less."

He shook his head in a mixture of irony and something that looked like grudging admiration, even fondness. "That old fox. Always telling enough truth to make his logic irrefutable, hiding enough to make himself too noble to be denied. So he kept his accounts in the present, didn't say why only I was considered worthy. Until I blew it big time, that is."

She sat up. "My conspiracy theory centers are all ears."

He laughed, lay back on the couch. She didn't follow, somehow. "It's not a conspiracy, it's worse. It's something far more petty. And far more damaging. You know it well. It goes by many names. Tradition, conservatism, ancestry, bloodlines. All I have on those two men is an accident of birth that made me eligible and eliminated them from the running."

Suddenly something clicked. "Durante? As in Durante D'Agostino, King Benedetto's estranged eldest son?"

He nodded.

"Whoa. The current king's son. The cardinal no-no."

He gave a vicious snort. "And even in their hour of need, the old farts can't bring themselves to overlook the letter of a law that should have expired when the need for it did."

"In their defense, that law has made Castaldini one of the most stable kingdoms in the world."

"And the most stagnant."

"And you took advantage of that law yourself," she retorted. "Seems you always thought Durante—your best friend—as good a candidate as you, yet you didn't make a peep about changing the law to give him an equal playing field."

He sat up again, his eyes spitting emerald fire. "And I'm ashamed that I didn't. I'm even more ashamed that I saw the error of my ways only when I had no choice anymore. But now that I have the choice again, I'm making up for being a party to such a backward practice. I'm daring them to *really* let the best man win."

"I do believe that's who they believe you are."

"I'm only the best man because I'll be more acceptable to the masses, who've been indoctrinated to accept only the old laws."

"Isn't that a huge factor to consider? Don't you factor in popularity and acceptability when assigning your CEOs?"

"If I ever take the crown, it would be to move Castaldini to the point where laws that no longer suit the times are phased out. I would start by seeing to it that the people come to decide who's best for Castaldini without ticking off a list of criteria topped by an outdated, demeaning and just plain prejudiced birth requirement."

She gaped at him as everything he'd said slotted in place. And she exclaimed, "You're a social reformer and a modernizer!"

"You say this with the same revulsion you'd say 'a womanizer.'"

"It's not revulsion. It's realization. I'm shocked. I was led to believe you were revolutionary, but not in that sense."

"In what sense, then?"

"In the establishment-destroying, eco-depleting sense."

"And you believed that?"

"Why not? You're ruthless in your takeovers and your enterprises are sprouting mega-size urban developments."

"So? My conquests are prospering. Go check with my longest-term ones and ask if they'd change a thing. As for developments, I build those where it suits the social and ecological climate, and after careful consideration of all ramifications. I don't go around haphazardly overdeveloping land and exhausting resources."

She somehow believed every word, no need to check. She should have let it rest, but she found herself adding, "And why should your being a womanizer revolt me? It's none of my business."

One formidable eyebrow shot up. "Really? Interesting." Then both eyebrows dipped into an ominous line. "And I'm not."

"Not what?"

"A womanizer. I have too many handicaps to be one."

"Handicaps?"

"Fastidiousness, wariness, allergies to pointless pursuits…"

"Don't men consider physical gratification the point?"

"Do you always go around dispensing general condescension on all men, or am I just blessed? And then, you're counter-asserting that women don't consider physical gratification of importance? The old paradigm that women want emotion while men want sex?"

"That paradigm has stood the test of time and the approval of the majority. That's not to say it applies to everyone."

"It sure doesn't apply to me. And physical gratification comes with a womanful of traits, whims, demands and trouble."

"In other words, it comes attached to a sentient being." His eyes remained steady, as if he was trying to read her mind. She let out a shaky breath. "Phew. The one way to avoid such nuisances is to…rent a companion. And I can't see you doing that."

His eyes turned lethal. "You always had perfect sight."

"Then how do you find any women who fulfill your criteria of being a non-imposition? And you think Castaldinians are unreasonable?"

"My criteria aren't affecting present and future generations, I can make them as unreasonable as I like. I don't need to make concessions, either, since feminine wiles no longer work on me."

"You mean they once did?"

"Oh, yes, all the way."

Her heart did its best to explode from her ribs.

He'd—he'd been…in love? All the way? Before or after her? And he was telling her all this…why? Warning her off while pulling her in? Was that what her tormentor was trying to do to her?

Suddenly he sat forward, thrust a hand into her hair. He let a thick lock sift through his fingers before he groaned, "Not that it doesn't suit you, it does, even more than your natural hair color did, but what made you dye your hair black?"

Leandro groaned again. He'd swerved from the vulnerabilities he was exposing, groped for the diversion of something that gnawed at his curiosity. And she looked as if he'd slapped her.

"Don't you mean why did I stop dyeing my hair blond?"

He gaped at her. "You're a natural brunette?"

"You didn't realize that? But then it stands to reason."

"What do you mean by that?"

"You knew nothing about me, apparently."

"I knew plenty about you. I bet I know everything."

"You're talking in the biblical sense? How original of you."

"I mean in every sense."

"Yeah? Okay, let's test this knowledge. Or are you going to plead memory holes due to the time lapse?"

"I have the memory of an entire herd of elephants."

"And the comparative rampage damage potential."

He harrumphed. "I never rampage."

"Of course not. You're too organized and premeditated for that. I should have said 'incursion.' That *is* your MO, whether it's on a personal or a global level."

"By definition, an *incursion* is hated, resisted. I remember nothing but…approval, encouragement. On a personal level."

"You have that effect on the people you take over—the super power of Stockholm syndrome. It took me a year and a half to realize what you did to me."

He went totally still. "What did I do to you?"

She looked at him as if he'd once strangled her cat and didn't remember it. She finally shook her head, let out a rough chuckle. "You didn't even realize I dyed my hair."

"And that made me…insensitive? Negligent? The hair on your head looked so natural with your tan. Thanks to your grooming habits, there was none anywhere else to give me a clue. What else did I allegedly do to you?"

She shook her head again. "You exist in a universe starring you, don't you? Other people are the bit players who exist just so you can bounce your lines off them."

"Why are you saying that when you know it wasn't true…then?"

"Listen, I'm not criticizing you or laying blame…"

"No? You have a strange way of *not* doing that. The way you tell it, I was an egocentric, exploitative bastard. Come to think of it, I do remember a comment you hurled at me on your way out of my life. About my so-called self-absorption. Is that how you rationalize the way you ended things between us?"

"'Things' would have ended between us sooner rather than later, and you know it. I did us both a favor—"

"Why don't you speak for yourself?"

"Fine, I did myself a favor by not sticking around to experience the deterioration of 'things' before their inevitably nasty end."

He stared into the twin storms of her eyes.

Was this her admission that there'd never been more than self-interest behind her actions? Or was it self-preservation? Her words *could* be interpreted that way. Had his rage at the time made her fear he'd take his bitterness out on her?

What was he *thinking?* Why was he debating this yet again? He'd admitted there was no way to find out the truth for sure. And what did it even matter? That was then. This was now.

He was taking now. And when the end came this time, he

wouldn't spend eight more years agonizing over the reasons why. The whys would be of his own orchestration. And his own timing.

It was time to set things in motion.

Phoebe felt like a cat who'd just streaked across an antiques exhibit and sent everything crashing to the ground. Hurling those bombshells of self-pity sure felt as if it had caused comparative damage. So what now? Back to square subzero?

Her heart clanged as he unfurled to his full six-foot-five and gestured to someone in the distance. Music at once drowned out the cacophony of memories, the tumult of this confrontation.

Then he extended his hand to her in imperious invitation.

"Dance with me."

He'd said the same thing the night they'd met. Before they'd even been introduced. She remembered only that he'd taken her in his embrace and that her feet hadn't touched the ground until he'd first kissed her and changed the course of her life forever.

Now was the same. She didn't know when she'd taken his hand, or how she'd reached the dance floor. All she knew was that he surrounded her like an extension of her own body, all her missing parts, moving with her, moving her, as if she shared his nervous pathways, as if he was in control of hers.

Suddenly her whole body shuddered on a shockwave. His whisper. Against her temple. "You learned to dance the guadara."

The guadara. That unique dance born of the inextricable Moorish, Amazigh and Italian folklores that formed Castaldini. She'd seen it performed in rural areas on romantic occasions and at celebrations. She'd never danced it before. She'd never tried.

She was dancing it now, the sensuous rhythm turning her body into a malleable instrument that merged with the demands and vitality of the beat, flowed into the power and beauty of his body, rode the grace and fluency of his movements.

But soon the dance morphed into something else —syncopated footwork, a full-body embrace, entwining legs, a creation of his own invention, and she suspected from the intensity coming off of him in waves, his own improvisation. And that she managed to follow his spontaneous lead, move as one with him…magic.

Suddenly he spooled her away, whirled her back, gathered her, back to chest, in a off-the-ground hug that had emotion blossoming into pain behind her eyes, threatening to burst into an outpouring of pent-up longing and heartache.

Before she could bring herself to struggle, he swept her around and into an embrace that no longer pretended to be about dancing.

She began to shake. Recollections of his possession were brutal, accomplices to his passion, to his eyes as they bore down, *burned* down on her. She needed a reprieve. She needed… *Needed.* "Leandro, I—I…"

He wouldn't let her find words. He lifted her, making her feel weightless, soaring. His arms fused her to his chest, where she'd once nestled for hours, under which she'd writhed in ecstasy, where she'd dreamed of being again every day of the past eight years.

She moaned her greed, her welcome. His eyes grew voracious. Volcanic. She wanted him to devour her, destroy her.

But he only watched her, singed her with the emotions fast-forwarding across his face. Why wouldn't he give anything to her? His lips, his breath, his possession? Did he want more than surrender?

She succumbed, gave him more, clutched his hair and pulled with all she had. A growl revved inside his chest, driving her to her toes, reaching for his half-open lips. She sealed them, took his scalding *"Phoebe"* and breath inside her.

He still didn't respond until she whimpered, *"Please…"*

The broken entreaty seemed to shatter whatever was holding him back. His lips crashed down on hers, wrenched hot, dark, desperate kisses from her depths. *Yes…yes…*Leandro…

Leandro. From the first moment, everything about him, everything with him, had been beyond reason, out of the bounds of right and wrong. He'd warranted one-off rules. Still did. And it had been so long without this…without *him*. No reason was good enough for that kind of deprivation. Had he suffered too? *Tell me…*

One of his hands answered in spasms of passion in her hair, the other pressing her where contact was a necessity. His legs continued the confession, rough, urgent, spreading hers for the relentlessness of his arousal. Her core wept, remembering, ready. His mouth told her the rest, every molten glide, every invasive thrust showing her how much, just *how much*…she'd lost.

Suddenly he tore away. She cried out as if he'd ripped her flesh off, surged up, needing his breath so she could breathe, his heartbeat so her heart wouldn't stop. He let her drag him down, only to bury his face in her neck, her breasts, growling jolts of molten agony to the very depths of her. Then he groaned, "I will do it."

She jerked as he pushed away, left her swaying without his support. "You—you mean you're accepting the succession?"

"We will have to wait and see if I'll accept it. But I will go back to Castaldini. On one condition."

Tremors wracked her. "I…*knew* you'd make demands."

"One demand. Do you also know what it is?"

She bit her lip, trepidation and temptation turning her body into their battleground. "Something concerning me."

"And what would that be, do you think? From the man who 'muddies the professional with the personal'? Come on, guess."

"You want me to…to…" She couldn't say it, damn him.

"What?" he prodded, a huge cat nudging its exhausted catch to entertain him some more. "Sacrifice your virtue for Castaldini?"

That turned her stone-cold steady. "How can I, when my virtue is something of the past? As you're best equipped to testify."

His face turned to stone, too. "Virginity is not virtue,

Phoebe. Or have you been on Castaldini so long that you've subscribed to its dated, narrow-minded views of morality?"

Her temperature fluctuated from a furnace's to a freezer's. "So what do you want? Me, as your secret lover again?"

His smile had her heart thundering with arousal…and dread.

Then he whispered, soft and annihilating, "Nothing so simple. Until I decide to accept the succession or not, I'm staying in my ancestral home in El Jamida on the western shores of Castaldini. My condition is that you live with me there."

Five

"Live with you?"

Phoebe was stunned to realize that squeak had issued from her. Her speech center was still functioning. Incredible.

Leandro was moving away. He stopped at a waist-high round quartz table sporting another buried-in-ice bottle.

He filled two flutes and flowed back to hand her one. "You object to the condition? Or is it only to the term 'live'? If so, I wonder why. We'd both 'live' while we're staying there. What would you rather call it? Exist with me? Survive with me? Occupy the same space-time continuum with me?"

"Okay. I'll call on you when I'm brainstorming my stand-up comedy routine…" She stopped, exclaimed, "Live with you…*openly?*"

The mockery in his eyes leapt a few notches higher. "You'd rather be my secret lover?"

"That was a question, not an offer."

He pressed the flute into her hand, engulfed the other in his and swept her to the table, where he hoisted her up on the gleaming metal and red-satin stool, had her feeling he'd perched her at the edge of a skyscraper. He dragged his own stool to touch hers, seared her left side with his body heat as he mounted it. She stared at him with the same fascination that people watched catastrophes in progress.

He gestured to someone, and lazy, sense-soaking music flowed over them. He took her hand, tilted his head at her. "How about being my guest and guide? I'm seeing no more than necessary of those who exiled me. You understand that I don't harbor nostalgic feelings toward them. But I am out of touch with Castaldini, and I'll need updates on its current situation. You know, the pulse of the street, the daily worries, the existing public opinions on everything from sports to politics. You are the perfect liaison to reconnect me with it all."

This was what he meant? What he wanted from her?

She wouldn't examine the jumble of relief and letdown.

Lobbing this ball back in his court was her only way out of dissecting her stupidity. "Why am I the perfect liaison? I can give you a list off the top of my head of a dozen people who'd be far better at it, born and bred Castaldinians who'd be only too eager to provide you with whatever you need."

"I want *you.*"

She choked. On her heart. On his intensity. On longing for what had never and would never be. He'd always wanted her for the wrong reasons. She'd bet he still did.

Instead of arguing against the far deeper wrongness of his reasons now, all that came out was a stifled, "Why?"

"Because most people think nothing of embellishing or outright lying to steer me to the decision they want me to make. Your bluntness proves you're the only one who'll give me unbiased reports, that you'll tell me only the truth. And I need that to come to a decision."

That didn't sound like a wrong reason. It sounded very good. Too good to be the truth? At least, the only truth?

Only one way to find out. Only one way to be with this man from now on. Head-on, full-blown confrontation.

"And besides needing my insights and whacks of candor upside your head, do you also want to pick up where we left off?"

"Yes." The word disrupted her nerves wholesale with its force. Then he made it worse. *"Si."* Then even worse. *"Aiwa."*

She spilled half of her flute. "I…got it…in one language."

He took the flute from her, took her wet fingers to his mouth, sucked them to a cinder. "It wasn't enough to tell you how much I want you in one language. It never was. I doubt anything will ever be. And if I had any doubt that you want me as much, those…fireworks put it to rest. The desire between us is not only as explosive as before, it has intensified. We're more complex people now, with far more extensive knowledge of ourselves and the world, and it has only deepened our attraction."

He let go of her hand after he'd decimated whatever reason or resistance she had. As he dried the puddle she'd made, she wanted to tell him to get something bigger. For the puddle she'd become.

He went on, intensity now morphed into matter-of-factness. "But I'm only declaring my intent. This time I'm not sweeping you away to bed. It's up to you when you decide to come to me."

So *über*-businessman was back, huh? With the need for driving his bid home over and said bid certain to be soon begged for?

"When, not *if,* huh?" He gave her a serene look. *Wanna contest that?* it said. And oh, how she wished she could. She couldn't. Not when the truth was *I wanna come to you…*right now.

She groped for something to say that wouldn't be a lie or made her a self-destructive fool. "And what about the storm of speculation this will kick up? You don't care what your possible future subjects think of your actions?"

"Of course not." He made it sound as if he'd care about the opinion of the island's population of monk seals first. "You will have an official job of the highest order. Whatever else we choose to be involved in is our business. We are both free agents and too grown-up to care what people think or say."

"That wasn't your position in the past, when you were obsessively secretive about our…liaison."

Something harsh flared in his eyes. Or maybe she'd imagined it. Her powers of observation weren't the epitome of reliability right now. "My reasons for secrecy no longer apply now."

Yeah, tell her about it. Worrying that their liaison would threaten his chances of capturing the crown wasn't a consideration now. They'd give it to him this time even if he kept a harem.

"And with the changes in circumstances and in ourselves, we owe it to what we have raging between us to explore it to the fullest, without the shackles our old situation imposed on it."

"So this is all about 'what we have raging between us'? It has nothing to do with having your way after all these years? Not that I know if your offer then *was* to 'live' with you, mind you."

His eyes turned unfathomable. "It was something along those…lines. And you think this has an element of payback?"

"Why not? You're a man who's used to having all your whims bowed to. Both Castaldini and I thwarted you then. You'd be getting even with both in one fell swoop."

"You still can't believe revenge is not my style, eh? No, Phoebe, this has nothing to do with asserting my will, over you or Castaldini. This is purely what I want. What I'm burning for."

She struggled to gulp down the heart that kept squeezing into her throat. "But if you're making it a condition of coming back to Castaldini, then it's an ultimatum that reeks of coercion."

"It's a statement of intent. And then, what reason do you have to say no? When it's clear no one you've been with has measured up to me?"

He paused. Waiting for a corroboration?

He'd have to wait another lifetime.

When she made no answer, he again decimated all projections of what he'd say next. "I haven't found anyone to hold a candle to you, either. And I felt that way when I held memories of your far less potent self. As you did of me. Now,

I can hardly imagine what it will be like between us. But I intend to find out. I need to, to get this out of my system, as you said. I believe you need it, too. And we should wallow in every second of it."

Okay. He had been lying through his teeth. He *was* out to exact revenge on her. The cruelest, most annihilating sort. She could feel months ticking off her life expectancy with each word. And whatever turmoil didn't consume, temptation would.

But she had to kick to the surface for one last breath before she sank to the bottom under the weight of both.

"And that's your position concerning me made crystal-clear. Great." She inhaled. "About your position on Castaldini. I admit I let prejudices form my opinion of why you'd be the worst thing that could happen to Castaldini now. But I still believe you would be more hazard than help. Don't get me wrong, I do think that, with the methods you used to build your financial empire, compounded with the views you gave me a glimpse of, you'd make a formidable ruler. But I don't think you're best suited to be Castaldini's."

And he laughed until she almost slumped off her stool.

He wiped his eyes, his laughter subsiding. "Ah, Phoebe, every word you say makes me more undecided. Are you being Castaldini's top negotiator, so devious you're saying exactly what will reel me in to the challenge, or are you being confrontational for the sake of it and as unprofessional as you accused me of being?"

"I'd love to lay claim to deviousness. But I can't." She shot him a sullen look. "Not with you around."

"So you're being confrontational and unprofessional?"

"Just appallingly, undiplomatically truthful. I think you're unbelievably powerful and proficient. But you're also driven and fixated on a certain mindset. You could make a magnificent king if you would consider other outlooks, if you would temper your views and methods. If you don't, you could put an end to the monarchy."

"And you wonder why only you will do?" He pulled her to

him again and robbed her of inhibitions and self-preservation. All she wanted to do was nuzzle him, inhale him, open her mouth over his pulse, taste his vitality and forget that a time when he wasn't filling her world had or would ever come. "So that's your opinion concerning my eligibility for Castaldini's crown. What of my eligibility to be your lover? Are you going to sacrifice your truthfulness and say I'm not the best man for that role?"

He wanted a verbal confession? Tough. He'd have to settle for her turning into estrogen goo in his arms.

"What I want to know is, is your condition a deal breake—?"

He didn't let her finish. "Definitely."

"And you say it isn't a coercive ultimatum?"

He pulled her almost over his lap, cupped her face in his large hand with such gentleness. Everything inside her surged, tensed. "You need to get one thing straight, Phoebe. I spent my first thirty years with one goal on my mind: becoming the king of Castaldini. Then, suddenly, it was not an option anymore. I no longer believe it's my destiny. I'm willing to give it a chance, but if you refuse my condition, I'll be relieved, since that will put an end to your mission. They'll be forced to go after Durante or Ferruccio and leave me out of it. And without the intrusion of duty, I'll make you mine again that much sooner."

"Then you're not giving the crown serious consideration," she gasped. "It's just a pretext for what you really want."

"I always give any undertaking my absolute best intentions and efforts to produce the best possible results, and that's what I will give the succession proposition. But you're right. *You* are what I really want. You once knew how much I can want. It's nothing to how much I want you now. I put duty and the world's expectations ahead of my desires before. But I've lived too hard and I know now what really matters to me. Having you, slaking my thirst for you, is my number one priority. It's what I *need*. Anything else comes second. Or not at all. Your choice. But whatever you choose, I'm making you mine again. It's up to you if I do it while giving Castaldini another chance."

Too much. What he was. What he said. What he did to her. "Resistance is futile, huh?"

He brushed his lips below her ear, along her jaw, to the corner of her mouth before sprinkling her quivering lower lip with what felt like a hundred kisses and a thousand volts. "You want to resist? Because you think you should? Why? To what end?"

Indeed. To continue living her excitingly barren life?

He knew as well as she did that she couldn't resist him. Didn't want to. That didn't mean she shouldn't make terms of her own. Something to stop her from exchanging inertia for a plummet from a plane. Sans parachute.

She stopped his tormenting lips with hers. Satisfaction splashed through her when he jolted in surprise, then shuddered in response. Then he took over the kiss.

Seconds from begging him to finish her, now, here, she tore her mouth away, settled for the words that just minutes ago she'd thought he'd have to wait a lifetime to hear.

"I want you, Leandro." She buried her face in his neck as she admitted this was far stronger than she was. That it scared her witless and it didn't matter. She wanted it. Against all reason. For all reasons. "And yes...I want you more than ever. But no rush, right?" She raised her face to him, knew what he'd read there. Vulnerability, nervousness, capitulation, excitement...greed. "I'm taking you at your word about that."

He groaned and crushed her to him for a moment before he loosened his embrace, let her slump back in its circle in a daze. "And I always keep my word, Phoebe. I won't sweep you into my bed. You will come to me this time."

She closed her eyes, let his spell claim the last corner of her sanity, and marveled at what a difference a few hours could make. She'd come here intending to deliver her arguments, stay the hell away from him, then run back to Castaldini to burrow out of sight until he'd made his decision—and bolt when he had.

Now—just look at her. Eager to go back to Castaldini with him, and the only burrowing she wanted to do was into his arms. As if he knew, as he'd always seemed to know, he stood up, lifted her from her stool and floated her back to the dance floor, taking her precisely where she wanted to be.

What felt like a few days of languorous, erotic torture later, she heard him rumble against her neck. "I have another promise, *bella malaki*." She threw her head back over his arm, waited for it, at peace, in torment. "I won't rush you, but there won't be a minute when I won't show you how much I want you in my arms and in my bed."

Six

Was it possible for a man to get older, to amass world-spanning experience and world-shaping influence, and not add one ounce of judgment or restraint? Basically, to remain a fool?

Leandro let out a shuddering exhalation as he stared at the source of all loss of control. She was presenting him with the elegance of her profile, the sootiness of her lashes shading her silver gaze as it turned sideways to the clarity and endless-ness of the horizon as they drove along the coast heading to the capital, Jawara, from the private airport where his jet had landed on Castaldini.

Such beauty. The only kind that had completely com-manded his appreciation, ruled his libido, wreaked havoc with his restraint.

Prince Overwhelming, indeed. Says Mind-Blowing Beauty.

He'd forgotten his plan to make her pursue him inside an hour. An hour? A *minute*. Within that time frame, he had barely stopped himself from dragging her down on that dance floor and taking her then and there. He'd not only succumbed to her "negotiations," he'd practically blackmailed her into letting him do so.

And he hadn't stopped there. Instead of ending that blistering night by taking her back to his bed after she'd admitted her desire, he'd sat there and promised he wouldn't.

And here they were, with the sizzling rules of their new liaison laid down, finally in Castaldini.

All through the trip onboard his private jet, she'd tried to keep their interaction flowing, to inject it with lightness and teasing, and he'd struggled to match her attitude.

But it had been no use.

There was too much tension and pent-up passion between them, too much anticipation, too much…everything.

And that hadn't been all. Something else had been happening. Something he'd been totally unprepared for.

The closer they'd gotten to Castaldini, and as the reality of his return there crystallized, the more his ability to keep up the pretense had faded. He'd looked down at the island as the jet had started to descend and had felt a pressure building inside his chest, around his throat, behind his eyes. It had escalated with every meter's descent. And it had had nothing to do with the pressure change inside the cabin.

By the time they'd landed and disembarked to the limo he'd had waiting, the imaginary pins holding up his smile had seemed to pierce his flesh. He'd had to relinquish the expression, as well as any attempt at communication.

He'd been relieved when she'd withdrawn into herself, too. For about fifteen minutes. Then restlessness had started to claw its way to the surface. How was it possible to miss her when she was within arm's reach?

He wasn't about to reinitiate dialogue. He couldn't. He had nothing to say—nothing he could put into words. But he needed to reconnect with her. Just…feel her. He reached for her hand.

She surrendered it to him with a squeeze that transmitted directly to his heart, and a smile that lodged there, too, before she resumed watching the scenery rushing by her window.

He dragged his eyes away from her, forced himself to look through his own window. He cursed himself for the reluctance, the trepidation that gripped his guts. It was just an island, just another beautiful country with magnificent nature and blessed weather. Looking at the scenery wouldn't hurt him.

But it did. He felt things splintering inside him. The once-severed and reattached tethers of his heart snapped under the strain, one after the other with each mile deeper onto Castaldinian soil. For eight years, he'd lived with the certainty—the hopelessness—that he'd never see this land again.

He hadn't imagined he could feel this way. He'd thought he'd long ago moved beyond such frailties as homesickness and nostalgia, that this land and all it represented had no more hold on him.

He might not have known, but Phoebe clearly had. She knew. Everything that was roiling inside him. He now understood what she was doing. She was trying to turn off her aura, her presence. She was trying to give him privacy. To sort through the chaos that returning to his homeland had kicked up inside him.

He felt something too warm for comfort swell inside his rib cage. Something achingly sweet. Gratitude. That she understood, gauged his needs and gave him the spiritual space and silent empathy that would soothe him, ameliorate his turmoil. And he just knew she'd also sense when he'd dealt with the first shockwave of response, would come back to him then.

He shook his head in self-deprecation as he succumbed, let storm through him the emotions he'd believed he'd never feel again—for the land that had exiled him, and the woman who'd deserted him.

Yes. A fool. In so many incurable ways.

Phoebe kept her eyes on the rushing by Jawara.

As capitals went, it was probably the only one in the twenty-first century that didn't have one building built later than the eighteenth. Its mixture of Gothic, Moorish and baroque architecture was considered the best-preserved in the world. Or it used to be. There'd been cuts in the restoration programs over the last twenty years, channeling of funds into venues of a more pressing nature. To her—someone who hadn't seen Castaldini before those times—the kingdom looked magnificent anyway, even with the disrepair. But Castaldinians said the decline had been noticeable. And though she hadn't been at her most observant of the outside world these past years, she'd noticed the deterioration deepening.

Jawara did still feel like a jewel, as its Moorish name proclaimed it to be, sparkling under perpetual sunlight, nestling between the banks of the Boriana River and the Montalbo mountains before giving way to rolling plains to the north and south. But it did look like a cracked jewel the closer you looked. Now it needed the help of its closest peak, the 2,010-meter Odesilia only a few kilometers from the city center, to augment the majestic feel that it was losing. And as they entered the oldest part of the city, which was dominated by the massive royal palace overlooking it on a hill between two smaller mountains, she drew the parallel for the first time.

The whole place was getting old and tired. Like its ruler.

That was why it was imperative for a new king to take over.

A powerhouse like Leandro could be Castaldini's salvation in so many ways. *If* he could see that Castaldini needed only revitalization, not reinvention.

For though he thought the country stuck in time, she saw it as a refuge from the invasion of modernity. Let the rest of the world join that parade. Castaldini felt like the last stronghold of times gone by. And no, she wasn't romanticizing those times by calling them the good old days. The "old days" had had their share of the bad. And the extremely bad. But though Castaldini wasn't perfect and was showing its age, she believed it had the potential to become the best possible combination of old and new, under the leadership of the monarch Leandro could be.

She looked at him now. She couldn't get enough of looking

at him. Never would. But right now, worry was a fist tightening over her heart. How *did* he see this place? Did it have the same magic and potential in his eyes? Or did he see it through the cast of bitterness and the critical eye of the developer? How did he feel as they approached the royal palace, the place she'd come to call home in the past ten years? The place he'd thought he would call home once, only to have his plans so viciously torn apart?

She hung on every nuance as his eyes, now as verdant as Castaldini's meadows, as clear and jewel-like as its shores, roamed the enormous complex of buildings comprising the palace.

They passed by the National Library, the Royal Museum, the ceremonial halls and government offices on their way to the royal apartments and the king's state rooms. It took a while to get there, as the palace grounds had a depth of ten miles and the palace itself lay over four hundred thousand square feet.

She hadn't been inside even one-quarter of its more than one thousand rooms during her stay. She'd only once visited the rooms most famous for their design and decoration, the king's and queen's apartments. It had been a chance visit with Julia about three years ago. Those rooms had indeed been something to see, even if the deceased queen's apartments had the stale feel of a shrine, and the king's had shown the most neglect she'd seen anywhere in Castaldini. She'd then thought the visit worth it just for the mural-framed study window from which the king waved to subjects and visitors in the Solarella Square on Fridays and Sundays, and the ceiling frescoes painted by masters who'd inspired Michelangelo and Raphael.

She regretted ever seeing the apartments. She now had an indelible image of the quarters that would one day be Leandro's if he accepted the succession—and those that would house the woman Leandro would marry.

She no longer had the least delusion she'd be that woman. She wondered how she'd harbored it once. She was certainly not queen material. But then, she hadn't thought of it that way in the past. She'd wanted only to be Leandro's. She'd never thought about what being his when he became crown prince, then king, would entail.

She could imagine both apartments revamped for the new, in-their-prime king and queen, saw the connecting room between them, with a king-size bed placed below the magnificent central dome, where Leandro and his…his…

She tore her eyes away from his face, her thoughts away from the images. But it was no use. She could still see him, caught in the throes of passion as he'd been with her years ago. But this time he was with a faceless woman. Leandro. Growling in pleasure, driven to ferocity by that woman's touch, that woman's body and hunger, his magnificent body spread over her, undulating in a fever of arousal, driving between the splay of her greed, roaring in completion, spilling…

She bit down to stop a surge of tremors. How stupid was it to feel this way, when she'd made a pact with him about the nature of their liaison this time? The kind designed to burn someone out of one's system? What she did believe she needed?

The limo glided to a smooth stop at the gates leading to the king's quarters. She was thankful for the bustle of activity as Leandro descended from the limo and came around to hand her down, as they were met by dozens of people pouring out welcomes and opening doors all the way into the king's inner sanctum.

Once they were alone, Leandro exclaimed, "*Per Dio,* this place is falling apart."

Phoebe frowned. The place *was* in bad shape. King Benedetto hadn't had any renovations—nor any repairs—done since long before she'd been here. Oh, the work needed to preserve the palace as a national monument had been done, but she now wondered if his total lack of interest in preserving his own living quarters was his way of mourning his wife's death and his eldest son's estrangement. And his decision to exile Leandro?

The king's secretary interrupted her musings. The king was waiting for Prince Leandro in the Throne Room.

As the man turned to usher him there, Leandro gestured for him to wait outside, gave the place another sweeping glance, his eyes heavy. "It seems dilapidation is now considered heritage to be preserved in Castaldini. You're going to have a tough time getting me to change my conviction that Castaldini is stuck in time. It might even change to going back in time."

She grasped his forearm, anxious to ameliorate his disappointment. "I do believe the condition of these rooms is a reflection of King Benedetto's state of mind. Not that that's good news."

"It wouldn't be as bad if Jawara wasn't suffering the same signs of neglect."

She could protest *that*. "Jawara is nowhere near this bad."

"I hope not, as this is… *Dio,* this is unacceptable." She found nothing to say to that. It was. "I hope you're right about this being exceptionally bad, that on closer inspection Jawara won't reveal the same level of deterioration, since you've been right about many things. Being Castaldinian whether I like it or not, for one. It hurt, physically, just flying into the airspace. Setting foot here again felt like stepping back into the worst days of my life—and that was nothing compared to driving through the streets, feeling the majesty of the place dimmed and seeing my worst projections coming true."

She had so much to say. That it wasn't that bad. That he could make it so much better. But she had no words. All she could think was that she couldn't bear to see him…*subdued* like this, almost dejected. Not her imperturbable, indomitable Leandro.

And she did something she hadn't thought she ever would. She threw her arms around him and hugged him. Just hugged him. A with-all-her-strength squeeze of empathy and compassion.

She was about to step back when he caught her back in a compulsive crush. When he let her breathe again, she blinked back her agitation as he touched his forehead to hers, like a lion butting his awesome head against his mate in affection.

Then his whisper seared her, with its softness, its sensuality. Its sincerity. "*Grazie, tesoro mabuba,* I needed that."

He left her struggling with a widespread nervous dysfunction at his endearment—beloved treasure—and with a shuddering inhalation, stepped away. Then he crooked his arm. She blinked.

He quirked one eyebrow at her. "You got them the prize they wanted—worthless as it is." Before she could protest, retract that piece of petty vindictiveness, she realized he was teasing. "Don't tell me you're letting it walk into their greedy hands unescorted?"

Seven

"Leandro, *il mio figlio, sede benvenuta*."

Welcome home, my son.

Phoebe winced as King Benedetto's words seemed to ripple in ever-expanding waves in the Throne Room.

He was underlining the significance and official nature of the meeting, his respect and appreciation of Leandro's presence and position by receiving him there. Big mistake.

She wished he'd met Leandro in his private rooms. And she wished he'd made it a closed meeting. With her new insight into Leandro's character and preferences—which was in absolute contrast to the opinion she'd previously held of both—King Benedetto would have put his best foot forward by approaching Leandro on a personal level. This man really didn't know what he meant to Leandro, even after all the enmity and estrangement.

And then he had to complicate matters further. *Welcome home my son* was probably the worst thing he could have said in the presence of the Council, who didn't have any measure of Leandro's affection and respect, whose injury was untempered by entrenched hero worship and memories of much better times.

She found herself holding her breath, dreading Leandro's response. What was he thinking? Feeling? She remembered his state eight years ago, the soul-permeating anguish at the amputation of his goals and identity. Would reinstatement, would welcome to what King Benedetto claimed to be Leandro's home, the palace, the whole kingdom, be enough? Could anything be?

Leandro crossed hands over heart in that gesture that was quintessentially Castaldinian. *"Grazie molto…"* he wiggled his eyebrows, once "…King B."

Gasps swept through the expansive hall, like a gale blowing through a forest of dying leaves. They couldn't have been more shocked if Leandro had made an indecent gesture. Everyone except the king himself. It was difficult to read his skewed face from this distance, but she felt his reaction. Relief. He must have been prepared for far worse than Leandro's irreverence.

Leandro gave her a sideways glance. Her throat closed. His eyes were eloquent, but she understood none of the things they were telling her. Were his wounds opening, his bitterness pouring out, overwhelming his restraint and his intentions to give the people who'd stripped him of too much a fair chance, the opportunity to atone? Was he deciding he'd made a mistake coming here…?

She gasped. He'd winked at her, slammed her with conspiring mischief and harsh-edged satisfaction—and the message that his desire was mounting, that nothing could take his mind away from it. Then he turned to King Benedetto.

"This place is stuffy. How about we reduce…" his gaze panned over the Council members "…carbon dioxide production?" More gasps ensued. He shook his head. "You'd better do something fast. Oxygen levels are plummeting with those spikes in consumption."

This time Phoebe's heart twittered with excitement. Enjoyment. All these years she'd loved and lusted after Leandro and she'd never suspected how deviously, deliciously witty he was.

She had eyes only for him as he stood in the middle of the massive space and extreme opulence, overshadowing it all, giving no outward reaction to the Council members' displeasure as they obeyed their king's silent gesture for them to leave.

When the doors closed behind the last grumbling member, he took her hand, walked them to the bottom of the crimson carpet-covered steps leading to the gilded, carved-wood throne and the man doing his best not to slump in it.

"You're looking good," Leandro murmured.

One of the king's eyes closed. She knew both would have if the other had obeyed his emotions. When both were open, they were brighter than before. His voice reflected his agitation, too. "I don't expect courtesy from you, Leandro. Certainly not kindness."

"I've been called many things." Leandro gave her a teasing look before looking back at the king. "Kind was never one of them. I expected you to be in bad shape, what with all the desperate cries for me to come back. Now I'm almost wondering why you brought me here. You look—hell, you *feel* vital enough to me. So what's your game?"

"I may be guilty of many things, irreconcilable things where you're concerned, Leandro, but if there's one thing I never committed with you, it's lying. I'm not well. You are here because I need you. Because Castaldini needs you."

Leandro shrugged, dismissing that. "Castaldini can as easily need Durante. Or Ferruccio. I'm not your only choice."

"You are our best one."

Leandro raised a hand in a "don't" gesture. "I have no ego to appeal to here anymore. I no longer subscribe to the letter of the ancient criteria. And it's about time you sift through them and keep only what works. You're just too afraid to propose them to the people, and the Council are a bunch of stuck-up snobs who can't force themselves to look beyond the birth requirement and lineage crap."

The king seemed to have trouble finding words. Then he rasped, "I have loved you since you were born, Leandro. Osvaldo would have been the proudest father had he lived to see you become who you are. But if I were unencumbered by the laws, by people's expectations, don't you think I would have wanted my own son to succeed me?"

"Sure. If you dared approach him. Which you don't."

"You judge our choice harshly. Won't you even consider another point of view of why we made it?"

"You mean there are reasons, apart from Durante's hatred, and considering me the lesser evil, even when I was once considered public enemy number one? And you haven't even mentioned Ferruccio. His stigma is the worst in your eyes, eh?"

"There *are* factors that make you, if not the best, then the most logical choice. You're the one who once believed it his destiny to be king, the one who worked not just to succeed but to succeed *me*. You were also a diplomat."

"Again…total crap. It's just easier to reinstate an errant prince who has all criteria ticked off, rather than to recruit a prodigal prince, or—God forbid—an illegitimate one."

Silence fell. Phoebe could almost hear incredulity whistling long and loud in her head. And puzzle pieces clinking into place.

She'd been scratching her head, thinking of a Ferruccio who fit the incredibly demanding bill of succession criteria. There wasn't one. Not a D'Agostino. The only man she'd seen on Castaldini who was on par with Leandro's demigodliness and who happened to be named Ferruccio was a Selvaggio. And now she knew he was a D'Agostino as well.

"No convenient rationalizations?" Leandro asked. "But let's say I give you the benefit of the doubt, that you do believe I'm the best man for the right reasons—"

The king interrupted, his voice the very sound of desolation. "Durante didn't even call when I had my stroke. He didn't care if I lived or died. He would never agree to be my crown prince." He brought himself under control with obvious difficulty. "And yes, Ferruccio's parentage makes him very…problematic. I don't know how you come to know about him being a d'Agostino—"

"Ferruccio sought me out and told me in confidence. He didn't say exactly who his parents are. I've been wondering if you would have the guts to send the laws to hell and ask him or Durante to be your crown prince. But you're taking the easy way out."

"It's not that at all, Leandro. It's one thing for it to be whispered that Ferruccio is a D'Agostino, another to validate it so that he can take the crown. It might be imperative to divulge his parentage for people to accept him. But exhuming buried secrets would have untold repercussions on the house he belongs to. The Council were reasonable to consider him our last possible choice, for the sake of those whose lives would be turned upside down if the truth came to light."

"I see." It seemed Leandro *was* seeing this in a different light for the first time. He still didn't like it. "So you don't think much of depriving him of what he deserves—the recognition of his family, and the crown—based on nothing but fear of disrupting the self-righteousness of some over-privileged D'Agostinos and the sensibilities of the holier-than-thou masses?"

The king seemed at a loss. He exhaled. "Compromises are never totally fair or acceptable. But the fact remains—neither Durante nor Ferruccio ever wanted to be king of Castaldini. By choosing you, I won't be depriving them of something they never wanted in the first place."

Leandro shook his head, wry, resigned. "You know, we can go around in circles forever. So let's narrow down the threads of discussion. What makes *me* salvation material all of a sudden?"

"You were always that, Leandro. But you know exactly why I was forced to implement the measures I did in the past."

"I do know exactly why. I pushed you against a wall."

"You amassed power too fast, Leandro, juggled over-whelming agendas and goals. You pushed *yourself* beyond your limits."

"Oh, so now you're maintaining that I was having some sort of breakdown at the time? But I was too powerful to risk letting me run around unchecked, so you performed damage control?"

The king gave a grave nod. "That is basically the truth. Though you had worthwhile concepts, you wouldn't take into consideration the hindrances of reality versus theory, or the suitability of planting what you were proposing in our socio-political soil. You wanted your way and you wanted it imme-diately, and you started acting with a volatility that shocked me for being so out of character. I dreaded your influence on the international community. You had its ears and hearts, and they started pushing for your policies to be installed, at once, for you to take over the crown. I never expected you to turn on me to get it."

Leandro's volley was ready, lethal. "And I never expected you to commit an injustice to hang on to it."

The king didn't contest the accusation. "It was one of the most difficult choices I've ever had to make. With your passion and power, what you were proposing was not so much a succession as a coup. You might think you would have been in control, but Castaldini's enemies would have capitalized on your revolutionary policies, would have entrenched them-selves into the kingdom by invoking the pretexts of global-ism. I feared that once you made me step aside, your reign would be the beginning of the end—and that once it ended one way or the other, Castaldini itself would be no more."

An outcome she'd told him he was capable of causing. And coming from his king, it silenced Leandro.

At last he drawled, "You really believed that? You really feared I'd be the end of the monarchy?"

The king's gaze was steady. Sad. *"Si."*

Leandro inhaled, shook his head. "What's different now? I'm still the same man."

"But you're not the same. Time has tempered you and the brutal prices and constant compromises of keeping your place at the top have taught you the multiplicity of points of view and the paramount importance of implementing what works, not what you personally think is right. I'm sure that now, even though your views remain unchanged, knowing the dangers, you will find a way to make your vision come true while keeping Castaldini sovereign. And intact."

Silence. It resounded off the soaring domed ceilings. The theatrical-echo effect gave Leandro's laugh, when it burst from him, the force of a gunshot.

"You're good. In fact, I think you're too good to step down now. You've got plenty more to give."

"You've always saddled me with worth beyond my true value, an image no one could live up to, and that was why you were so bitter in your disappointment in me. But forty years of tests are catching up with me and I'm holding on only until I can pass the baton. Take it now, Leandro. I have earned my rest. Let me have it."

Leandro gave him a challenging look. "As long as you're not talking about the final, in-peace type that involves digging."

The king smiled. The first real smile she'd seen since his stroke. Leandro's drollness had that effect. She would have, too, if what she'd witnessed between the two men who meant most to her in life wasn't threatening to open the floodgates of her control.

Leandro's smile vanished, but his eyes remained almost… gentle. "Let me make my position clear, my plans clearer. I'll take care of any immediate threats, even though you make it sound as if I have the damage potential of a nuclear bomb. *Then* I need to consider your views with fresh eyes. I need to know what taking the baton from you—even temporarily—would mean, to Castaldini and to my other interests.

"But though you've managed something I thought impossible—made it almost a…pleasure to see you again—you'll see me again only if I accept the role of crown prince and/or regent. If I decide not to, I'll just leave. I would come to say goodbye properly this time, but you pack quite a wallop still, King B, and I've discovered I'm still as susceptible to your influence as ever. Seems I am as predictable as Ernesto always laments."

Then he turned to Phoebe, extended his hand. She clutched it, desperate to reconnect with him, to siphon off the turmoil she could feel roiling inside him, even when he hid it so perfectly.

He pulled her close as he turned to the king again. She gulped as she felt herself melt into his hold. The intimacy in his touch, in the way he hugged her to his side, was unmistakable. He was demonstrating the nature of their relationship for the first time ever.

Self-conscious, tongue-tied at this unexpected move, she met King Benedetto's eyes as she murmured the greetings she hadn't had a chance to utter before. Before she had a moment to wonder what the acceptance, the approval she saw in their shrewd depths meant, Leandro said, "I do have to thank you for one thing, though. Knowing your business so well, you sent me Phoebe. She's the only person who could help me make a sound decision. The best decision for all concerned."

He exchanged a long look filled with a lifetime of meaning with the king, then gathered her closer to him, turned her toward the door. "That's one hurdle out of the way, *ariana 'yooni*."

A tremor passed through her. He'd called her his silver eyes. Did coming up with another of his unique endearments mean he wasn't as disturbed as she feared over this face-off?

Then he dropped a whisper in her ear, reminded her of what was coming, sent her world churning. "One more left, then I'll have you to myself for as long as I want."

As she walked out with him, she wondered just how long that would be. But did it matter, when she had no choice? And her lack of choice wasn't because he wasn't giving her any. If she walked away now, he'd let her and still give Castaldini a second chance. His condition had been just to show her how much he wanted her.

But she didn't want to walk away. She *couldn't*. She'd take anything she could have with him. Even if only one more time.

The real problem would be when she had no choice *but* to walk away. Again. This time, forever.

Eight

Leandro was used to winning. *Maledizione,* he'd come to demand nothing less than victory. In anything, over anyone. And he always started by triumphing over himself.

He was losing big-time right now.

His evil thoughts were in control, tossing his emotions wherever they pleased. He threw all his vaunted self-mastery at them, tried to loosen their grip. He didn't want to infect Phoebe with his tension.

Too late. On the way to their destination, he caught glimpses of them in the massive mirrors placed in strategic spots. He looked like a man with serious damage on his mind. Phoebe looked like a woman walking to the guillotine.

And it was all about that next hurdle, the one that was left in the way before he could have Phoebe to himself. Her sister.

Phoebe had insisted she couldn't move into his home and call Julia after the fact. She had to inform her sister of her plans, explain the situation and arrange this separation face-to-face.

It was the "arrange this separation" that made him want to

haul that tyrant from the chair from which she ruled her sister's life and shake some consideration for others into her. He would extract Phoebe from her clutches, even if he had to cut off her tentacles while he was at it. He owed that woman a lot of pain.

He believed that a big part of Phoebe's rejection of him in the past had been caused by true panic at the idea of leaving her sister. He'd scoffed at Julia's need then, but he'd long accepted that Phoebe believed that need to be real. And endless.

Oh, he might try to tell himself that Phoebe had gained a lot by sticking by her sister, but he only bought that when he was on one of his bitterness binges and needed to paint Phoebe as dark a shade of exploitative as possible. What he'd spent years needing to believe didn't mesh with reality. Reality said Julia had it all, and Phoebe, the strong one, the capable, nurturing one, had ended up living in her shadow, everything in her life a reflection of what filled Julia's.

He'd met Julia twice. On both occasions, he'd bristled with animosity. He hadn't known why until he'd realized he'd been in the presence of tyranny of the weak in a wraithlike, female form.

And they were two corridors away from said monster's lair.

Phoebe felt so taut she might snap. *Maledizione,* was she so deeply conditioned to put her sister's so-called needs ahead of her own that she dreaded leaving Julia even for a short time…?

Short time. Did she think it would be that? Did she want it to be? Did he? How could he, when he'd never get enough…? *Never?*

Never. But…what about closure? Closure…

The word churned in his mind, sickened him. And he had to face it. He didn't want closure. He never had. All he wanted was a continuation. And he was no longer putting a definition or form to that continuation. Something as elemental as what they shared abided by no rules but its own. But that was how he felt. What about her?

What if this tension wasn't all about her mother complex

over her sister? What if there was still an element of coercion here? What if being with him was what she wanted, but also what she'd rather not do? What if she felt cornered by both her need to help his kingdom, and her need for him? He couldn't bear that he might be contributing to her turmoil.

He reached for her, pulled her through the nearest doorway.

The couple going about their business in their own quarters looked as if they'd been caught trespassing, started babbling apologies. He winced as he requested the kindness of the use of their quarters for a few minutes. They streaked out.

The moment the door closed behind them, he took Phoebe by the shoulders. She stared up at him, her eyes alarmed, confused.

He groaned. "I take back my condition. And my promise. I'll stay in Castaldini and draw on your opinions and guidance in coming to a decision. We'll work out a way to collaborate while we're on opposite ends of the island."

The deluge of emotion that flooded her eyes inundated him. She seemed to stop breathing. She seemed...hurt? More...stricken?

His lungs burned as he waited for her to put her reaction into words. They finally came from her lips, but felt like a trembling caress in his mind. "You don't want me...to come with you anymore?"

The barked laugh gashed something on its way out. "If I wanted you more, we'd have a medical emergency on our hands."

Her lower lip trembled. His whole body rioted. "Then why are you taking your invitation back?"

"Because I didn't exactly make it an invitation."

Her eyes—those eyes that dominated his fantasies—bombarded him with so much emotion, everything in him tensed. His thoughts and heart and guts and loins. Then she upped the ante. Comprehension, followed by delight, turned her face from the sum of his desires to the end of life as he knew it.

She slowly, so slowly, imprinted her body on his, slid up

against him, her lips open on pleasure-laden breaths until she whispered into his mouth, "Then make it one."

He was a super hero. He didn't devour her. Or maybe he couldn't. Because he was dying here. Not that rigor mortis would stop him from obeying her. He groaned.

"Will you come with me, Phoebe? Unconnected with anything but what we both want? Will you bestow on me the pleasure of you?"

"Yes." The S lingered as she pressed all that reason-annihilating femininity against him. The world faded as the sound did, as she nestled her face into his open shirt. His heart did its best to tear open his ribs for a direct rub. "Now promise me again."

Was this survivable? He frankly didn't care. "I'll let you come to me. But I'll keep showing you how much I want you to, how mind-blowingly better than ever it will be when you do."

Her giggle was a cocktail of distress, mirth and yearning. "This I have to experience to believe."

He still kept his hands to himself. Somehow. "You will. Experience. And believe. When you make up your mind."

She trembled as she leaned on him. He swayed. As they said in his hometown, *sandadet ala haita mayla*—she sought support from a collapsing wall.

"Oh, my mind's made up. It took you a whopping twenty-four hours to make it up for me. I need longer than that to follow conviction with action."

"Your pace this time. I might not have given you reason to believe that, but my stamina is legendary." He paused, groaned. "And that sounded like so many famous last words."

Her laugh shook him. It contained something he'd never heard, not from her. Carefree cheerfulness. Its power was total. "Oh, you gave me every reason, in *that* sense. As for the one you meant now, I hope my stamina lasts long enough to give yours a workout."

"And I'm at once hoping it lasts as long as it takes for you to feel right about coming to me, and hoping it will crumble within the next three minutes so we can cut to just *living* this."

"Forty-eight hours ago I wouldn't have believed it. But I've been hearing it with my own ears nonstop, so I have to sanction the verdict. You talk good. Too good. As I'm sure you know."

His lips twisted. "You'd be surprised what I don't know."

"I don't know…" she ran a finger of fire down his sternum and marked him for life yet again "…about you, but I want to get goodbyes out of the way. I'm dying to…see your home."

"And I'm dying—probably literally—to see you in it."

She hooked her arm through his. "Then come on."

Feeling like he could indeed sprout wings if he clucked hard enough, as she'd once said, or that he'd already sprouted them, he shared unfettered smiles with her as they hurried to her sister's apartment. The sister he no longer felt like strangling.

Until he laid eyes on her.

The tinier—and in his eyes, off-putting—loosely-based-on-Phoebe variation was sitting in her wheelchair like a queen bee surrounded by her workers. Paolo, her doting idiot of a husband, the brood of children she'd shackled him with—and from the shape of her belly, she wasn't done smothering him, not by a long shot—and an assortment of nannies and maids all flitted around her.

As soon as they entered the sunset-drenched family room of the apartment that occupied a hefty part of the palace's left wing, the two girls and the two boys, all dark-haired and healthy-looking, hurtled toward their aunt, yelping at her like excited puppies. Paolo targeted him with a smile.

A tall, slender man with an eternally boyish face, Paolo looked younger than his thirty-one years. Until you looked into his eyes. There you could see the toll of being a father four times over, with the fifth—or only Julia knew how many more—on the way.

Paolo had kept in touch with Leandro over the years. Not that they'd been close before, but he'd become a better friend after the breach than before it. Leandro had appreciated that. Even if he didn't appreciate Paolo's choice of wife. When that choice had led to Leandro's meeting Phoebe, he couldn't have endorsed it enough. Not anymore.

"Leandro! So good to see you back in Castaldini." Leandro let himself be pulled into Paolo's hug and kissed on both cheeks. Paolo pulled back but kept both hands on his arms as he beamed at him. "I hope this time you're here to stay."

Leandro smiled as he extracted himself, trying to make it seem a natural move. He was bursting with impatience to get this visit over with.

He got right to the point. "That's still up in the air. And it's why we're here." He explained his plan and Phoebe's role in it.

As he finished his explanations, a sense of oppression came over him. Her eyes were on him. Had she wanted to do the explaining? Had he made amends only to commit a worse offense?

He tried to gauge her reaction as she stood there, covered in kids, and the sense of oppression deepened. They looked as if they were extensions of her life force, made of her flesh. As they were. Partially. So many of the desires he'd repressed since she'd walked out on him besieged him, forced him to look, acknowledge. Things he thought he'd never have, because she'd left his life. Now, seeing her this way, the thought of her growing bigger with…

Paolo moved into his line of vision, interrupting his fevered musings. "I really hope you come to the right decision. You know what I think that is. You'll make a helluva king, Leandro."

"No need to kiss up to him yet, Paolo. We don't know if he's going to be crown prince this time or if he'll blow it again."

Silence fell like acid rain in the wake of Julia's vindictive comment.

Then Paolo's laugh boomed. "*Mia moglie cara*—my darling wife, the consummate diplomat. Guess Phoebe sucked that trait right out of your family's gene pool and left you with none."

"Yeah, and I don't envy her the job it landed her with."

Julia didn't even try to disguise the glare she impaled Leandro with. To his delight. It gave him license to glare back.

But instead of teaching his nemesis that Phoebe wasn't an

extra in the play starring her, he just wanted to snatch Phoebe away. And never let her return.

"Say, *caro,* how about you and the kids show Leandro around?"

Leandro bared his teeth at Julia in a parody of a smile. "Thanks, but no thanks. We have to get going."

Julia's full lips thinned. "Okay, since you won't take a hint. I want to talk to my sister. Alone. Do you mind?"

Phoebe couldn't believe that Leandro had submitted to Paolo's cajoling and left her and Julia alone. She'd thought there'd be an explosion. A belated one between the two most important people in her life who'd detested each other on sight. Probably more proof that she and Leandro weren't meant to be.

Now accusation simmered in Julia's eyes as she stopped her chair a couple of feet away. Then she stood up.

Phoebe winced. The effort it took Julia to stand always left her feeling traumatized. The two steps she took to come nose to nose with her were even harder. Julia really wanted to lay into her. And she could guess why.

"So that's your secret," Julia hissed, her voice rough with anger and hurt. "The reason you've been frozen ever since we came here, the reason you do anything you can to avoid having a personal life."

"I have a personal life, Julia. I'm a person, and I'm alive—"

"Don't. Just *don't,* Phoebe."

"Uh-oh. If I'm *Phoebe* now, things must be dire indeed."

"Phoebe, shut *up.* I'm so angry I could kick your stubborn ass. You still think I'm just an invalid, don't you? You still think you have to protect me from even a moment's discomfort? What can I do to make you realize I'm not the clingy, needy mess I once was? That I can support the people I love? Support you? When will you stop giving and accept that I have something to give back?"

"Darling, of course you have…"

"Don't you dare placate me, *Phoebe*. This isn't about me, dammit. I'm not the center of the universe, so for God's sake stop putting me in the center of yours. This is about you."

"What about me, Jules? I have a wonderful, ever-growing family, you rabbit, an incredible job, a palace to call my home, and the fact that I haven't yet found the man for me—"

"But that's the problem, isn't it? You think you found him ten years ago, and that's why you never gave anyone else a chance. Even Armando, that droolicious hunk of a human being. You blew it with him, big time. And it's all over that ex-royal pain in the rear, isn't it?"

Phoebe's lips twitched with distress and amusement. "He's royal again as of this afternoon, by the way."

"You're not glossing over this, do you hear me?"

"I think the whole capital can hear you, sweetie."

"Don't *sweetie* me or I swear…ooh. And all this time you kept me in the dark, you overprotective, suffering-in-silence…*rat*."

"Who said anything about suffering—"

"*I* say. I *felt* it. And I should have known what it was about. At my wedding when that hunk of rock almost made love to you on the dance floor and then dragged you out to the terrace and you came back looking turned inside out, I was sure he'd kissed you senseless. And that you, Ms. No Man Ever Gets Past the Inspection Stage, *let* him, worried me sick. I spent half my wedding night interrogating Paolo about him. He said he respected Leandro as a prince and a businessman, but that as a man, he thought there was no colder fish in the known universe. I laid into you the moment I returned from my honeymoon, but you were all, 'I haven't seen him again and nothing happened that night.' But you were seeing him all the time, weren't you?"

"I wasn't exactly seeing him all the time, Jules. He didn't live on Castaldini, remember?"

Julia staggered around, threw herself back into her chair with a furious screech. "You threw me off the scent so well, and I believed that not even that Roman god could fool you!

I was in a bad way at the time, and I just dismissed the whole thing. Whenever your tranquil act cracked, I'd say, nah, not that, not Phoebes. Paolo did wonder how Leandro could afford to come to Castaldini so frequently during his campaign. But he was coming back for you, keeping you like a dirty little secret, forcing you to lie to me and to everyone, wasn't he? And now he's back and he wants to play some more, that… that…*bastard*."

So she hadn't been a good enough actress. Oh, well. Time to come clean. She sighed. "You're talking as if I was a minor who was seduced by a dirty old man, Jules. He didn't coerce me into anything."

"But he's coercing you now, isn't he? Tell me he is. You can't be that stupid twice in a lifetime with the same man."

"He's not as bad as you think, Jules. In fact, I'm discovering that he's very, very good."

"Oh, no, he's messed with your mind again already."

"Maybe. But as totally moronic as it may sound to you, I'm excited about this. I get to be his bridge back to Castaldini, and I believe I can do both him and the kingdom a serious service."

"That's not the kind of service he's looking for from you!"

She laughed at Julia's venom. "Oh, that, too. But one thing you don't have to worry about is him forcing me into anything."

"I get the feeling it would take force to pry *you* off *him*."

Phoebe laughed again. Leave it to Julia to hit her over the head with the truth. Half the truth here, though. When it was time to let go, she'd walk away. She already had that routine down pat.

"What's so wrong in being with the one man who ever got—and as it turns out, who'll ever get—my motor running?"

"You want me to point out all the mistakes in this picture? One, you're not on a level playing field. He wants entertainment, you want serious, and commitment, and forever—"

Phoebe snorted. "You make me sound like so much fun, Jules."

"Okay, Phoebes." Julia's tone switched from exasperated to coaxing. "I understand, honest. I mean, I'm deliriously in love with Paolo and I still got the wind knocked out of me when Leandro walked in with you. Then he came closer, spoke…and whew. What I'm saying is, he has some serious brain-shutdown powers, even in completely committed women's cases. So I totally sympathize. But you must resist the pull of the dark side!"

"So now I'm facing the return of the Jedi?" Phoebe hooted. "Oh, Jules, I'm sorry I didn't confide in you. But this is my choice now as it was then. I want this. And when I'm gone, don't you dare take your frustration out on Paolo, hear? Don't go around being discontented, not over me this time. Or I'm sending Stella to scare you back to your best behavior."

Julia's gaze turned hot at the mention of the woman who'd once tried to wreck her marriage, the woman Phoebe had most minded seeing Leandro escort in public during his and Phoebe's affair. "You're a master at subterfuge, aren't you? And to think I never suspected it."

"I have many hidden talents."

"So when are you going to stop hiding them?"

All temper evaporated from Julia's eyes, all feigned lightness from Phoebe's. This was it, then. Moment of truth.

And the truth was, she'd overstayed…maybe not her welcome, but her usefulness in Castaldini. One of the reasons she'd ended her ill-advised engagement to Armando had been that she'd recognized it as an attempt to revive the need for her to stay there. Julia had adapted to her condition, hadn't needed Phoebe's support for years now. It had been her who'd stuck around, avoided facing the facts that her purpose had dwindled to nonexistent and she was going nowhere staying in Castaldini. King Benedetto had created a job for her where she *was* needed. But she wasn't indispensable. Not to Castaldini, not to Julia or the children. Not to…anyone.

The one thing that had been keeping her there was being at a loss as to what to do next, where to go. She'd always put everyone else first, let their needs dictate her course and choices. First her mother, then Julia, then Leandro, then Castaldini. And her use had expired for each, one way or the other. Now she had to get a life of her own.

And Julia was calling her on putting a time limit on getting one.

Phoebe looked her sister square in the eyes. "How about now? And I'll start by going west with Leandro, taking every day as it comes."

"You're not fooling me. You did that once before with him."

"Oh, it was different then." She'd jumped in blind then, had had her eyes opened the hardest way. Now she saw exactly what she was getting into. "This time I'll finally get the running start I need to launch into the life I should have started living years ago."

Before Julia could volley and take the conversation deeper, Phoebe swooped her up in a bear hug, then made her escape through the door where Paolo and the kids had kidnapped Leandro.

And there he was, at the end of the immaculate gardens, the one thing she craved. If she didn't already know it, the tension radiating from him even from that far, the way his gaze was pinned to the door he knew she'd exit from, would have told her she was on top of his list of must-haves, too…

She blinked, gasped.

Exiting from the massive columned promenade, his formidable frame etched in stark light and deep shadow in the setting sun, was Armando. Her ex-fiancé. Heading toward her on an interceptive course.

Nine

Okay. This was unexpected. Which meant…Julia.

Matchmaking again? This time not to save her from spinsterhood, but from depravity? But how could she have gotten him here this fast?

She sensed Leandro's tension rising as his dash toward her was aborted by Paolo and the kids. Armando had already reached her, and Leandro stood there like a volcano about to erupt, letting the kids jump all over him with Paolo evidently talking his ear off.

Armando stopped before her, all male and beautiful with bronze hair, eyes and skin, radiating vitality and steady power. He bent, kissed her cheek, had her asking herself yet again why she couldn't feel the tiniest twinge of desire for him. A question the answer to which was standing right there in the distance.

"You're looking beautiful, as always." The smile didn't reach his eyes. They were serious, intent. "I asked Julia to let me know the moment you were back. She informed me only half an hour ago, and I'm thankful that I wrapped everything up and ran here, since I was just informed you're flying out again immediately."

And Julia hadn't said where or with whom? Seems she hadn't. *Weird, but thanks anyway, Jules.* "Yeah. How've you been, Armando?"

"I've been thinking about us…" *Uh-oh* "…regretting that I agreed to end our betrothal. I know you have to go, but just hear me out, think it over while you're away. I might never love again as I once loved, and I don't inspire your passion as you feel a husband should, but with your serene and steady temperament, our relationship could be powerful and enduring. Towering emotions—trust me—are distressing and addictive, and they bring little, if any, happiness."

Yeah, tell her about it. This was heavy. And very untimely. But she respected Armando too much not to give him all due consideration. She exhaled. "You can have that kind of relationship, Armando…with anyone else. I'm not the one to build something powerful and enduring with you. I'm so much the opposite of steady and serene, it's painfully funny hearing you call me that."

"How can you underestimate yourself, when you've been such a stabilizing influence in so many lives since you first set foot on Castaldini? Without you, Castaldini would have gained many new enemies and wouldn't have been able to prevent a few old ones from gaining ground. Without you, your sister's and my cousin's marriage wouldn't have lasted one year, let alone ten."

"Whoa. Don't go overestimating me to counteract my alleged underestimation of myself. Paolo and Julia love each other."

"And their love, like mine and Donatella's, could have been total chaos, until one or both couldn't bear it anymore."

"You never told me it was like that with Donatella."

"It was so intense, it sometimes left us gasping for breath. The good times were heaven, but the bad times were hell, and, regretfully, they lasted longer. Both of us were older and stronger than Paolo and Julia, and we weathered the hellish parts and would have done so forever had she lived. But I fully believe that without your support and counsel, the intensity of Paolo and Julia's love, muddied by his impetuousness and her insecurity, would have pushed them apart in less than a year. They have a beautiful marriage, and Julia is that giving, nurturing wife and mother now because of you."

"Oh, no, you're not handing me all the credit here. Julia struggled long and hard, and Paolo did and still does everything in his power to do his part and more. Even though I may have helped, she would have done the same for me had the situation been reversed."

"So you think your role isn't to be admired or thanked?"

"I don't care one way or another for admiration or thanks. But whatever my role, as you call it, was, it's over."

"Exactly. And you're free now to start a new phase in your life. To live for yourself at last."

Everyone must be fed up with her. They were all bringing it up. She huffed. "Yeah, now I've run out of excuses not to."

"*Causes*, Phoebe. And you'll never run out of those to champion. I ask only for the honor of sharing your life while you find more lives to enrich. You and I, we're kindred spirits."

"We may be, Armando, but I have nothing to offer you."

Suddenly he winced, his eyes flashing gold. "*Dio*—how didn't I see this before? It's another man, isn't it? A man you loved and lost, but not like I lost Donatella? This man hurt you, didn't he? But you still can't move on. You are still waiting for him."

She gave denial a second's consideration, especially since she wasn't *waiting* for Leandro as he intimated. She just nodded.

The flare in his eyes and the step closer he took seethed with urgency. "Don't let that man claim more of your life."

She shook her head wryly. "I'm done letting people, or life, do things to me. I'm taking charge, as of now."

"I'll hold you to that. And Phoebe…" Her heart dropped a beat at the harshness that suddenly blazed on his face as he cast a look behind him. "It's Leandro, isn't it?"

This time she didn't consider denying it. She even told him how things stood. She was done hiding things.

Armando digested this with a frown. "He might be the power Castaldini needs now, but he always was like a force of nature, unstoppable and indiscriminate on his quest for greatness. Now that he's fulfilled his potential…" He suddenly caught her by the shoulders. "Stay away from him, Phoebe."

Her eyes escaped his, clung to Leandro. "I can't, Armando."

"If he hurt you before, he will destroy you now."

"Don't worry. I'm not a silly twenty-year-old anymore."

"It's because you're a mature and very sensible thirty-year-old that I *am* worried. What you felt when you were barely an adult will pale in comparison to what you're capable of feeling now."

She touched his hard cheek, loving him, but knowing she'd never be *in* love with him. She had terminal one-man-woman disease. "Here's another possible outcome to all this. That I'll put things in perspective, purge them and move on."

He clearly wasn't buying that. Then he gritted his teeth. "I may not be as powerful as he is—yet. But if he ever hurts you again, I'll destroy him. Tell him."

And with that he turned on his heel and strode away. She stared after him, stunned. Who knew Armando was capable of all that passion? Evidently it had taken his late wife—and Leandro—to rouse the sleeping tiger. Not her. Thank God.

Speaking of tigers, an even more impressive one, *the* one for her, had gotten rid of his human shackles and was stalking toward her with danger and desire blasting off him.

"That was quite a conversation," he drawled.

She cocked her head at him. "Yes, it was."

"Nothing more to say?"

She sighed. "You like to say that, don't you?"

"I can't think of anything I dislike saying more. You have a habit of forcing me to say it."

"I'm making the poor mogul prince do things against his will?"

Emerald fire leapt in his eyes. "You could make an army of mogul princes jump in the air and stay there until you say 'down.'"

She exaggerated a flutter. "Whoa, I must be super potent."

"And how. And you are super exasperating, too."

She gasped in mock innocence. "What have I done now? Besides ignore another of your infringing allusions?"

He snatched her hand to his lips for a compulsive kiss. "How many years will it take you to get enough of saying that to me?"

He was telling her she had…years? Figure of speech, girl. "What you're saying is, find some fresh lines, huh? Drat. I loved that line. I was so proud of how pompous it sounded. I churned it up to give you the benefit of all those important-sounding words I learned in law school."

He growled, bit into the flesh at the base of her thumb. "You talk too much, yet say nothing. The sure sign of a master lawyer."

She gasped at the pleasure shooting from her thumb to her core. "Says the master mogul-cum-diplomat."

"Phoebe, *voi shaitana bella*, you beautiful devil, tell me what Armando had to say that took so long and looked so serious."

"Why don't you ask him? You are related, after all."

"*Si*, and I used to even like the man. Now you're really putting *il bastardo* in harm's way."

She giggled. "What a coincidence. He thinks of you just as highly and feels as much goodwill toward you."

"*Infischio di lui*—I don't give a damn about him or what he thinks of me, or whether he'd like to have my head on a pike."

"Ooh, such aggression. Has anyone told you how absolutely beautiful you are when you're caught in a fit of hostility?"

"*Porca l'oca*—damn, Phoebe, you'd test Gandhi's restraint."

"I'm so glad you think so." Before he could answer, she reached up and pressed her mouth to the throbbing pulse at his corded throat. "But with the way *you're* prevaricating, I'm beginning to think you really don't want to take me to your home."

He rumbled something that zapped her nerveless, snatched her up, took her lips to within a hair's breadth of sanity.

When breathing became an emergency, he let her go, left her clinging, panting. "Don't stop…"

"Have to…I started this…again…and I promised…"

Yeah, and she'd made him do both. Start this. And promise. This time, there'd be no one to blame but herself.

Ten

"Why didn't you ever tell me you lived in paradise?"

Phoebe stretched up on her tiptoes, arched her back, opened her arms wider as if to encompass the beauty around her.

Layer upon layer of natural and man-made wonders stretched as far as she could see, drenched in the Mediterranean sunlight and swathed in the western sea breeze.

She'd read up on this place when she'd learned it was Leandro's birthplace. No wonder Moorish poets described it as "pearls set in emeralds." That was exactly what this place and the town and countryside it overlooked resembled. Pearly buildings set in emerald nature. They should have added the sapphire, aquamarine and gold of the sea, sky and sandy beaches to the setting.

The palace complex sprawled in multiple levels over the mountainous site, the park around it overgrown with wildflowers and grass and teeming with roses, orange trees, myrtles and dense elms. Its resident nightingales had been filling the night with songs on their arrival, but now the silence was penetrated only by the sound of water surging in fountains and flowing in cascades.

Leandro came up behind her, stopped millimeters from touching her, creating a force field of screaming sensuality between them, his lips hovering in a path of destruction from her temple to the swell of her breasts. Then he took the same path up. This time he breathed, exhaled his hunger over her. "Would it have gotten you here sooner if I had?"

She collapsed back against him, knowing what a phoenix felt like, burning to ashes only to be recreated, over and over. "How much sooner than forty-eight hours could I have been here?"

"Forty-eight minutes." His murmur thrummed inside her in a path that connected her heart and core, sending both gushing. "Forty-eight seconds. I should get my R & D department working on teleportation. All that commute time was pure torment…"

His voice plunged on the last word, lurching through her with enough power to whirl her away from him. "You should talk about torment. You invented it."

He surveyed her, giving new meaning to lord-of-all-he-surveyed. "If I did, you must share dibs on the patent."

"Okay, from one tormentor to another, how about we do something else for a change? Have a truce and explore your paradise?"

"The one I've been cast out of, you mean?"

His tone was unchanged, that teasing, tempting burr. But she felt it. Eight year's worth of damage and disgrace. It wrung from her the now second nature urge to ease his hurt, to defend him against the pain of the past. She took a breathless step forward. "The one you can now live in again, if you only desire."

"Oh, I desire." He aborted her movement, hungry strides backing her up across the huge stone terrace until he had her against the three-foot-high balustrade. His gaze swept her, from piled-up hair to white wedge sandals, practically setting her on fire. "How I *only* desire."

"Truce, remember?" She pushed past him to search for air.

"*Va bene.* I'll honor it, even if it was a one-sided deal." He leaned his hips against the balustrade, shoved his hands in his pockets as if they itched, stretching his pants over a sight that almost had her dropping to her knees in worship.

He beckoned to his house staff, who immediately got busy setting up an outdoor café for them. He watched them for a minute then swept a moody glance around. "This place is the one thing I regret about being who I am. My life has always contrived to keep me away from all this."

And "all this" was something huge to be kept away from.

She walked back to him, the need to connect with him physically in a non-sexual way overwhelming her again. She took his hand in both of hers. "I'm sorry you had to sacrifice being *where* you wanted to be for *what* you wanted to be."

"Funny, eh? To succeed to the point that I don't get the things I really want." Her heart no longer had distinct beats, buzzed like a hummingbird's wings. Did he include her in what he wanted and couldn't get? Before she asked, he sighed. "But being away from here was out of my hands at first. The funny part is, when it was in my reach, everything I did took it away again."

She blinked back agitation. She treasured that he was exposing his inner self, letting her in, but she couldn't stand to see him vulnerable or morose. "You can change all that now."

He looked at her as if attempting to chart her brainwaves. She felt he must have succeeded by the time he looked back at the preparations. Then his expression changed back to scorching flirtation. "Let me feed you. A tour through my paradise is hard work."

She scampered behind him to the table his people had conjured up, a dream in crisp white, luscious cream and deep emerald. Silver and crystal flashed and sparkled in the sunlight that hurtled through the canopy's sighing folds. He dismissed everyone, then sat down in one of the *fer forgé* chairs. She moved to her own chair, only to be pulled down onto his lap.

She settled on the hardness she was molten for. She gasped, wriggled, wrenching a growl from him as one hand pressed her down harder to meet what felt like an involuntary thrust.

She gulped around the need to crash her lips to his, to straddle him and take him all the way in, to her heart. "So this is what they mean by the lap of plenty? Or is it luxury?"

"Don't move, or it will be the lap of injury," he groaned.

"Let me up and no one needs to get hurt."

"Just don't move, and I'll still get to feed you and walk out of this with intact equipment."

She wriggled more until he thrust back with a long rumble, his hands circling her waist, raising her as he once had during exhausting rides to extremes of ecstasy. She made use of the boost to stagger up to her feet and whirled around to flop down in her chair. "I've been feeding myself for some time now, thanks."

He mock-scowled. "Who'll lick my fingers for me?"

"So that's what you wanted? No free rides, huh?"

He tossed his head back with a guffaw. "If I didn't dread another lecture about criminal excess, I'd tell you what I'm willing to pay for one finger lick right now."

She leaned over, picked up his hand. Then, holding his eyes, she sucked his middle finger into her mouth. She almost fainted with the spike of arousal. Was turnabout supposed to turn on its perpetrator? But at least she was causing him equal distress.

When he snatched his finger away with another string of language-blending curses, she murmured demurely, "Write the checks. I'll give you a list of my favorite charities."

He grunted a laugh. "You'd better stand over my shoulder when I'm writing the checks, or I'm liable to sign my fortune away."

"For just one lick?"

"But what a lick. So that's what 'getting licked' means, eh? We keep finding out the real meaning behind common expressions."

He lifted a silver cover bearing a repoussé cartouche.

The sight of dewy chicken and vivid vegetables and the scent of spices she couldn't guess at knotted her stomach with hunger.

She exchanged unabashed smiles with him as he served her, feeling like an eagle that had just discovered she could fly.

Then she breathed, "Tell me."

He didn't ask what. He just raised his eyes to hers without raising his face, his expression almost…loving?

As she backpedaled from that interpretation as if she'd landed in shark-infested waters, he lowered his gaze, started to eat. He swallowed his first bite, then began.

"I've never stayed here, or on Castaldini, longer than a few months at a time since I was seven. After my mother died, my father was inconsolable. My maternal aunt, who lives in Venice, took me to live with her for two years. I came back for a few months when my father fell sick. Then he died. I was passed between my immediate family members—who happen to live all over the globe—with Ernesto in tow until I was seventeen. Then I struck out on my own. No wonder I'm not much of a Castaldinian."

She'd been finding it harder to swallow as she imagined him, an only child, being orphaned at an even younger age than she'd been. That last remark had her almost coughing out her food.

"You're the best sort," she cried. "You have an uncanny ability to analyze problems and tailor solutions. All you need to do is fit your powers to Castaldini's needs."

"You really think so?"

"I'm providing uncensored thoughts, remember?"

"You're providing a life-saving service. And your uncensored thoughts are a blessing to me and to Castaldini."

"Which makes me a blessed angel, not a wicked devil, as you always claim," she quipped, escaping his intensity. "Tell me about this place. It's…amazing."

He pushed away a clean plate. When had he finished it? "It is. Castello del Jamida—yes, an Italian/Moorish name—

is what its name proclaims, an enduring castle. It was completed by King Antonio himself, but there is no record of when it was started. Its walls enclose an area reaching down from the Indara up there—" she followed his pointing finger "—the highest place in the El Juela mountains, down to the sea. A lot of the palace was rebuilt during the second Moorish period of occupation of Spain in the early fourteenth century, after its near destruction during a re-conquest of Gibraltar."

She digested the sweeping historical details. "It's mind-boggling. I can't begin to imagine how big the central castle is."

"The castle rests on a plateau that measures about three thousand by one thousand feet."

"That's as big as the royal palace!"

"It *was* the royal palace for four centuries, before King Arturo moved the capital to Jawara in the seventeenth century."

"So you're the direct descendant of King Antonio?"

"I inherited this place. It's an indication I am related."

She narrowed her eyes. "You're on shaky ground here, mister."

"Not 'mister.' You may call me Your Royal Highness again now."

"You may not live long enough to be called anything."

"You're right. Overexposure to toxic levels of beauty and sensuality is making my survival chances iffy."

She turned up her nose at him. "Flattery won't get you anywhere. Since there are no more places left for you to go."

"I bet I can show you places you didn't dream existed." He stood up, came around, pulled her up. "And I'm starting now."

She giggled and exchanged quips with him as he took her at a run to the ground floor of the castle and outside to begin the tour, all the time pointing out details with the thoroughness of someone who truly loved and cared about a place.

"This palace was built in the Mudéjar-Romanesque style, a symbiosis of architectural syles from cultures living side by side, which on this side of the island were Roman, Andalusian and Moorish with some North African influences. It's characterized by geometric patterns in which accessorizing is everything, from elaborately worked tile to wood and plaster carving to ornamental metals."

When they were far enough into the park to get an overall picture, he stopped. "The majority of the palace buildings are quadrangular, with all rooms opening onto central courts. The complex reached its present size by gradual additions of more quadrangles connected by smaller rooms and passages. And though the exterior was designed to be plain, even austere, the interior of each new section followed the theme of the core buildings."

"What's that?"

His grin burst like a flash in her eyes. "Paradise on earth."

She whooped. "I knew it!"

"You're a genius. Or maybe the columned arcades, fountains, indoor gardens, reflecting pools, sun and wind passing freely from ingeniously positioned and decorated openings, plus a feast of color touched by gold and bronze and silver gave you a clue?"

"You saying I was stating the obvious, Your Royal Wryness?"

He chuckled at her ribbing, pulled her into a run just as her breath evened from the last sprint. At the end of the park they ran down a steep descent leading to the biggest fountain yet. They slowed down as they passed through two gigantic gates.

"That's where we access El Jamida town. The first gate is Cancello di Cielo, and it dates from the fourteenth century."

"It's an honest to goodness triumphal arch!" She gaped up as they passed beneath the dwarfing construction. "Hey, what's that hand above the gate? I saw a key in the same place on the inside."

"That's the Hand of Elaya, with fingers outstretched as a talisman against the evil eye. That's why it's outside. The key is the symbol of authority, a reminder to those inside." She laughed at his villainous tone as they passed beneath a massive horseshoe archway surrounded by a square tower.

"And this is the Cancello di Giudizio, which was once used as an informal court of justice."

"Gate of Heaven, Gate of Judgment. Divine delusions galore. But okay. You make a good guide. You may live."

His laughter rang out again, and continued to do so as they walked.

They soon happened on a long queue of vegetable and fruit peddlers on their way to the palace complex to sell their fresh produce.

When they saw Leandro, they freaked out like a posse of hungry cats in a fresh fish market. Suddenly she couldn't see Leandro in the maelstrom of human bodies and eager cries.

He finally managed to include her in their excitement, only for her to find herself and Leandro being dragged onto the leading cart and heading at a gallop into the streets of town.

All the way, people ran beside their cart, deluging Leandro with questions about the time since they'd last seen him.

Everybody in town knew Leandro, clearly loved and respected him. And missed him. The excitement of the situation soon turned to poignancy as she watched the reunion between the people and their estranged lord.

They were offered the use of every home, the food on every table. Leandro, unwilling to turn anybody's generosity down, arranged for offerings to be taken back to the castle.

It was deep night by the time the townspeople let them go, and then only after Leandro promised they'd return in two weeks to celebrate the Merraba Feast.

By the time Leandro walked her to her room, all she wanted was to drag him inside and just end the torment. At the twelve-foot door that had survived eight centuries, he loomed over her for a heart-stopping moment. Then he lifted her in silence, plastered her against the door, opened her body around his bulk and took her lips, drank her, drained her, ground her between his unstoppable power and the immovable door until there was nothing left of her.

Then he let her down, stood back, vibrating. She saw his

fantasies, imagined each dig of fingers and nip of teeth and flay of breath as he hauled her over his shoulder, stormed into her room, flung her on her bed and ravished her.

With an explosive oath, he turned and strode through the arches of the vast corridor until darkness claimed him.

She didn't run after him. Something she couldn't—didn't *want* to—define overpowered even the mind-numbing hunger.

She stumbled through her door, fell onto her bed fully clothed and prayed for sleep.

Eleven

Leandro had been right.

This new hunger far surpassed the mindlessness they'd once inspired in each other. It was also so different in nature, in texture. It was vast and powerful, not grabby and frantic. It wasn't just making them tense, it was making them buoyant, exhilarated.

But he'd been wrong about something else. She had been, too.

This arrangement was no longer what they'd agreed on. It wasn't an all-out fling to exorcise their hunger. The past week had followed a pattern of escalating enjoyment and rapport, each moment creating trust and understanding and appreciation between them—things that had been grossly lacking in the past.

It made all the difference in their relationship. It was as if each hour was a continuation of a long history of harmony.

But it wasn't a continuation. This was a beginning. This was magic. Powerful, pure, compelling. She had no doubt it would be ongoing.

And there were more wonders.

As Leandro steered his vast business by remote control, as he handled two threats Castaldini faced, one internal and the other external, she had the chance to analyze his methods and views firsthand and find out how wrong she'd been about them. It was a delight to discover they shared the same belief in the power of logic and the art of the possible, embraced almost all the same convictions. It was exhilarating to explore how alike they were, both negotiators and intermediaries in their own way, when they'd started out so differently in life.

Every day, true to his promise, he made use of her knowledge of Castaldini, probed her insights, sought her opinions, discussed current internal affairs, everything he'd never found out through his investigations into the state of the kingdom. Then he returned the favor, taking her through more magical explorations of the seemingly endless palace complex, the district under his family's rule and protection that was now under his.

During a conversation over breakfast, she discovered that he had never ceased to be El Jamida's prince.

"My grandfather finally put an end to the expansions," he was saying. "That turret was the last addition. Ironically, it was the first thing to go—it was decimated by lightning six years ago. But as it was restored, I had a closer look taken at the structure and wound up totally overhauling the outer walls, towers and ramparts."

"Six years ago?" she exclaimed even as realization dawned. "So *that's* what Ernesto was doing here all those times!"

"Yes, all those times when you saw him." She poked him and he only sighed long-sufferingly. "Seems Ernesto is a double agent. Never telling me he'd seen you, while never telling you why he came back to Castaldini. That must be why he's all but disappeared since we arrived. He realized we'd compare notes sooner or later and expose him. Hmm. I think I need to have a word with him."

"Leave poor Ernesto alone. So you maintained this place? And from your popularity within the towns and villages, I bet you had a hand in their picture perfection."

He shrugged. "The district is under my protection. It's my responsibility to maintain it to the best of my abilities."

"And since your abilities literally are the best, this area of Castaldini is probably the luckiest place on earth."

"It's one of the reasons I couldn't hate the king. He might have exiled me, but he didn't deprive my district's people of my services, or this place of my preservation efforts."

"And would you offer your services and preservation efforts to the rest of Castaldini if you become crown prince?"

"I will even if I don't. I will see Castaldini returned to its former glory. But I won't just throw money at problems and send others in my stead. Now I'll again be able to inspect work progress myself, to shake hands with people, listen to their complaints and work with them on solutions."

She stared at him, her heart doing jiggles that she knew hearts weren't supposed to do. She was almost in tears, and in stitches, all at once. "You're not just any Castaldinian, you're a patriot. And not only are you a social reformer and modernizer, oh, my God, Leandro, I suspect you're a democrat, too. What will we *do?*"

He bounced to his feet, pounced on her, swung her high in his arms. "We're going to keep it a dark secret, that's what. And since you've wheedled all those out of me, I guess it won't do more damage to tell you one more—a family secret."

She clung to his neck, beamed at him. "I'll take it to my grave. If I don't volunteer it to the first passerby, that is."

He pinched the buttock filling his hand, his smile widening. "I told you the complex consists of three main parts…"

"And you showed me only two! The Eddar—the administrative area—and Elkasar, where we are. What's the third part? Is it a catacomb filled with skeletons? A labyrinth teeming with the treasures plundered by your marauding ancestors?"

"It's a harem."

"No way," she squeaked. "On Castaldini? You're *kidding* me."

"Alas, no. But the pity is, it fell into disuse for over a century until my mother took a shine to it. It was abandoned again after she died. But I've since restored it. If you take a fancy to it, you can stay there. And I'll stay in my quarters and fantasize about you in one of the bedrooms, shrouded by tulle screens, wrapped in miles of satin and silk of vivid reds and blues and golds, *bianco-e-nero amar elaty."*

My black-and-white moon goddess. And why wasn't she asking him to take her there right now? Take her until he finished her?

He strode out with her still in his arms. She thought she heard whispers and saw people dashing out of their way.

"And to damage myself for life, I'll imagine you in the main chamber. The one that's open to the elements. I'll imagine you as you float in a hot tub, the water massaging all your secrets, or lying on a marble platform, overheated and flushed and wet, writhing as you think of me, as the sun latches hot lips on your arms and breasts and thighs, as the wind strokes greedy fingers over your nipples, up your legs, between the lips of your—"

Her lips silenced him. Stemmed the flow of torment.

She thought she heard giggles and murmurs of approval.

Suddenly he tore his lips away, put her down on her feet, whispered in her ear, "And here's another secret."

He walked away. And away. Turned out, they were in a humongous elliptical domed gallery. When he was across from her on the other side over two hundred feet away, he turned. She saw his lips move.

"Jaan per voi, Phoebe."

She lurched. *I yearn for you.* Oh, dear God…

A whispering gallery. She'd heard about them, but never thought they could be that…effective. It seemed impossible, how his whisper had reached her across the space, as if he'd poured it into her ear. Into her brain. And she could swear it wasn't only his voice. She felt his thoughts possessing her, his breath on her lips, his scent filling her lungs, his heat, his fingers, his tongue…

A wave of longing rushed through her, seemingly ripping things inside her as it rippled out. She was in heat. Coming apart.

All she had to do to put an end to this torture was walk up to him and offer, take. Everything.

But now she faced it. What stopped her. Dread. Dread that once they became locked in the insanity of passion again, their magical rapport would end. He'd again be the driven man who devoured her without a word, except those of hunger.

And she loved what they shared now, couldn't get enough of the fluency of their interaction, the purity of their connection. She loved *him*. Like Armando had said, the love she felt now made the younger version—which had impacted her so hard she'd never been able to move on—seem flimsy, foundationless. And she feared that if she changed their status quo, all would be consumed in the conflagration. She couldn't go back, couldn't risk it. She had to be sure first that this would continue. She couldn't lose him again, in any way, now that she knew for real and in detail how much there was to lose.

She had to wait. Even though it was killing her.

She leaned on the wall behind her to keep herself from collapsing to the ground, whispered, "*Jaana per voi, anche,* Leandro."

Her whisper seemed to rip through him with the same force his had through her. He jerked as if under a flesh-splitting lash. And he waited. For her to follow through on her answering confession.

After about five minutes of staring at each other across the space, chests heaving, bodies trembling, he turned and strode out.

"So what is the Merraba Feast?" Phoebe shouted to Leandro over the din of galloping hooves and whistling wind. "I found no mention of it on the Internet."

"I would have been stunned if you had," he shouted back, his smile eclipsing the sun. Who needed the star when he lit up the world?

After that fraught face-off a week ago, he'd sought her out, apologized for walking out, begging testosterone intoxication. And even though their yearning had taken a turn for the distressful, they'd resumed their rapport, even better than before.

"It's a feast unique to El Jamida, and it's exactly what its name implies. A jam-making feast."

"Oh, I didn't know that word. Back to hitting the books for me…" She paused, frowned, sniffed. "Leandro, do you smell a—?"

His shout drowned her words. *"Fire."*

She saw it then, on the far side of the village. A black cloud rising over the horizon. Then the first tongues of flame broke through the darkness of roiling smoke. God…it was *huge*…

Leandro got out his phone, called in a firefighting and emergency medical operation of mammoth proportions. Then he turned to her.

"I'll organize the efforts. You go back to the castello. I'll call you as soon as it's under control." Then he raced away.

She sat on her whinnying horse, stunned, until he almost disappeared. Then she was galloping after him, screaming for her horse to go faster. But nothing was fast enough. She reached the scene to see Leandro hurtle into the burning barn.

And the fire seemed to reach out and drag him in.

Twelve

Seeing Leandro walking into the fire made Phoebe realize.

She wouldn't die without him. But she would die for him.

What followed was something she would always find difficult to remember. The terror and heat and suffocation. The exertion and smoke and screams. It was too much to take in, to process, to retain. So she kept her eyes fixed on her goal. Leandro.

She ran after him into the inferno, ran back out when the hellish heat almost fried off her skin. But she'd seen enough.

He was helping others. Children who were caught inside and kept climbing higher to escape the flames. Parents who'd run in only to be overwhelmed by smoke or set on fire. Others who'd followed to help and met the same fate. Only Leandro had protected himself so he'd be of use to those he was walking through the fire to rescue. He'd smothered himself in soaking wraps, was breathing through their barrier. His eyes were covered in sunglasses. She screamed for people to provide her with the same protection.

Then she walked into the fire after him.

* * *

Leandro had never known what terror was. He now knew.

It was seeing Phoebe with flames lashing out at her, dragging her into their incinerating arms. It was imagining her body consumed by their indiscriminate cruelty.

Terror had a taste, a texture. He retched on its foulness, shredded his sanity on its lacerating talons.

He roared his soul bloody as he waded through the inferno, gathering small bodies and hurtling to her, as she mirrored his actions. Then, in the depths of the macabre scene, everything stilled. Fright no longer drove him mad, desperation no longer paralyzed him. Instead they infused him with strength, to demolish obstacles, with clarity to do only what would see her safe.

He *would* see her safe. With his last breath.

Every breath felt like his last. Every shudder felt as if it would tear his muscles off his bones. His mind couldn't process it still. It was over. There had been no loss of life, but injuries were varying in degrees. One was…bad. Horrific.

Not Phoebe. Not Phoebe.

There was only that thought, nothing beyond it as quakes intensified, reaction crashing down on him like a caved-in ceiling. Phoebe filled his arms, alive. Unscathed.

He'd had her checked for injury, then rechecked. Dread rode him. What if her injuries manifested later?

He was assured, over and over. And over again. She'd bolted out of hell with minor respiratory irritation. So had he.

He couldn't stop crushing her to him. Terror still roared through him. Hide her. Keep her safe. He railed at her, for coming after him, for endangering herself. He'd never— *never*—get over the memory gouged into his psyche. Those minutes as he struggled to save her without abandoning the children he'd retrieved would be the bottomless mine of his nightmares.

But she hadn't needed saving. She'd saved with him, helped him, survived with him. *She was safe.*

He clutched her to his chest, pushed open the door to her room, entered and walked to the bed, stared down at it. Saw flames raging across its crisp immaculateness. He folded her into him until they both gasped for breath.

Among the gasps there were whimpers. "That boy…he's Alessandro's age…oh, God, Leandro…"

The boy with the worst injuries. He held her harder, merged their quakes. "I'll take care of him. For life. And all the victims and their families. I promise you."

She nodded frantically against his heart, wound herself tighter around him. She believed him.

Then she was pushing at him, struggling against him. She wanted to regain autonomy, and he couldn't bear the separation.

He bit down hard on his needs, gave in to hers. He unlocked himself, let her thrashing form spill from his hold.

She tackled him with all her strength, took him down on the bed. Writhed all over him, tore at his clothes, at his lips, sank her teeth into them, her nails into the flesh she exposed.

His response overtook his ability to register it. He blanked out. Catapulted into his first out-of-body experience. He saw himself tearing back at her, tackling her underneath him, nothing but a mass of instincts and frenzy.

He tore her sooty, damp clothes off her, madness deepening as she rewarded each rip with a fiercer cry, a more violent tug on his hair, a harder grind of her flesh against his hardness, a more blatant offering of herself to do with as his voracity dictated…

It hit him then, what he was doing. What she was seeking. He froze. Her cry was one of panic as she clenched around him.

But he'd come back into his mind. And he couldn't do this. Not to her. Not to them.

He exerted all the gentle force he needed to unlock her from around him, felt things shattering inside him as he swayed up to his feet and tried to move to the other end of the room.

She was there before him, dragging him back. When he resisted her, she climbed onto him, stormed his resistance with her passion, the pressure of her urgency bursting his heart.

"You didn't start this," she panted. "You kept your promise, you don't need to pull back. This is me coming to you."

"Phoebe…" He caught her hands, turned his face away from the blatant need in hers, felt control slipping like the first boulders heralding the avalanche. "This is PTS talking. This isn't how or why I want you to come to me."

She wrestled her hands free and clutched his head, pulling him down, sobbing into his mouth. "Then I've been suffering from it for eight years. I walked away then and have been pulling back ever since, for all the damn wrong reasons. But there is no reason good enough not to take what I can have with you, to live this. Maybe it took thinking we'd both die to get over my stupid fears. So I'm human, sue me."

"Phoebe, I want you so much, it scares me."

"Just take me," she cried. "I need you inside me… *please…*"

It was that *please.* It made him a beast. One that wanted to wrestle his mate to submission, mount her, pound into her until she disintegrated around him and he erupted inside her.

Growling, out of his mind, he bundled her over his shoulder, strode to the bed, threw her down, watched her as the last pillars of his restraint were reduced to wreckage as she arched like a wave, breasts jutting in the air before the undulation traveled down her body, offering him herself in a thrust that blanked his mind with carnal rage.

He descended on top of her, impacted her, would have torn her legs apart if she hadn't wrenched them wide, maddened for his invasion. He didn't need to make sure she was ready. Her readiness steamed his lungs, scalded his skin, slashed him down to his primal elements.

He tore inside her. Her answering scream tore at the tethers of his soul. The scream of woman, of long pent-up needs bursting. He penetrated her essence, the molten flesh that poured around his shaft. It was like forging through lava, as he invaded her to the womb, as she accommodated him in a liquid vise of flame.

This flesh. This being. This. He'd been without it for so long, had thought he'd be without her forever. The despair had worn away at him with each breath. And with each exhale, he'd braced himself, for her absence, the impossibility of her return. For the next inhalation when it would all start again. And again. Until he stopped breathing. And stopped yearning.

But she was here. He could breathe again.

He withdrew then drove back, all his power behind the lunge. Her scream this time deafened him with its unbridled provocation, its lashing challenge. More, it shrieked at him. Harder. All. She was a twisting pillar of fire beneath him, more destructive than the blaze they'd barely walked out of hours ago. She was bent on consuming him, and he was bent on pounding her out.

As pleasure rose, and rose, like the flames had, the smoke of the past—the bitterness and the pain and the separation and aloneness—gathered, suffocating, a cloud that needed the gust of a release that might leave them too damaged to dispel it. He rode her hard, felt her folds clinging to him, wringing him, her scent intensifying with her pleasure, her cries sharpening, lengthening, until they became one long wail interrupted by tearing intakes of breath.

He bellowed, over and over, with every lunge, forging deeper inside her. She augmented his force, arched, driving her heels and shoulders into her support, struggled against him in a reverse tug of war, as if striving to make their two bodies one. His movements grew frenzied, giving her the friction she needed to unravel, nerve by nerve.

Then he felt the orgasm tear through her. Its force forked through him, ripping at him in turn, wrenching on his shaft until he felt as if she would take his entire body into herself. Her paroxysm was the final stimulus. His body detonated, his buttocks convulsing as he unleashed himself into her, jet after jet of searing liquid propelled deep into her womb. His body quivered with the recoil as he filled her, poured his pleasure into hers, attempting to put out the fire before it reduced them to ashes.

It only raged hotter. His groans echoed her sobs as pleasure hit a plateau, left them straining at each other like two electrocution victims, helpless to break the circuit of destruction. It felt as if they wouldn't survive it. He didn't mind...

At last, the brutality of sensations leveled, declined. Had mercy. He melted into the puddle of enervation she'd become.

His heart pressed to hers, banging to the same drummer's madness, the pain of it telling him this encounter could have easily been fatal.

As it should be. Nothing less could have been fitting after all this waiting, all this craving. All this...love.

Yes. Love. But...no. Not love. He needed a new word, a new *language* to convey the magnitude of his involvement, the magnificence of melding with the mind and spirit of a being so kindred. But until he formulated the words, he'd use *love.* For real this time. He'd thought his past feelings for her had embodied life's most powerful connection, but compared to what he felt now, they had been juvenile, reeking of infatuation, lust and possessiveness.

This new feeling, while it possessed even fiercer coveting and carnality, was also selfless, pure. Total.

It also wreaked total havoc. If another fire broke out now, he wouldn't be able to move—not if it meant moving away from her. He could only adjust their positions so that she lay on top of him.

Her eyes reflected his devastation, his surrender. Then they faded, dragged him into another dimension of oblivion...

Thirteen

"Are you ready to be surprised?"

Phoebe kept her eyes closed as Leandro's murmur flared through her.

She sank in the luxury of sensations he evoked, in the beauty of his presence. Lying face-down, she felt ever more boneless. "Keep talking."

"What kind of answer is that?"

She felt the bed dip under his weight, like her world did at his approach, sighed. "The kind of answer your contradictory question deserves. Now just talk. If you run out of things to say, get the phone book. Not El Jamida's, though. It's too short."

He said nothing. She moaned her impatience. Then gasped. His teeth sank gently into her left buttock. Her moan deepened as she pushed back at him, giving him a better bite. He rumbled something wordless then mounted her, all that glorious bulk and maleness.

She dug her knees into the mattress, thrust her hips up, inviting his invasion. She'd thought after three weeks of marathon lovemaking, her in-heat state would level out. Instead, it was escalating. She had only to breathe to want him. She breathed all the time.

She wanted him to take her now, from the back, so she couldn't see his face as it seized with the savage pleasure of possessing her except in her imagination, feeling nothing but the force and size of him dominating her, stretching her to that point where pleasure and pain became howling mindlessness.

Then she'd turn on her back and beg him to take her again. Like she had that first night.

That night she'd overcome her fear, had made the leap of faith that what they shared this time wouldn't be consumed by the flames of passion. And she'd been right. Everything had blossomed instead, evolved. Beyond her misguided notions of perfection.

If the world ended tomorrow, she'd only feel thankful for having experienced so much with the one and only man she could ever love.

If only he would hurry up and let her experience more. She writhed her hips against him, opening herself over his clothed erection. He lunged, pinning her down, his teeth anchoring her by the neck, like a lion in a mating frenzy. He still said nothing.

She couldn't bear it. "Talk. And take me, dammit."

He started to shake. He was…he was…*laughing*.

She struggled beneath him until he flopped on his back beside her, exposing her to his beauty as he surrendered to the throes of unbridled amusement. She twisted around, lunged over him, gulped his laughter into herself, reached for his hardness, stroked him until he was grunting and thrusting into her hand.

She purred against his lips, "Still feel like laughing?"

"If you mean the laughter that indicates happiness, I do. Like a hyena, *albi coraggiosa*."

She giggled. "Your brave heart? We'll never hear the end of my heroism, huh?" She bit his jaw, dipped her tongue in his dimple, pouted. "Not feeling heroic right now."

"Feeling hot and bothered will do for now." He surged up, turned her onto her back, ran hands and eyes heavy with appreciation and hunger over her, until he reached her core. Then he slipped two fingers between her folds. She mewled, threw her legs wider, thrust up for more. He gave her more, pumped her with his fingers, his thumb pressing and circling her nerve bundle, bringing her to the edge. Then he withdrew. She shrieked in frustration. He laughed again, licked his fingers, growling his enjoyment. "Now I know you're ready to be surprised."

"I could have told you *that*."

"I asked. Nicely. You had to go ask me to keep talking. I'm a man of action." He submitted to her playful thump in blatant pleasure, then in one move, wheeled over her, sprang to his feet, had her wrapped in her sheets and up in his arms.

She squirmed when she found him striding out of his quarters, which she'd been sharing with him since the fire. It was one thing for everyone to know she was sharing his bed, another for them to see him hauling her around half-naked. He soothed her as he forged through connecting chamber after columned arcade, passing by fountains and winding through corridors lit by torches. She should have known he wouldn't embarrass her that way. The place was deserted.

"Is that the surprise?" She looked up from the comfort of his shoulder, trying to stem the pounding between her legs. "You sent the twelve hundred people populating the complex to buy you a soda? So we can make love any- and everywhere while they're gone?"

"While that is a brilliant idea for another time, which part of *surprise* don't you get?" He turned another corner, then started to ascend a spiraling stairwell lit with lanterns.

She gasped at the drapes hanging from its top down. A hundred-foot cascade of heavy damask in such vivid colors and intricate patterns they seemed to leap out in three dimensions against the stone wall.

She tried to wriggle down. She was no lightweight. Not that

he seemed at all exerted. When he pinched a buttock and told her to be still, she sighed. "Seriously, where did everyone go?"

"To buy me twelve hundred sodas, where else?" He kissed her lids closed. "And no peeking. Until I tell you to."

She didn't peek. It only sent the rest of her senses into hyperdrive. Scent, bypassing his smell to overload on the mixture of frankincense and musk, burning candles and night air laden with sea salt and jasmine and a hundred flowers and fruits. Hearing, skirting his heartbeats and breaths to lose itself among the sensuality of water sounds, trickling, lapping, the flow of music that seemed to originate inside her head, the trill of a lute, the hypnosis of languid percussive instruments.

Then touch took over. He slid the sheet off her body and it caressed every tight inch that begged for his ferociousness, slipped between her trembling legs, over her throbbing core. She arched into his assuagement, but he put her down and her feet sank in coolness…sand!

She panted, her toes dipping in the sensation as he urged her on. After two dozen steps, the medium beneath her soles suddenly became soft as down…grass. Then two dozen more steps and she was wading in warm water over the massaging smoothness of stones.

He was exercising his power of sensory overload on her. And she was too inflamed, too wide open. She couldn't take it anymore.

She begged. *"Please…"*

He scooped her up from behind, until she straddled his arousal. "Don't say *please* again. Tonight is for you. Say please tomorrow, when things will be back for both of us." He put her down, stepped away. "Open your eyes, *hebbi preziosa.*"

He might have let her go, but she felt his words hugging her again. *My precious love.* Another unique combination in his ongoing quest to tell her in how many ways and to what levels he loved everything about her, about them. Putting everything that filled her being into words. Words she'd been unable to rival. Her lion man was too inventive to keep up with.

Joy mushroomed inside her again as she opened her eyes.

She blinked, to make sure she wasn't imagining the sight before her. Not that she'd ever imagined so much.

This had to be the harem. She saw a gigantic chamber, at least two hundred feet across, with a towering, complex system of domes for a ceiling, with openings of uniform sizes near the top of the opposing walls below which galleries supported on arched columns were reached by two spiraling wrought-iron staircases on opposite ends of the chamber.

And in between ceiling and ground—the latter divided into areas that seemed to represent earth, reflecting pools for seas, sand for deserts, and grass for meadows—there were a dozen levels made of marble steps, slopes and platforms that seemed to represent mountains and valleys. There were couches and chaise lounges in the same vivid colors as the drapes of the stairwell. There were sunken tubs and massage platforms. And through all the levels was a winding path where water ran like a miniature river. Incense burners hung from macramé holders, and everywhere there were candles. Thousands. Flickering in the circulating night breeze.

Everything engraved itself on the pages of her mind.

"You sure kept this place maintained," she whispered.

"It looked nothing like this before I was done with it. This is all for you. But in case your feminism objects to the concept of what it used to be, this wasn't where a king kept wives and concubines. This was for all royal womenfolk, children and female servants. It fell into disuse when women wanted their own domains, even if smaller and less opulent. Which turned out to be to my advantage." He started running his hands over her back, fingers pressing into all her triggers. "Now I can do everything I want to do to you in every corner of this place that's been designed to pamper a woman."

"As opposed to a man?" She moaned, leaned into him. "Bet I can do everything to you here as easily."

"Shush. Tonight I feast on you, savor you, drain you of every spark of pleasure your lethal weapon of a body is capable of. I'll play with you, torment you, madden you, make you beg, then stop your heart with more pleasure than you can stand."

In response to his erotic threat, she twisted around, rubbed herself against him, purred low with aggressive surrender. "That's nothing special, really. You do that every night. And day."

"I'll show you nothing special." He took her wading into the pool that reflected the columned arches and the candles that crowded the walkway beneath them. They emerged to walk below those arches, their shadows dancing in the illumination coming from every direction.

At one arch he stopped. She squinted up. "Uh…Leandro, I think whoever hung that swing had no idea what you wanted it for."

"I hung that swing. And I know exactly what I want it for."

Then his large hands circled her thighs above her knees. She gasped as he raised her with unbelievable steadiness and strength until her hips hit the swing's seat. She clutched the silken ropes, shimmied into place, looked down as he kneaded her thighs apart. And she got it. His head was level with her core.

His hands did everything, went everywhere but where she was combusting for their touch. He waited until she clamped her thighs around his neck, arched backward in the swing, open, abandoned, mindless, then gave her a sharp flick. With his tongue.

She cried out, the pleasure a slash through her system.

She tried to press her mound to his mouth, but he unlocked her thighs, kept only her heels around his neck. Then he pushed her away. She swung back the length of her legs before her hooked heels brought her hurtling back. To his waiting tongue. It found her opening, slipped inside her. Her cry was sharper, louder this time, the stab of pleasure too much, over too soon. Now she knew why he'd emptied the complex. With the way this place was open to the outside, her screams would be heard for a mile.

She receded from him on the swing's next excursion, and

every time she came back, he did something worse to her. When she was begging him to finish her, he let her gather him tighter, making her swings shorter, her return to his torture faster, harder. Then he took over, held her hips and began rocking her back and forth on his plunging tongue, until she bucked, ground herself against his mouth, convulsed in furious rhythms, choking out his name, her eyes streaming with the force of her orgasm.

He lapped her to quivering satisfaction. Then he repeated the torture using his fingers alone, then again using a combination until she collapsed in a backward arch across the swing, her legs dangling on one side, her head and hair on the other. With a whirr, the swing descended, bringing their loins level.

He pulled her up, began a striptease that stopped maddeningly with his shirt. She tried to touch his ridged flesh but he caught her, produced satin ribbons from his back pocket and tied her hands to the ropes. She wouldn't fall back now if she fainted. And she felt she was about to. He was drinking her, rubbing her inflamed nipples with his hair-roughened flesh, undulating against her. Keens spilled from her. Arousal roared inside her again at her helplessness to reciprocate the exquisite torture.

Then he painted her with honey and kneeled before her, licked it all off starting from her toes, working his way up until he burned out all her stimulation centers. When she couldn't writhe anymore, cry out anymore, he tongued her to another climax.

And instead of being sated, all she wanted was him.

She struggled from her slump, croaked, "Leandro…if you really want this night to be for me, you'll give me you…in every way."

He looked deep in her eyes, his own emerald in the candle-light, supernatural in beauty and influence. Then he smiled and everything collapsed in a domino effect inside her. He undid her satin shackles, carried her to one of the sunken tubs, rinsed her off, then took her to a couch as deep as a double bed.

He stood between her legs, his erection level with her

mouth. His bass rumble shook her insides. "This is for you, remember. Use me for your pleasure. I'm yours."

He was indeed hers. Her fate. "Too bad you're going to enjoy it, too, huh?"

He smoothed his hands over her head, massaging her. "You may not believe me, but I enjoy your orgasms more than I do mine."

"I believe you. Same here. *So* selfish in a roundabout way."

She reached for him, kneading and nipping him through his pants, and he rasped, "Release me."

She undid his zipper with shaking hands. Her mouth watered as he sprang forth, hit her waiting lips, a work of divine beauty.

She explored him, smelled and tasted and touched, lost in sensory nirvana, unable to believe that she could take all of him inside her. She circled him. Her hand wouldn't close. She traveled up and down the silk steel shaft, rubbed her lips around his head, suckled it, her tongue shuddering all over his satin hardness with the pleasure he intensified with his uninhibited vocal response. Then she had him, all his power and virility, filling her in yet another way. She took all she could of him inside her mouth. He groaned his mounting pleasure, the sound creating another rush of liquid desire between her legs. It felt as if he was making love, so gently, so languidly, to her mouth, to *her* through it. But soon each thrust was another stab of need, until the emptiness where he wasn't occupying her started to hurt her.

Suddenly, his hand in her hair stopped her. But she wanted it all, his seed, his pleasure, his abandon. "Come for me, darling."

"I feel it. You need me. Say 'please' now, Phoebe."

"Oh, thank goodness. We're back to pleasure for both of us."

"Only because it's what you need now. Then it's back to only you"

"I'll just keep saying…*please*…"

"Then I'll please you until you can't say please anymore." He propped himself at the back of the couch and stretched out the miles-long power of his legs on its width. He was still following his "for her" theme, inviting her to use him for her pleasure. And she couldn't draw another breath if she didn't.

She trapped air inside her lungs as she slid over him, slithered down until she felt his width at her entrance. He held her eyes, her waist, caressing her, his massive body trembling. She should torment him like he did her. She couldn't.

She sank on him in one downward stroke, losing sight for a moment with the blow of pain and pleasure. He seemed to fill her whole body. He did fill her whole being.

He buried his face in her breasts as he lay buried inside her, and they trembled together for a long moment, just savoring the connection, the reciprocal submission and domination.

He suckled her nipples in turn, soft pulls that grew hard then harder, each tug shooting straight to her core, making her pulse around his invasion, shifting her up and down his shaft. She pulled his head up when she couldn't bear any more, captured his lips. He drew her soul right out of her, infused her with his. His endearments grew thicker, more explicit, the words she longed for, the voice she lived to hear.

As the pulse of pleasure threatened to burst into the convulsions that would shatter her, he felt it, swept her around and under him and gave her the pressure she needed to spill over, screeching, into intoxicating climax. She felt his jolt of answering ecstasy, was scorched by his seed as it pulsed over and over into her womb, bathing it, filling it, until the pleasure eddied in a downward spiral so violent her consciousness flickered.

She came back into her body to his caress, to the feel of him still filling her. He was poring over what she knew was her ravaged-by-emotion-and-satisfaction face. His was gentleness and possession personified.

"You would send a man to his grave with a smile on his face and a fervent wish to rise again only so that he could die once more at your hands. You'd make him want to do anything to deserve your esteem and respect. You make me want to be the best man I can be." He took her lips in what felt like a pledge. "So yes, Phoebe, I will become crown prince."

She cried out her pleasure, for him, for Castaldini, surged up to fill his cherishing and indulgent embrace.

Throughout the rest of the night, they planned and projected and shared all the exquisiteness that was only theirs to share, a steady supply of which would fuel all her tomorrows.

And if something in her deepest consciousness fidgeted, wondering why he hadn't exactly asked her to be part of his future, it settled back into serenity with the certainty that he soon would....

Fourteen

They stayed two more weeks in paradise.

They would have gone back to Jawara the day after Leandro made his decision, since he'd refused to have a succession ceremony. He wanted no fuss, no media, no delegates bearing congratulations. He was taking the oath then getting down to business. But the king's illness had postponed his instatement.

On the day they did return to the capital, she went out. She bought something. She returned to the palace, entered her bathroom and came out. Transfigured. *Pregnant.*

She'd planned on taking the Pill before she and Leandro become fully intimate, but their intimacies hadn't been planned. She'd started the Pill the day after the fire, but the power of what they'd shared that climactic night hadn't only brought them back to life, it had sowed new life inside her.

It felt like a miracle. It was one. And more.

Before Leandro had come back into her life, she'd been resigned to live a life devoid of passion, had assumed that, to fulfill her hopes of having a child of her own, she would have had to go the sperm donor way. But now…

She was having Leandro's baby.

The only baby she wanted.

The discovery rocked her, the knowledge tore her apart.

With joy.

The reality, the significance, the beauty expanded through her in a paroxysm of mindless delight. The news trembled on her lips, shuddered through her limbs with the need to tear through the palace and fling herself into his arms.

One thing held her back. Something just as momentous. The historic occasion of Leandro taking on the mantle of power. And even though she felt her heart unraveling with impatience, that event had to take precedence right now.

But after he did…blood frothed and tumbled through her system in a boil of expectation and glee.

Then, as she got ready for the succession ceremony, her whoops and whirls around her room decelerated, her simmering blood cooling. Then it gradually…chilled. With the sedimentation of frost. Of uncertainty.

He had been beyond loving to her, beyond magnificent, beyond memory or imagination, as he'd promised. But he hadn't promised her a future.

Oppression bore down in degrees, until it started to cut off air and blood flow.

Did he want a future? Wouldn't he have said something during the past weeks if he did?

He'd told her everything, from his earliest memories to how he loved everything she'd ever touched. But he'd said nothing about taking back his original pact—the one she'd once agreed to wholeheartedly. What if he'd been gorging himself on all they could have, like a man would at an all-you-can-eat buffet, to turn craving into a permanent glut? He might have been living a totally different experience from the one she'd been losing herself in, believing they were in agreement. And she would be the one guilty of changing the rules midstream, believing her own fantasies, and imposing them on his every word and look and touch.

More nightmares blossomed, billowing like the smoke that had heralded the flames that had almost claimed their lives.

His old accusation mushroomed inside her. That she'd wanted him as a stepping-stone to royal status. What if he considered her pregnancy a ploy to entrap him? Even if he didn't—if he hadn't thought of a future with her, did *she* want one if he felt obligated to offer it now that she was carrying his child?

The dream world she'd been inhabiting for the last seven weeks started to distort into something macabre. A place where any move might end in devastation.

Stop. *Stop.* What was she *thinking?* This was Leandro, and this was the present, not the past when everything had gone wrong. They *had* a future together. If she couldn't believe he loved her after all they'd shared, when would she? So he hadn't mentioned future plans. Yet. He had that tiny matter of taking on the destiny of a whole kingdom on his mind. She should just shut up her insecurities, and go watch her man— her love—enter history.

She rushed to put on the dress he'd asked her to wear. Feeling the fumes of insecurity blowing over, chalking them up to the aftereffects of the life-changing discovery and pregnancy hormones, she ran out to the Throne Room.

Despite Leandro's wishes, there *was* a ceremony of sorts. The representatives of the D'Agostino family and the Council gathered in their fineries to witness a succession, something most of them hadn't witnessed. But Leandro wouldn't let them force him into changing his plans by much, didn't give them the spectacle they were congregated to watch.

Looking light-years beyond spectacular in his crown-prince uniform, colored the deep crimson and gold of Castaldini's crest, he walked up to the king, knelt on one knee, recited the oath, barely gave Benedetto time to tap his shoulder with the scepter before rising, turning around and thanking everyone for coming, clearly telling them all to scoot. It was over in less than five minutes.

But it was still something she'd remember forever. The sight of the only man she'd ever love in the middle of the fairy-tale setting as he took on the mantle of power and privilege he'd been born to, that he'd worked all his life to deserve.

He was now glaring at the crowd. He seemed to want a private audience with the king. And he wanted it now.

Everyone, disappointed, succumbed to Leandro's influence, learning from the outset they had a regent who got his way. She met Leandro's gaze over their departing bustle. Those eloquent eyes of his said so much, with such intensity. Such emotion.

She almost ran to him. She told him instead. In their whispers. The ones they no longer needed the whispering gallery for. *Me, too. Oh, my love, me, too.*

She suppressed the impulse to dance all the way to her room. She thought she might have scared a few people with her blaring smiles.

She'd just flung herself down on her bed when the venomous words hit her.

"You think you've got him now, don't you, you American harlot?"

She closed her eyes. She knew that voice. She didn't want to acknowledge the malignant manifestation that wore the body of a stunning female.

She opened her eyes, sat up in slow motion. And there she was, as majestic and flawless as ever, wrapped in the perfection of the emerald chiffon creation she'd worn during the ceremony. Stella the Serpent, as Phoebe and Julia called her.

Phoebe got up, circled the malevolent presence. "I wish I could say the same to you, Stella. But 'harlot' would be a huge compliment. And I certainly don't owe you any of those."

Stella's perfect face was stained with the nastiness of her

nature and intentions. "Save your pathetic attempt at cutting wit, you low-born trash. Your sister might have caught a minor prince—"

Phoebe interrupted fiercely, "Caught *and* kept. In spite of all your efforts to take him away, you high-born waste of DNA."

Stella's lips thinned. "Paolo was a child when she trapped him. And I let him go because he's pathetically attached to the brood she's saddled him with. I wouldn't play mother to her rats."

"Yeah, keep telling yourself that he didn't see the evil spirit infesting your beautiful body. *He* ran from *you,* not the other way around. And we all know it. Notice the 'all' part?"

Stella smirked. "Go ahead, delude yourself. But there's another who won't run away."

"You mean Leandro, right? Of course you do. Why chase the current king's son when you can go after the future king himself?"

Stella stiffened, her eyes shooting over Phoebe's head, her composure cracking.

Then it hardened again, the maliciousness in her eyes growing maddening. "I know this tactic. Women like you, climbers and moochers who have nothing but an easy body and a scheming mind, go around accusing others of what you're doing yourself. *You're* chasing after Leandro. You think if you compromise him enough, he'll be honor-bound to make you his queen. But I'm not letting you disgrace him or black-mail him into making you anything."

Exasperation and animosity finally morphed into rage. "And how will you stop me? Will you run to Leandro and tell on me? Tell him how I've been entrapping him with only one goal in mind?"

"Yes, I will. I'll save him from the user that you are."

"You mean you'll save him for the user and abuser that *you* are? Well, good luck, sister. It's your word against mine. Who do you think he'll believe?"

"He means nothing to you at all, does he? This incredible

man, and all you see is your ticket to royal status. You're so certain of your power over him, think him so under your spell, you believe he'll give you everything you've been after."

"Yeah, my power over him is total, and it has no chinks in it for pathetic schemers like you to enter through. So go ahead, try to get him out from under 'my spell.' Knock yourself out. Preferably literally."

Stella's voice shook, but her eyes were stone steady. "You…you vile manipulator…even if you manage to deceive him now, I'll help him see through your act one day."

"Yeah, yeah. Save your breath for *your* act. Break both legs."

Stella gave her such a look, Phoebe's blood stopped in her arteries. It was…demonic. Then she sobbed and ran out.

The moment the door slammed after Stella, Phoebe began to shake. But it had been worth it, dammit, to turn that viper's attack against her.

Suddenly tears were streaming down her cheeks. It was…too much. The paroxysms of emotion were taking their toll.

Seemed it was going to be one hell of a pregnancy.

And she couldn't wait to experience each tumult and discomfort. And each breath of life with Leandro.

Leandro's fury mounted. Even now that it was all over.

The moment he'd declared he'd accept the succession, the damned Council had dared demand—again—that he take their choice of queen with the crown. They claimed they were conveying the king's will, since his illness had robbed him of the ability to speak it. The bastards even insinuated they'd take it up with Phoebe. They were sure that as an official of Castaldini, she's see the exigency of having the crown prince marry, for his kingdom, a woman versed in all the demands of a queen's life and duty.

He'd blasted them. He was marrying—for himself—a woman who would put any queen in history to shame. It was nonnegotiable. Otherwise, good luck with Durante or Ferruccio.

He'd stuck close to her during the last couple of weeks in fear that someone would get to her, try to pressure her into leaving him to his "greater destiny," distress her for one second behind his back.

Out of respect for the king, he'd given his word that he wouldn't declare his intentions until he'd informed Benedetto of them. They probably thought the king might still sway him. The fools.

Not that Phoebe needed declarations. She knew he was hers. She didn't need words to solidify her ownership. Still, she'd have them now, like she already had everything that he was.

After the ceremony, he'd arrived to find her door open, and his sprint had faded. She always closed her doors. She probably wasn't inside.

He'd been about to go tearing through the palace searching for her, to make a very public fool of himself when he'd…heard.

Her voice. As he'd never heard it. Cruel. Cold-blooded.

Stella had accused her of entrapping him for the sole reason of becoming queen. And… *Dio*… Phoebe…she'd admitted it, gloatingly sure of her power over him.

Stella had dashed out of Phoebe's room in tears, not noticing him standing there, dumbstruck. Echoes of her voice and Phoebe's still shrieked their vicious catfight in his brain until it felt like pulp.

He means nothing to you at all, does he?

Yeah, my power over him is total.

His own thoughts battered him. Taunting. Jeering. *You believed she wanted you for yourself? That that made more sense than her wanting to be queen?*

His worst nightmare. Again. A virtuoso act. In the past, and now, far worse. She'd used reverse psychology so he'd rise to the challenge, do whatever it took to be perfect in her eyes. As he had. And all that time, everything that had appealed to his tastes and logic and healed his wounds and ensnared his mind and spirit—unreal. Every word and glance and touch,

a yank from a master puppeteer. Everything—*everything*—
they'd shared, a lie.

His feet moved, taking him inside her room. She lay on
her bed. Everything. She was everything. And she'd left him
with nothing.

She suddenly jerked up and looked around. "Leandro,
darling…"

She looked…overwrought. She'd guessed that he'd over-
heard her confessions. Was thinking how to perform
damage control.

He felt something within him give, like the steel foundations of a skyscraper moaning as they collapsed.

He heard himself saying, "I've chosen a wife, Phoebe."

He stopped, torturing himself with every nuance of her
masterful act. Such expectation on her face. Such trust.
Such adoration.

And he lost whatever shred remained of his control, his
sanity, in the conflagration that consumed his soul.

"You want to know who she is? The only woman to suit
me, the woman worthy of being my princess, my future queen,
mother of my children, my heirs, owner of my heart and soul?"

He waited again. Saw the dawn of absolute delight.

Then he drawled, "A pure, noble, Castaldinian woman."

He opened himself to the shock wave razing through her
until the agony of it decimated his last shred of humanity.

And he taunted, "What do you think of Clarissa
D'Agostino?"

Phoebe stared at Leandro. The man she loved with everything in her. The father of her unborn baby.

He'd turned into a stranger. And he'd said…he'd said…

This had to be some trick. But he didn't have a sick sense
of humor. And this was beyond sick…this was…was…

The banked panic began to rise. "Don't, Leandro. That's
one thing that just isn't—isn't…"

"Funny? You think I'm joking? I'm not. Can't you see

that? So—how does it feel now? To be led on until you think you have the world in your hand, only to be cut down in one vicious stroke? To know that you mean nothing?"

She wanted to close her eyes. She couldn't see this. That face. Demonic in beauty and evil. Far worse than Stella's. Than anything. But she couldn't look away. She was paralyzed. Beyond agony. Beyond shock.

All this time, he'd been building up to this moment? When she'd believed in him, lived and would die for him? He'd done this just for the pleasure of slamming her down? This was his revenge for her daring to run away from him once? Was there cruelty like this?

There was. And worse. It was him, looking at her with that mad gleam in his eyes, a feline hunter waiting for its kill to twitch so he could batter it again. And again.

But she wouldn't curl up and play dead. She had to fight back. If he was the monster he was showing himself to be, she wouldn't just expire in silence.

She could say nothing. The truth was sinking its talons into her guts, preparing to wrench them apart.

"So what do you think of my choice, Phoebe? As the king's daughter, Clarissa is everything my wife should be. And she was such a vision tonight. Don't you agree? Come now, Phoebe, tell me. You know how I value your opinion."

Every word was one more slash, tearing everything she'd believed they'd had apart, everything she'd thought would sustain her for the rest of her life.

"I wouldn't have believed that even you had the nerve to ask something like that, to…to…"

"To…what? *Mat'ooli,* don't say…you expected me to choose *you?*"

She could only stare into his malice. So there truly was no end to one's capacity for suffering.

She wondered if pain could kill. It should. Nothing should be this cruel without an end. "Isn't that what you wanted me to expect? What you worked so hard to lead me to expect, when I started this relationship with no expectations? Beyond feeling blazingly alive in your company, in your arms? Isn't this what you planned? What do you want to hear now—how completely you've taken me in?"

Hot tears corroded her eyes, scouring down her face, splashing down her chin to spread darkness on her red taffeta dress, his choice. Had he planned that, too? So that she'd look down and see the stains spreading like oozing blood? *Were* those tears, or was her pierced heart bleeding out?

More needed to gush out of her. "Have you appeased your monstrous pride? Have you taken your revenge on me for once daring to escape your abuse? Are you now satisfied that you've damaged me beyond repair? And you're asking my opinion on your 'pure woman'—me, the woman whose innocence you took, whose pride and heart you destroyed and who you're reviling for it? But I can't blame you. I set myself up. Again. I got what I deserved. But though I now know that my opinion—and I—mean less than dirt to you, I'll tell you I believe that Clarissa would make the best queen. I just wish for her sake you weren't the one who'll be king."

Run. She had to run. Pride had nothing to do with it—it was maternal instinct. The baby inside her was the one thing that gave her the strength to get away, to survive.

She passed him, reached the door when she turned. "I once told you we owed each other no hellos. I owe you one thing now, a wish…" He was standing there, chest heaving, eyes scary, his focus that of a madman. Pain ruptured her heart all over again, crushed it in its own blood. "I wish for you to go to hell, Leandro. The same one where you sent me."

Fifteen

I take it all back. Every word I said was an unforgivable lie. I was cut open and bleeding and I went mad. Forgive me.

The pleas looped like a broken record inside his head.

They hadn't made it out of his mouth.

He'd stood there, mute, as she'd turned away, looking like everything inside her had been crushed. He'd stood there until she'd disappeared. Then he'd collapsed to his knees and remained there for several mind-destroying hours, reliving every word she'd said, suffering every pang she had, burning at every tear she'd shed.

Then he'd launched himself after her. But it had been too late.

A murderous Julia railed against him with the rage of a lioness on the scent of blood. She had a formidable ally in an outraged and disgusted Paolo. Among them, they made sure Phoebe's trail was stonecold.

That had been three months ago.

He'd gone stark raving mad within three hours.

He'd become dangerous. Everyone was regretting pursuing

him so hard to take on the succession. Having an insane crown prince, one with all this power, was a recipe for disaster. He might yet be the end of the monarchy and Castaldini, much sooner than the king's worst fears.

He *needed* Phoebe. He had to find her, prostrate himself at her feet, beg her forgiveness, take back every word, erase every hurt, to remain sane. He couldn't. So he…rampaged.

Just this morning, he'd thrown a delegate out during a televised negotiation session. Bodily. Right there on the live feed, he'd lunged at the offensive weasel, bundled him up like a soiled sweatshirt, marched him, kicking like a cat about to be dropped in boiling oil, down the stairs and out the palace door. It made world news within minutes. Along with the details of the brewing international incident.

He hadn't even missed a beat before he'd stalked to his jet and gotten the hell out of Castaldini on another search for her, following the last lead he'd gotten. It had been another false one. He'd just finished putting the investigative agency who'd supplied him with it out of business.

"When will you stop your never-ending tantrum?"

Ernesto's disapproval jolted its icy tranquility through him.

"*Not* a good time, Ernesto," he barked. "Not a good *life*."

"She doesn't want you to find her. Why don't you move on?"

"Why don't *you*, Ernesto? Before I throw another 'tantrum'?"

"As long as getting violent makes you feel better."

"Nothing will make me feel better. Ever."

"Finished being melodramatic? I never thought I'd say something like this, but if she left in such a condition that made her family wish you dead, maybe you don't deserve to find her."

Leandro closed his eyes. He was only hanging on because she was there, and safe, somewhere in this world. But he didn't deserve to find her. That was why he hadn't. Ernesto was right.

Then the moment of sanity passed and frustration sheared through him again, tearing his eyes open. "No, Ernesto, I don't deserve to find her. But I have to, if only to offer her the chance to finish me herself and take her revenge."

Ernesto pursed his lips. "I fail to imagine what you could have done to her this time. If she left you, left Castaldini and her family, evidently never to return, then you've hurt her beyond repair. Even worse than the first time, when she left because she felt she meant nothing to you."

Incredulity boomed out of him. "Where did you get that piece of unadulterated crap? Are you claiming that she told you—?"

"She told me nothing. She never did."

"So that is *your* interpretation? That she meant nothing to me? *Dio,* Ernesto, how can you think anything so insane? You saw how much I needed her. You yourself, who advised me not to spend crucial time with her, saw how unable I was to even consider your advice."

"What I saw was a young man in the throes of an all-consuming passion, but *that* didn't indicate any true or lasting emotions. Many times as I escorted her to you I found myself aching for her. She was so eager to come to you, so amenable to your decree of secrecy. But I always felt her pain. You might have been blind, but I saw her face many times when you passed her at a function with another woman on your arm. My sympathy must have started to color my expression, because she once asked—with such shyness and trepidation— if I was reluctant to play the role of go-between. When I assured her I wasn't, she persisted. She felt my disapproval. Did I fear she was distracting you? Harming your campaign for the crown? Was I offended by her behavior? I vehemently denied it. But I realized later, I *did* disapprove, I *was* disappointed and offended. By *your* handling of her and the situation.

"I did recommend that you leave her alone, not because I thought the crown was more important than her, but because you were not giving this exquisite woman the respect and consideration she deserved. And I started to fear you were incapable of giving them to her. You might have decreed the secrecy a necessity, insisted that you hated it, but to me it started to look like you were having your cake and eating it, too. At her expense. And if I can suspect you, do you wonder she had no faith in your intentions toward her?"

"*Dio,* how could you have doubted me?" he groaned. "I would never treat even a woman I disrespected with anything but dignity, but Phoebe… Didn't you see the power of my involvement?"

"I did, but I had no idea of its true nature. I even feared it for its very power, for being unprecedented. You were behaving out of character, and your next steps became a total mystery to me. But then, there was only one projection, really. You'd worked for the crown since you took your first steps. And I believed that if you had to take it at the cost of casting Phoebe aside and taking the wife it came with, that you would have done it."

"How could you have been so wrong about me?" Leandro exploded. "I only kept her a secret because they wouldn't have given me a fair chance at the crown if they'd known beforehand that I wouldn't marry the queen they wanted beside me on the throne. But I had only one plan—to make Phoebe my princess, my queen, at any cost. And if I couldn't have both her and the crown, I would have chosen her. But I had to give the chance to get them both all I had first."

"And you told me that? You certainly didn't tell her."

"You know I don't discuss my plans before they bear fruit. I couldn't promise her what I didn't yet have to give."

"And she was supposed to…do what? Just know? Trust you?"

"*Yes.*" This was bellowed.

"I never thought you had unreasonableness in your makeup, not even when you were knowingly going against everything Castaldini stood for. You had every right then, according to your set of beliefs. But to demand that she trust you based on intentions you never declared, that goes beyond perverse."

"What's perverse about expecting the woman who trusted me with her heart and body—*Maledizione,* her *life,* when she came to me with no one knowing—to trust me to be a man of honor?"

"But that was probably why she believed she didn't have any place in your heart or life—because she believed you are one.

A man of honor who wasn't honor-bound by the promises he hadn't made. A man of honor who had a momentous destiny, one that from every possible indication, didn't include her."

Leandro's heart stampeded. His skull seemed to squeeze his brain until he felt it would crush it. He couldn't… He never… He didn't…

"And when you saw how her desertion devastated me, you still didn't realize how much she meant to me?"

"How could I have known you weren't devastated over the other catastrophes that had taken place at that time? How could I have guessed, when you seemed to remember her only four months later, sent me to fetch her without a word, and two hours later she ran out, begging me to take her back? I never saw anyone more miserable."

And he howled. "*Dio*…how can this be? How can I have behaved in such a way that I misguided you both, the man I value most, the woman who means everything to me, so totally about my emotions and intentions?"

"You were always the best at everything except the one thing you had no practice in. Relationships. But I understand now. A man of your capacity for commitment and passion, in love for the first time, at the most trying time of his life. You had tunnel vision, leading to your goal, couldn't perceive anything from anybody else's perspective. And both Phoebe and I were guilty of perpetuating that problem, catering to your every whim and accommodating your every demand, giving you the impression that all was well."

"But even if I was a fool who gave her no indication of my feelings, that was before I was exiled. When I brought her to New York… *Dio,* I told her I *needed* her."

"As what? And why only then? And how do you think she should have handled that out-of-the-blue admission? It might have been a precedent for you to admit you needed anyone, but to her it could have meant something very different. That you needed her as the ever-faithful, ever-accommodating lover who would provide a convenient outlet for your tumultuous emotions at the time. How could she have done anything but refuse to be that, to walk away before you destroyed her?"

"*Dio…Dio*…she couldn't have believed that…. She would have had to think I was unscrupulous, heartless…a *monster* to believe that."

"Not really. Just a man who'd suffered a grave injury and was looking for the best salve for his wounds. It still didn't mean you wanted her forever."

"What about the time I sent you to her again? That was five *years* after she walked out on me. What did that action signify to you, if not my continued commitment?"

"The day I arrived and learned she'd announced her engagement, I thought you were dangling yourself again to get her to break it off with Armando."

"You thought I was being a spiteful son-of-a-bitch? A dog in the manger? Don't you know me at *all*, Ernesto?"

"I did think of other reasons, but after a five-year silence, none of them was in your favor. I saw her whenever I could, and it always broke my heart to feel her still hoping for a word from you. A word I could never deliver. You were busy playing the martyr, it seems, in your own version of reality."

"She did accuse me of living in a universe starring me…" He dropped his head into his fists, pressing with all his strength against his temples, to stop it from exploding.

Ernesto went on. "But that was then. What did you do differently this time? Besides desire, what emotions did you confess?"

"*Everything.* I showed her in every way the depth of my involvement, which is a hundred times stronger than my past love."

"You probably only *think* you gave sufficient proof of your emotions. You believed the same in the past, and you were totally wrong. Is it any wonder she left you again?"

"That's not—not what happened… *Dio,* Ernesto, everything was beyond perfect and I believed in her again, would have never believed any evidence against her, but when the evidence was her own words…*Dio*…I *heard* her, Ernesto."

Ernesto's frown was spectacular. "You heard her? Saying what? In what context? And to whom?"

"She was gloating about her total power over me, to Stella—"

"Stella?" The name was an explosion of disdain and revulsion.

Leandro understood too well. After his exile, he'd discovered what a vile creature she was. *"Dio, si...*anything she said to Stella had to have been provoked, no doubt a defense against the acid that drips from that witch's tongue. But I—I think I lost my mind. All I could think was that my worst nightmares were true, that she'd been manipulating me from day one, never wanted me for myself and I—I told her I'd choose a wife, but never her...and more...and by the time I regained my senses, she was gone."

He stopped, retched at the memory of the vile things he'd said, at realizing the enormity of his crime against her yet again. At the look in Ernesto's eyes.

"I struck you only once, Leandro."

Leandro shoved a fist against his heart, wanting to punch through his rib cage and snatch it out. Maybe then it would stop battering his insides to a pulp. "I might have been only eleven then, but if you think I can ever forget the slap that sent me hurtling to the ground, think again."

"In case you've rewritten history in that intractable mind of yours, let me refresh your memory. You accused a servant of stealing and he was punished, only for me to discover later that you built your case against him based on nothing more than that it 'made sense' to you. You've used that same kind of senseless sense again on Phoebe. And not only have you accused her, you've condemned and punished her. And you dare to seek her now? You think no one can ever look beyond your assets to want you for yourself, so you keep superimposing your suspicions on everyone's actions. I think you've gone too far this time. And you've lost the woman you failed to deserve."

Leandro exploded to his feet. "No. I can't lose her, Ernesto. I came to my senses without needing proof. I was mad to suspect her, and it will never happen again. I would die in atonement, I would die anyway for her, without hesitation, but I'd rather live for her, spend every minute of my life making her happy and fulfilled."

Ernesto looked at him as if he was giving him a total mind and psyche scan. Just as Leandro felt as if he'd start destroying the place in a fit of helplessness and frustration, Ernesto nodded, as if coming to a decision. Then he said a clipped, "You *may* deserve another chance."

The bark that exploded from Leandro's depth felt as if it cut a sac of bitterness open inside him. "*Grazie*. As if your opinion matters. It's hers, and only hers, that does."

To Leandro's shock, a wicked smile spread across Ernesto's lips. "Oh, but my opinion does matter. If you'd failed to change it, I would never have told you where to find her."

Sixteen

Leandro stood at the end of the driveway of the delightful one-level detached house that Phoebe now called home. She wouldn't call it that one more day. Even if it killed him.

Suddenly his senses flickered.

The emanations were unmistakable. Hers.

He swung around. And there she was. In white slacks, a loose turquoise top and ponytail, she was so unbearably precious, so brutally missed, a convulsion of emotion ripped through him. Her face was frozen with the same look of horror and devastation he'd last seen on it.

He whispered, "Forgive me, *mi galia amore.*"

After their long sessions in the whispering gallery, they no longer needed its medium. He knew she'd heard him.

And she ran. Tried to escape into her house.

He wouldn't let her lock him out, his heart splintering for having to exert any force against her.

She suddenly backed away from the door, let him charge in under his unopposed pressure.

As soon as he closed it she hissed at him. "What do you want? More games? Sex? You decided you don't want to get married immediately, so you'll toy with me again until you do?"

"*No...no...per Dio,* Phoebe...no."

"You don't want sex? You've found a new nympho? Or is your harem already full of them?"

"*Li imploro*...I beg you...I only want to beg your forgiveness—"

"Why? You think maybe I didn't deserve having you tread on me like you did? That you should have been a tad less brutal? You're having conscience pangs? Do you even *have* a conscience, Leandro?"

"I don't have anything, without you."

She lurched as if he'd backhanded her. "You...*bastard*. Why are you doing this? What reminded you of me again, all of a sudden?"

"I've been looking for you, to beg your forgiveness, your return, since the day you walked away."

"*Liar.* Every word you said, every smile, every touch, every moment, you lied. And you're still lying. You showed me your real face that day. A monster's. If you think I'll ever forget it..."

"Did it look like the face of a monster or a madman, Phoebe?"

"I don't care. It wasn't the face of the man I thought I knew, the man I loved. It was the cruel, warped, sick..."

She choked on emotion and he urged her on. "Yes, Phoebe. Call me names, scream at me, shred me with your rage."

She swayed away from him, escaping his begging hands. "Get out. And I don't care if you are a crown prince or the most powerful man in the world. Come near me again and I'll make you sorry."

"No, Phoebe, you must give me another chance—"

"Get *out,* Leandro. If you don't want to spend your time at the dentist implanting teeth from now till your coronation."

"I'm not going anywhere. Ever again. So do it. Hit me, Phoebe, vent your outrage. I misjudged you and mistreated you and tormented you. I took from you and never gave anything back. I made you feel like nothing, like less than nothing with the way I hid you in the past, and the way I flaunted our intimacy in the present. I gave other women my public respect, showed you you're only good for providing entertainment, then when you gave me all of yourself, I took it all and told you that you meant nothing to me, that when I chose a wife I'd choose a woman of good reputation and high social standing, that you had neither—"

A lash cracked.

He barely felt the blow fall on his cheek. He was too numb with pain and dread already.

Her chest heaved, her paleness evaporating in a tide of crimson. "Can't you leave me with something to look back on as clean and beautiful… Can't you leave me… Just *leave!*"

"I'm *never* leaving you. Hit me again, Phoebe. Harder. Do some real damage. It doesn't matter that none of what I just said is true, that I didn't mean to make you feel any of it. What matters is that I did."

"Yeah, and I'm not giving you the chance to ever make me feel any of that again, unintentionally or otherwise. And no, I won't hit you again. I only did that to stop your rant."

"Nothing will ever stop me from proving to you that the only lies I ever told you were that madness I struck you with. I'll spend my life atoning, reminding you of the magic we shared, reviving it until you believe that you *are* my life. Take it, *mi tesoro hebbi,* it's yours to do with as you please."

The horror on her face only mounted as tears became a thick cascade drenching her trembling lips. "God…you know, don't you? That's what this is all about!"

The sight of her anguish made him stagger. "Know what?"

She started sobbing until he could barely understand her. "How did you find out? It has to be your armies of informers and investigators. It can't be one of my family who told you."

"*Per Dio,* Phoebe…what are you talking about?"

"I can't bear to see you. I never want you near me again…
and I'm damned…if I'm letting you near…my baby. It's *mine,*
do you hear me? It has nothing to do with you."

Baby?

Agony clamped him with the force of a heart attack.

He reached for her, ignoring the pain. Only defusing hers
mattered, defending her. Healing her was the one thing he'd
do before he died. "I swear, offering my life has nothing to
do with…*Dio santo,* I didn't…*hebbi preziosa*…I didn't even
know…you were…were…"

"Of *course* you'd say you didn't know…you'd say
anything to get your hands on your heir…"

"*Giuro su Dio*—I swear to God—I swear by everything,
by my love for you…" And he caved in under the brutality of
it all, dropped to his knees before her, caught her around the
hips, frantic to stem the tide of her anguish. She struggled,
pushed him away, her sobs rattling through them both. He
clung, his own agony dripping down his cheeks. "I'm only
here because I never knew what love was before you, what
needing another was. The first time around, I plunged wholly
into loving and needing you. I was so submerged that I didn't
realize how I was messing up. I loved you so much more
deeply the second time around that I messed up far worse,
because I depend on you to the point of total vulnerability.
When I heard you talking to Stella…"

She stilled so totally that if she hadn't been standing, he'd
have thought she'd lost consciousness. She realized.

When she finally spoke, her voice was lifeless. "You loved
me so much you gutted me the moment you heard something
you misinterpreted."

"And my crime, after all you gave me, after all I knew of
you, is irredeemable. I can only beg your understanding. I
reacted so viciously because I *have* been in the hell you
wished me to go to, for eight long years. Then we were
together again, and though I didn't I realize it, I was living in

dread of losing you again. A word from you can cast me into heaven or into hell. When I heard you, I went out of my mind with pain, with the dread that I meant nothing to you and that I'd plunge into purgatory again, this time forever. I came to my senses the moment you disappeared, and there was no way I could have known you were pregnant then. Ask your family, ask Ernesto. They didn't tell you I was tearing up the world looking for you because they believed you were better off without me, because they thought I deserved to lose you. I'm here for *you*, and only you. I'd do anything for you. Remember the night of the fire and you'll remember I will brave burning to death for you. Just like you would for me. Have mercy, on both of us, Phoebe and forgive me. Be mine and let me be yours."

He stopped with a huge gasp, buried his face in her abdomen, where their love was taking a life of its own.

Then he told her everything about the past, things he now understood fully, thanks to Ernesto. His life depended on her believing every word.

She finally sagged in his hold, allowed him to have her again, hugged him back into her, let him breathe and let his heart beat again, blessing him with her resurrected belief and passion.

And he told her about the present. And about the future.

"You made me understand myself, *hebbi*, you opened my eyes to what I must be. And you were right from the start. I am not the right king for Castaldini. I cannot change to the extent the kingdom needs, and it sure can't handle my modernizing, expanding ways. But I'll remain regent until they make up their mind to pursue Durante or Ferruccio. I hope to God one of them accepts. And then I'll return to doing the best job I ever did on behalf of my kingdom—being its ambassador to the world. And I want only the best negotiator, the best deal-maker, the best diplomat I've ever known to be my partner, not only through life, but also in representing Castaldini, in bringing it what most suits it from the world. You. My love. My life."

* * *

The import of Leandro's words sank like depth charges in Phoebe's mind. Then they exploded.

She pounced on him, dragging him by the arms as if to pull him back from the edge of an abyss. "What have you done? What have I done? I convinced you you're wrong for Castaldini? God, Leandro, no! I was only trying to make you adjust your expectations and take it easy in your integration-into-the-world plans. You'll be the best king Castaldini ever had!"

"No, I won't. I'm too much of a capitalist democrat, remember? But I can be of much use in other capacities. You were right. About everything. *Everything, mi galia tesoro.*" When she kept squirming and protesting, he suddenly hugged her off the ground, his reddened eyes gleaming wickedness and worship. "Does it disappoint you too much that you won't be queen?"

"Don't you dare joke now, or I'll hit you, as you so wanted me to."

He guffawed as he spread himself to the hands flailing on his chest. "You *are* hitting me. And I love it. Hit me some more."

She oohed. "I *knew* you had an S-M streak!"

"And I hope you'll exploit it to your imagination's content." He gathered her up and she immediately melted into him. "That's my one regret. And was half my reasons for accepting the succession. I wanted to give Castaldini the best queen ever, to make you the queen, as you deserve to be."

She hit him again, hugged him. "I deserve only to be loved by you. Are you getting that, or do I need to use more force?" He drowned her in another kiss, chuckling in elation and relief. As he wrapped her around him and carried her off to bed, she murmured, "I want you to rest your mind on this point, for as sure as I knew I'd never love another, I never thought I was queen material. But you *would* make the best king!"

"I want only to be king in your eyes."

"In my eyes, you're everything."

It was still after much debate and tears that she came to accept his decision, to believe she hadn't caused a huge loss to him, to Castaldini, that the path he'd charted was the best one.

Then he knelt before her at the foot of the bed, produced an embossed silver and gold box from the pocket over his heart.

Phoebe stared as he opened it. A ring, and a pendant.

In Castaldini, she'd seen what she'd believed to be the most stunning creations in the world. These surpassed them all in taste and craftsmanship. But it was the significance of the design—her name wrapped around his and his family's crest—that had tears bursting from her eyes.

And he pledged. "This is you owning me and holding in your hand and near your heart my future and that of my family. Will you be queen of my life, keeper of my heart and destiny?"

She fell to her knees before him. "I'll be anything you want me to be. Take all of me, my love. You already own it all anyway."

He swept her up, and to bed, rejoined them, mended forever what had almost been sundered, what could never be parted again.

"It's a boy?"

Phoebe snuggled up to Leandro. Boy, he was big enough for her to drape herself over in extreme comfort. "So far."

He tugged a lock of hair gently. "What do you mean 'so far'?"

She rubbed herself over him, every cell bursting with the delicious soreness of satiation. "I feel I might get pregnant again after what you just did to me."

He guffawed, turned her to her back, luxuriated in feeling his unborn son under his hands. "And you might well be. Our lovemaking did feel…supernatural this time. I'm amazed how much pleasure I can endure. But I don't think this was a one-off, because of the urgency of almost losing each other. I think this is going to be the norm from now on. It's the…certainty."

She hummed in agreement. Yes. Certainty. It was indeed a super power. A magical one.

Suddenly he rose above her. Her heart gave that clutched pause it always did whenever she realized again how much she loved him, just how beautiful he was. Which was so often her heart was developing a new rhythm.

"I shouldn't ask, but I don't ever again want to have anything on my mind that I don't resolve with you. You mentioned that you thought you'd never love again. Does that mean you…didn't?"

"Are you going to be very disappointed or hurt if I…did?"

"I won't lie. It will hurt like hell. But it wouldn't change a thing. In any way. And I didn't deserve your fidelity. It would even be fitting punishment for all the pain I put you through if you…did when *I*…didn't."

"Oh, you're more deserving than you think. Eight years of pining that would've become a lifetime of such. But then, one time with you *is* worth a lifetime…" She stopped, gaped at him. "Are—are you telling me you…*abstained?*"

He shrugged. "Why so surprised? You did."

"I didn't know men could do that," she blurted out.

"Do you know just how sexist you sound?" He nipped her nipple. Wonderful chastisement. "And I'm not 'men.' I'm me. I had sex until I found you, then I had passion. I couldn't go back to sex and I knew I'd never find passion again. As I don't have any say in being Castaldinian, no matter what, I'm a one-woman man."

She collapsed under the enormity of his revelations. "Leandro, oh, God…you mean you didn't even try…"

"Try how? Besides the handicaps I told you about, those accompanying the one-woman-man syndrome, I'd sustained a crippling injury, remember? That tiny matter of a smashed heart?"

Tears flowed again. "I was the one you fell for all the way."

"Did you even have a doubt?"

"Oh, I had nothing but. Oh, God, Leandro…it's so hard to imagine…you're such a sexual being…"

"Look who's talking."

"Oh, God, don't look. Not now. I think my eyes are dissolving." She hiccupped. "Oh, Leandro, all that time? No sex?"

"You talk as if I'm some sort of sex maniac. Okay, so I am. But it's only with you. Aren't you the same with me?"

"It's just you're so…incredible at it…"

"And you thought I had plenty of practice? You still don't realize I'm just a superior talent?" She charged him in a ferocious kiss. He took it all, let her have her fill before he drawled, "All it takes to be a great lover is to love you so much that giving you pleasure is the only way I can find pleasure myself. And then, *you* were a virgin, and as soon as you dropped your inhibitions with me, you became a lover I hadn't known could exist. All it takes to find perfection is to give it your all. As I give you. As you give me."

She tackled him on his back, rained tears of love and gratitude all over him.

He wiped them away, teased, "But I had sexual relief, if this is what you're wondering. You do know the concept of self-help in this area, don't you?" She poked him, collapsed on his chest in another fit of weeping giggles. "I became quite the guru. And I have to thank you for my expertise in the field. The memory of you—and your photos—were quite the inspiration."

She rained kisses and bites all over him, igniting again at imagining him pleasuring himself to her image. She just had to watch him do that. A lot. "Any time. And then you know how eager I always am to give you…a helping hand. Or tongue. Or body. Or whole life, you unbelievable man, you." She came up on her elbows. "Say, can we stay on Castaldini longer than you did before? Or at least return more frequently?"

"We'll do anything that ever crosses your mind. Though I don't have to stay on Castaldini to be regent, I will so you can be with your sister as often as you please." Then he muttered,

"Maybe the wretch will stop wanting to carve me open and eat my heart."

"Oh, my love, it's all a misunderstanding. She thought you were hurting me. She turns vicious at times like that."

"*Si,* I got that impression. That woman could wrestle an alligator with just a stare. But since that ferocity is on your behalf, she's my new best friend. We'll form a league, with Ernesto and Paolo, call ourselves Phoebe's Fabulous Fearsome Four."

"Mmm, I'll supply the superhero names and costumes." She chuckled, wriggled deeper into his embrace. "But really, Leandro, Julia outgrew her need for my nearness long ago, and though I'll always want to see her and the kids as much as possible, that isn't why I wish we could go to Castaldini more often. I want to spend the rest of my pregnancy in your home, have our baby there. I want his first breath to be of the sea air, want him to bond with the magic of the land from his first moment."

Leandro's arms convulsed around her. "So bursting with pride and emotion isn't such a far-fetched notion, after all. Whatever you wish for, *amore,* always consider it done. And it's *our* home."

Her sigh had to be what bliss sounded like. "Our home. So, how about going back there at once? I have countless fantasies that are unfulfilled yet, each and every one in your… *our* paradise."

Leandro jumped up at her demand, streaked to fulfill her wish. He arranged a journey home in record time and bounded back to fill her waiting arms.

"In eight hours we'll be there," he said against her lips, luxuriating in her, in everything they were together. Then he groaned, "This is too long. I will have to get that teleportation enterprise underway."

She shone up at him, made him feel like only she could, invincible, incomparable. Loved to his last spark of life.

"If anyone can do it, it'll be you. But then who needs tele-portation, when we can have instant wish fulfillment?"

She slid down his body, beamed him up into the first of many. As he reciprocated, he knew how right she was.

Who needed anything more than this?

There was nothing more than this.

This, her, them, was everything.

* * * * *

OLIVIA

THE PRODIGAL
PRINCE'S SEDUCTION

BY
OLIVIA GATES

To my husband. To my daughter.
Both of you, my one and only.
More and more, I wouldn't be doing all this
without you. Thank you for being who you are.

One

"I want one hour with you."

Prince Durante D'Agostino froze at the foyer's threshold.

That voice. Coming out of nowhere. So low he shouldn't have heard it over the live jazz music blaring its infectious energy from the ballroom where the charity function was in full swing.

He heard nothing but its softness. As if faders had been hit, boosting it, dousing every other sound. More. As if it had been generated inside his head, a caress of a thought, making all else recede from his awareness. An awareness that bristled with responses so tactile that every hair on his body rose as if he were caught in a field of static electricity.

He frowned. What was all this, over hearing a woman's voice? Over yet another blatant invitation?

A scowl seized his face as he swung around to the offending entity. And everything receded farther. Disappeared. He felt as if his blood stopped in his arteries even as everything else hurtled through him. Heat, sensations. Urges.

Eyes. From the shadows behind the foyer's door, they transfixed him. Pieces of heaven. Staring up at him from a face that was what the offspring of an angel and a siren must look like.

Then the impossible creature spoke again. "One hour. I'll pay one hundred grand for it."

His eyes dragged away from the clear skies of hers to the lips spilling that offer. Dimpled, dewy and flushed as if she'd been sucking on bloodred cherries. They were still again, slightly parted. But he could see them as they'd wrapped around each syllable of her spell, could imagine them nibbling and suckling their way down his body…

He shifted, stunned to feel himself hardening, zero to one hundred in two seconds.

Aroused? Here? From just a look and a few words?

He expanded his chest in an effort to draw in more oxygen, to drive blood to his head instead of his loins. He managed only to suck in her scent—clean, with a tinge of jasmine and a deluge of pheromones. Every cell in his body twitched, revved.

Then she stepped out of the shadows and he forgot any intentions or delusions of subduing his body.

This might not be happening anyway. He might still be in the back of his limo, dreaming this apparition as he dozed off on the way to the charity event he was sponsoring. Thirty-six sleepless hours must have taken their toll on his nervous system. It would explain *her*, the epitome of his every far-fetched fantasy. From hair the shade of fire he'd once seen in a painting and wondered if it truly existed in nature, a waterfall of silk his fingers itched to twist through, to a complexion of such clear olive that it offset the vividness of her hair and the lightness of her eyes, to features sculpted and aligned in such an unusual way that they screamed character and whispered sensuality, to curves and swells in the abundance and the distribution to answer his every specification.

But she was no figment of his overworked mind. She was real.

What was unreal was her effect on him. Women had been throwing themselves at him since he'd turned seventeen, and even then he hadn't operated on hormones. Then had come this woman.

She'd aroused everything in him just by breathing those words, by being near. Now, by just looking at him, she had his imagination flooding with images and sounds and sensations and scents, of drenched silk sheets and hot velvet limbs, of cries rising in the dark along with the aromas of arousal and satisfaction.

Was this it? The overtures of the breakdown Eduardo and Jade claimed he was teetering on? Was this surreal reaction the first crack before a chasm tore his psyche wide open? Not that he cared. If this was a breakdown, maybe it was exactly what he needed.

"I have a check right here." She fumbled inside her evening purse. "Make it out to the charity or cause of your choice."

He watched her supple hands, with those neat, short, unadorned fingernails, found himself imagining grabbing them, sucking each finger until she was begging for his lips and teeth and tongue elsewhere…everywhere.

He took a step toward her, maybe not to translate fantasy into action, but to feel her—any part of her—against him, to confirm that she—and what she evoked in him—was real.

She stumbled back. He surged forward to stop her, only to become trapped in the swarm of people who'd materialized between them.

Maledizione. He hadn't even heard them approach. Now there was nothing but the cacophony of their intrusion, the encroachment of their self-interest.

"Prince Durante! You're finally here!"

"Prince Durante, this way."

"You must come this way first, Prince Durante."

"I have someone who's dying to meet you."

"Me, too, and you'll definitely want to meet him first."

He was suddenly sorry that he'd left his bodyguards outside.

He fought the urge to signal them to disperse the throng who'd so rudely fractured the pristine intensity that had cocooned him with *her*. But they might rush to deal with the situation with inappropriate force. They'd been jumpy ever since Jeremiah Langley had stabbed him a month ago.

Apart from bellowing for everyone to get the hell away from him, he had no recourse but to let them sweep him along, watch her recede as she remained standing where she'd first intercepted him in that evening gown that could have been spun from the hues and radiance of her eyes. The last thing he saw of her before the ballroom doors closed was her arm falling to her side, the check held limply in her hand.

He buzzed his head bodyguard, muttered an order to keep track of her if she left. He couldn't risk losing her.

Only then did he start playing the evening's sponsor, burning to wrap everything up so he could do what he really wanted to do. The first thing in years that he couldn't *wait* to do. Seek her out, give her whatever she wanted and experience that eagerness and exhilaration she'd inspired in him, something he hadn't felt in…ever.

Gabrielle Williamson's eyes clung to one thing among the ebbing wave of people. The man they'd swept along, the one who towered above them all.

So *that* was Prince Durante D'Agostino.

She'd thought she knew what he looked like from endless photos in newspapers and magazines, including her own publications. She'd known nothing. Every photo had downgraded him to the man who deserved every letter of his reputation as the world's most notorious, eligible and panted-after royalty.

In reality he was a…a god.

And she'd approached him—okay, ambushed him more like—with her pathetic offer. A hundred grand felt ridiculous now. But what would an hour with a god rate?

The ballroom door closed, severing the mesmerism of those azure twin stars he had for eyes.

A tremor hit her. A second hit harder. Then a deluge broke out, until she was shaking like a rag in a storm.

What was wrong with her? She was the one who was supposed to surprise him into agreeing to give her that hour. To make a solid pitch *before* he asked questions. Especially about who she was. She'd wanted to eliminate—or at least postpone—the prejudice her name had already elicited from him. She'd wanted a fair hearing.

But seeing him in the flesh, even from the back, had almost blanked her mind. Then he'd turned, and everything had vanished.

She'd forgotten where she was, what she was supposed to say, could only stare at him. She'd moved only when the tractor beam of his will had forced her forward for his inspection. And boy, had he inspected. She'd felt…inspected down to her cellular level.

Then, those people had charged him, saved her from doing that rag-in-the-storm impression in his presence. They'd also taken him away before he'd said yes. And he'd been about to. Or she could have been imagining that, along with his surreal impact on her.

Imagining shimagining. She was a thirty-year-old divorcée who hadn't had fantasies even as a young girl. Being the only child of parents whose marriage had sunk daily into the dark realities of bankruptcy and depression hadn't been conducive to flights of fancy.

That was part of the convoluted journey that had brought her here today, on a mission to save her own company from bankruptcy, while repaying the man who'd supported her family during those desperate years. King Benedetto of Castaldini—Prince Durante's father.

After her father went bankrupt, the king, a friend and former business associate, had convinced him to move his family closer, to Sardinia, so that the king could be of more help. And he had more than helped, had continued to do so after her father's death six years later. He'd supported her and her mother and financed her education until she'd graduated from journalism school.

She'd since insisted on repaying her family's debts with interest. But while she'd needed to settle the financial debt, she'd always cling to the emotional one.

It had been because of that bond, along with what had been solid financial advice at the time, that she'd invested heavily in stocks and assets in Castaldini. It was partly why Le Roi Enterprises, her publishing company, was in trouble now. The kingdom had been hit by a steep recession after the king's stroke six months ago.

His condition had been hushed up until his recovery hadn't conformed to his doctors' optimism. His grim prognosis had leaked out, and Castaldini's stock market had crashed like a meteor.

He'd called her a couple of weeks ago, requesting a video meeting. He'd said he had a solution to all her problems. She remembered that call…

She'd waited for the meeting to start, contemplating how to turn down his offer of more help. It was one thing to settle her father's debts and see to their household upkeep, but another to float a company with multinational subsidiaries. She didn't think he could afford anything of this magnitude now. And she couldn't be so deeply indebted again, even to him. She'd been so driven to repay her family's debt that she'd done something as crazy as marry Ed. But…could she afford to turn down help, when hundreds of people depended on her for their jobs?

Then a stranger came onto the screen. It was several dropped heartbeats before she realized it was the king. The incredibly fit and virile seventy-four-year-old man she'd last seen seven months ago at her mother's funeral had metamorphosed into an emaciated, hundred-year-old version of himself.

Tears surged behind her eyes, at seeing him like that, at the acrid thankfulness that her mother's illness had been quick and merciless so that she hadn't suffered his fate, hadn't lasted long enough to see her beauty almost mummified.

"It's good to see you, *figlia mia*."

The wan rasp that used to be the surest baritone forced a tear to escape her control. She wiped it away, pretending to sweep her hair back. "I-it's good to see you, too, King Benedetto."

His smile was resigned, conciliatory. "No need to tiptoe around me, Gaby. I know that seeing me must be a shock for you. But I had to speak to you face-to-face as I ask you this incalculable favor."

He was asking, not offering, a favor? She didn't see how that could solve her problems, but the very idea of being of service to him infused her with energy and purpose.

"Anything, King Benedetto. Ask me anything."

"You once wanted to approach Durante with a book offer."

She frowned, nodded. She'd asked him how best to approach his elusive son with an offer for a motivational biography, when the enigmatic media-magnet had turned down every offer to publish anything about his life. The king had told her to forget it.

That had been before her mother's death and she'd since forgotten about it, along with every plan she'd had, lacking the drive to pursue anything new that required focus and determination. Her grief was dulling to a pervasive, crippling coldness, and there was nothing and no one to ameliorate it.

She'd made no friends since she'd returned to New York, seemed to have made only enemies. She had colleagues and employees, was on good terms with most, but she hadn't forged a real closeness to any of them. Her uncles and their families lived states or continents away and she'd never been close to them anyway. From the men who hunted her for the fortune they thought she'd inherited and the one she'd acquired, to the disaster of her marriage, to the disappointment of her attempts to wash away its ugliness in other men's arms, to the women who treated her like a succubus who'd drain their men of life, it felt as if she'd lost one bond to the world after another. Her mother's death had cracked the last link. *Why bother?* was the one thought left echoing inside her.

Only the employees who'd lose their jobs and the causes she'd be unable to contribute to if she threw in the towel had kept her going, just enough to keep her head above water.

"I feel responsible for your company's problems."

The king's rasp dragged her back to the moment. She blinked. "Please, don't, King Benedetto. It's not your fault."

She bit her lip on much more. Her company's decline had started with the discovery of her mother's terminal illness, and its slow death had begun when a part of her had died with her mother, a part she didn't know how to resuscitate, didn't feel like trying. Castaldini's recession had just been the last straw.

But she could see how he'd think that, because she wasn't alone in her decline. Many smaller corporations heavily invested in Castaldinian stock were floundering. Even though the new regent, Prince Leandro D'Agostino, had stepped in and floated the economy, the original hit had been bad. She'd heard that Leandro would work his way down to companies at the level of hers, but doubted her company could last until he did. And then, even with his power and financial clout, as regent only, he didn't promise the market the long-term stability a king would. Advisors had urged her not to await rescue, said Leando might even let lesser interests go under to stabilize the big picture.

The king went on. "Durante could revive your company, either with a bestseller or in other ways if he so wished."

That was what her advisors had said. That only a guaranteed bestseller or a merger with any major player would buoy her company. Prince Durante would have answered both criteria. But previously, the king had said Durante wasn't an option. Which meant… "So he'd be amenable to an offer now?"

"I'm not saying he would be."

That stymied her. "Then what has changed?"

"Your situation. And mine."

She didn't understand what her situation had to do with his, only that he thought a positive result might be obtained now. She should jump at the opening. Yet she wanted to do nothing but say goodbye and sit staring into space. It seemed that her lethargy wasn't about to let her challenge-tackling abilities escape its somnolent grip. She sighed. "I'll give it some more thought—"

"I'm *asking* you to do it, Gaby." The king interrupted her. "And I don't just want you to sign a contract with him. I want you to insist on being his editor or ghostwriter or however you get such books written. I want you to work as closely as possible with him so that you can convince him to come back to Castaldini." Gabrielle adjusted the screen, as if that would help his words make sense. He elaborated, ending her confusion. "He left five years ago, saying he'll never return as long as I live. And he's kept his promise. He didn't even call when I had my stroke."

Something trickled through the clotted mass of indifference inside her. Emotions. Surprise, indignation…anger.

What kind of monster would do that to his father, and a great man like King Benedetto, too? And to think Durante had been the one she'd admired most among all Castaldinian princes, his self-made success intriguing her far more because it didn't have the crown as its goal. As the king's son, Durante was the one prince who was ineligible for the crown. And then, *success* didn't describe what he'd achieved. He'd become one of the world's richest, most powerful men, starting with investment banking, then branching into just about everything, garnering a worldwide reputation for being unstoppable, as well as inaccessible. But it was one thing to reject intimacy as evidenced by his misanthrope/heartbreaker reputation, another to reject the man who was his father and king.

"Why all this…antipathy?" she asked.

"Durante blames me for terrible things, things I haven't been able to prove I wasn't responsible for." Okay. So it was more complicated than she could imagine. She really couldn't form an opinion here. She shouldn't. It had nothing to do with her. And she wanted it to stay that way. "But it doesn't matter what he believes. He must come back, Gaby. It's not only that I need my son—Castaldini needs his power and influence."

Scratch the no-opinion status. No matter Durante's reasons, he was a callous creep if he not only didn't care about his father's incapacitation but also about Castaldini's troubles. And *she* was supposed to make him care?

She asked that, and the king nodded. "I know you can. You'll come in with a fresh slate and views, with legitimate business offers and concerns. But give me your word that you'll never tell him of our connection. That would make him send you straight to hell. And none of us can afford that. The situation is grave, and I must be clear. I want you to do *anything* to make him come back."

His words had echoed long after their goodbyes. What he'd meant by *anything* was so glaringly clear, it was blinding. Seduction.

She was resigned to her femme fatale reputation. But it hurt that even the king thought seduction was one of her weapons, her only one, even. Still, she excused him. He was old and sick and desperate to resolve his problems, to secure his kingdom's future.

And then, what he'd proposed *was* a worthy cause. If she succeeded—seduction certainly *not* on the menu of maneuvers she'd use—everyone would come out a winner. The king would have his son back—a reconciliation that was bound to make said son happier, too—Castaldini would get a heavy-hitter to help its regent pull its fat out of the fire, and she'd stabilize her company.

But the damned prince hadn't even acknowledged her messages. She could think of only one reason. His initial background check on anyone who approached him must have accessed the usual slander. Seemed he'd thought such unsubstantiated filth enough to condemn her.

Furious, she'd called in a favor with one of his insiders and gotten his schedule for the next week. Besides being impossible to get hold of, he was also known for badgering the privileged into doing more for the world. This function was one of his traps where he wrung what he could get out of them for his favorite causes. She'd intended to intercept him, make him an offer he couldn't refuse. At least, that had been the plan.

So far, all she'd done was stammer three sentences and got nothing out of him but that disconcerting stare.

She needed results, but she had to restart her own volition first. Or at least the autopilot that had steered her for months now.

One or the other must have kicked in, because she moved at last.

She leaned on the door as she opened it. The exuberance of jazz and the forced gaiety in the overcrowded ballroom slammed into her. But what almost knocked her off her feet was the power of his gaze. He'd been watching for her, as if certain she'd follow him.

Not that she could. Those people who had the same idea as her—of ambushing him here—left her no chink to get through.

He left her no air to breathe as his gaze drilled into her across the ballroom. She began to think it might not be a bad thing after all if she didn't get a chance to talk to him alone.

She was a seasoned businesswoman who'd been through a battlefield of a marriage and divorce, who'd before and since been pursued by men, had thought she'd seen and tried all kinds, to her crushing dissatisfaction. But Prince D'Agostino fell far outside what she'd thought to be her inclusive experience. To lump him under "man" with those she'd had experience with was as accurate as lumping a top-of-the-food-chain predator with a jellyfish. Something very sure of itself told her she shouldn't get closer. For any reason.

She should leave. Now.

She had to pry her gaze—her will—from his first.

Somehow she did, was at the door when a rough velvet whisper hit her between the shoulder blades. "Don't run off yet."

Logic said that omnidirectional/internal sound effect was the surround system's doing. But there was no logic here. There was only the influence the voice exercised, the reactions it ignited. The certainty that it was talking to her.

She swayed around, found him on the dais in front of the mic, his gaze still cast on her like a stasis field.

"Ladies and gentlemen," he said. "Thank you for paying the ten-grand admission fee. But because you're getting…restless, I'll fast-forward to prying some *real* contributions out of you. You have the auction list, but in light of a certain…development, I have made some changes. Now the first item on auction is… myself."

Two

If Prince Durante D'Agostino had announced he was Superman and launched into the air to circle overhead, there wouldn't have been a more drastic reaction to his announcement.

Not that it would have shocked her. He did look like some superhuman being as he dominated the scene just by standing there, the rugged nobleness of his features and his leonine forehead accentuated by the swept-back mane of raven satin, the jacket of his sculpted designer charcoal suit casually pushed back by the hand resting on his hip, his white shirt stretching across his torso, detailing the daunting power beneath. He looked like a modern god swathed in the trappings of the times that equalized other men but that didn't begin to contain the influence he exuded, to disguise his in-his-own-league nature.

His gaze panned the ballroom yet somehow managed not to release hers. That alone kept her heart practically dropping to the polished Carrara marble floor. But what restarted her tremors was what she saw in those eyes—an intensity untouched by the cynical amusement with which he watched the mayhem he'd kicked up.

"Before you get too excited," he finally said. "I'm not auctioning off all of me, just my ear. Considering how in demand it is, with so many of you attempting to talk it off, I'm offering one hour of its exclusive use." His lips tugged into what had to be the most arrhythmia-inducing weapon ever deployed on susceptible females. And it had her in its crosshairs. "I already have an opening bid. One hundred grand."

Now she knew how *mamma mia* had been coined. It had to have been a woman who'd first exclaimed it, as a brutally gorgeous male plucked her strings.

And she did feel like a marionette, compelled to obey his every tug, any reluctance or misgiving evaporating in the excitement his mischief sent through her. She walked back under the pull of his challenge.

When she stopped at the fringe of the bidding crowd, he put his lips to the mic, implanted hot, wild images and sensations straight inside her, pitched his voice an octave lower. "Do I hear one hundred ten?"

Over three-dozen people, mostly women, raised their hands. She'd beaten them all in speed of response.

His lips spread in satisfaction, his pose grew more languid, a conqueror certain of his victory, indulgent in his triumph. "Thank you. Do I hear one hundred twenty?"

Her hand was up in the air before she could will it to be there. Seemed he'd jumpstarted her competitiveness. More. He'd sparked the first sign of life in her since she'd witnessed her mother's being extinguished.

He kept raising the bid, and her competition dwindled. Soon suspense was fast reaching the point of overload.

When a dozen hands still shot up in the air when he reached the four hundred fifty grand mark, her stamina snapped and recoiled like an overextended string.

She blurted out, "I bid one million."

A hush fell. Everyone turned to gape at her.

He straightened, his eyes losing all lightness, singeing hers through the charge that filled the space between them. "Now that's a nice round figure. Anyone willing to top that? No? Fine, then. I have one million from the lady in blue. Going once, going twice—"

"I bid *ten* million."

Durante saw shock seize his mystery woman's face before he registered the words that had caused it. Only then did he drag his eyes and senses from her and search out the new speaker.

His every muscle tensed. How had *he* gotten past security? How had Durante not noticed him before?

His security had messed up. As for him, all his faculties had been converged on *her,* everything else skimming his consciousness without leaving an imprint.

And there was the now-gaunt, wild-eyed Jeremiah Langley. Staring at him like a drowning man would at a lifeboat. A month ago he'd looked at Durante as if at his own killer, before attempting to stab him. Durante couldn't imagine how Langley had ended up blaming him—and not the investments he'd made against his advice—for his bankruptcy, but he'd hushed everything up, not wishing to add criminal charges to the distraught man's troubles. He'd also postponed announcing Langley's bankruptcy until he sold shares that would leave the man with minimal debt. But he'd made it clear to Langley, and to his security—he didn't want to see the man again. Not in this lifetime.

No one knew how things stood between them, or that Jeremiah didn't have the ten million he'd bid for Durante's leniency. He couldn't call Langley on it without outing him. Langley had cornered him into accepting his so-called bid as the winning one.

And *that* was his worst crime.

She had already accepted defeat. This time, she *was* walking away. He might not have more of her. Not tonight. Unacceptable.

He would have more of her. And if he had his way, as he always did, he would have all of her.

Gabrielle felt all animation drain from her system.

The moment her bid had burst from her incontinent mouth, she'd launched into feverish calculations to determine how she could part with that much cash in one lump sum in her current situation. Then that ten-million-dollar sledgehammer had fallen, pulverizing both worry and hope.

So that was it. She'd bid and lost. And he was no longer looking at her. Ten million dollars would distract even him.

So what was that tightening behind her ribs? Disappointment?

How stupid was that? This scheme wouldn't have worked anyway. She didn't know how she or King Benedetto could have thought it might. All her moronic endeavor would achieve was to give the scandal sheets fuel for the coming decade. She had to leave before the paparazzi he'd banned from the event got wind of this and ambushed her. *Leave. Now. And don't look back.*

She managed that, but still felt as if she were wading through quicksand. His gaze had latched on to her again, robbed her of dominion over her own body. Desperation to get away kicked in.

In minutes she was in the parking lot, running to her car.

She remote-opened her door, was reaching for its handle when a boom cracked the silence of the night.

"Stay."

She dropped her keys. Her purse. Probably a few months' to a couple of years' life expectancy, too.

She slumped against the warm metal and glass as if pressed there by the presence closing in on her. She heard nothing but the blood thundering in her head. The presence expanded at her back, pinning her to her support, squeezing her heart.

She fumbled for the door handle. She'd managed to open the door when that voice hit her again, a quiet rumble this time.

"Stay."

She clenched her eyes shut, pitched forward, her nerveless weight closing the door with a muffled thud. That one word.

An invocation. Deeper and darker than the moonless night.

She turned around, leaning on the car. And there he was.

The good news was that he kept a dozen feet between them. The bad news was that it made no difference. And why should it? He'd been dozens of feet away in that ballroom and had still overwhelmed her.

"Stay?" Where was her voice? She'd addressed him before in a breathless whisper. This time it was a husky rasp. Both were nothing like her usual crisp tones. "What am I? Your poodle? What's next? Roll over? Beg…?" She winced, stopped. Where were her brakes?

"How about 'stop,'" he drawled. "Before you inflame my already-raging imagination beyond control."

His voice wasn't the same as what had flowed from the sound system earlier. It was so much more layered and modulated and hard-hitting, the prominent r's of his accent far more intoxicating. Hearing it without distortion delayed her comprehension of his words. Then it hit her and she almost went up in a puff of mortification.

She couldn't *believe* she'd said something so provocative, just begging for misinterpretation. He'd never believe she hadn't meant anything beyond sarcasm.

But wonder of wonders, his eyes weren't stained with that knowing derision she was used to from men. His emitted only pure excitement. "Would 'stop' be less open to unfavorable interpretation? How about 'don't leave'?"

His voice sluiced another rush of heat over her. She quivered. "Still orders, both of them."

He tilted his head. Light ignited the azure depths of his eyes and carved dimples in his sculpted cheeks. "At least they don't have canine connotations, if my idiomatic English serves."

And she did something she'd thought was beyond her, now and forever. She giggled. *Giggled.*

His eyes widened as if she'd electrified him. He retaliated with something far more debilitating than electricity. He chuckled.

She struggled not to melt into the ground. "You're pleading less-than-perfect English skills to explain the inappropriateness of barking 'stay' at me across the parking lot like that?"

"Barking? Still going with the dog motif, eh?"

"You did bark," she mumbled in embarrassment. "You frightened me out of my skin. I think it's still pooled on the ground."

His eyes swept down her body, until she felt it was her dress that lay at her feet. "From where I'm standing, your skin is still enveloping you like a glove and, propriety notwithstanding, you can see what the sight does to me."

More heat splashed through her as she fixed her gaze on his so it wouldn't stray to "see" anything. "See? Perfect English skills."

"I'm sure my English tutor would love to hear that the ulcer he swore I gave him has ultimately been validated."

"You gave your teacher hell? You're pulling my leg."

"Again, do watch what you say to me, or I might succumb and tell you exactly how and where I want to pull both your legs."

Images slammed into her. Vivid, tangible. Those large, perfectly formed hands dragging her by the thighs, opening her around his bulk as he bore down on her…

"I've changed my verdict," she choked. "Your English skills are not perfect. They're horrible. Evil. *Sietto un uomo cattivo.*"

Suddenly the sounds of the night were amplified in the stillness that echoed between them. Whoever had said one could drown in another's eyes must have been describing Prince Durante's endless azure seas and the submersion of their focus.

Just as she felt her lungs using up the last tendril of oxygen, he exhaled. *"Mia bella misteriosa…parlate italiano?"*

She realized she'd said he was a wicked man in Italian. It had once come to her as unconsciously as English did. She used to talk and think in an inextricable mix, a habit that had faded since she'd returned to the States. This was the first time in many years that she'd reverted to the second-nature practice. It felt as if a missing part of her had clicked back into place.

Then more registered. He'd called her his mysterious beauty, asked if she spoke Italian.

"I lived in Sardinia and Italy from age five until I returned to the States to enter college at seventeen."

These revelations were way beyond the simple *yes* his question warranted. But he made her want to do unknown things. Flirt, tease. Confide. It had to be the premium royal testosterone overexposure.

After a long moment when he looked at her as if at a gem with a thousand facets, he breathed, "*Dio Santo,* what are you?"

"What…? Uh, yeah, I haven't exactly introduced myself yet."

"No, you haven't. Exactly or otherwise."

"Umm…yeah, there's sort of a reason I haven't. You see, I'm—"

"You are *mia bella misteriosa,* who's done what no woman has ever done—offered money to spend time with me."

"Now *that* I find impossible to believe. I bet women offer anything and everything for time with you. I bet most wouldn't mind if it wasn't even one-on-one."

"You think so? Because of who I am?" Her gaze wavered with uncertainty. He elaborated. "Rich and royal?"

Her laugh morphed into a snort that would have made a sailor proud. "Are you kidding? Or are you fishing? Women would throw themselves at you if you were a penniless nobody."

His eyes flared. "Coming from anybody else, I'd think that a worthless exaggeration, but from you, I know it's how you see me. For it's how I see you, too. As for the one-on-one basis, that is the only way I would accept to have time with you."

A moan of stimulation stumbled over her croak of embarrassment.

Hell, the man was reducing her to a pubescent state. But he was doing something even worse.

He was obliterating the distance between them.

Mesmerized, she took in the control and power that permeated his every move, the breadth of shoulders and chest that owed nothing to padding, the sparseness of waist and hips, the hardness of thighs rippling beneath exquisite fabric as he prowled toward her, a majestic creature by birthright and by merit. Now *this* was a man to make her revise her stance on swearing off men forever, a pledge she'd made happily years ago.

Which was a crazy thing to think.

Crazier would be to act on such insanity.

She stood there waiting for him to reach her with the same fatalism she'd watch a collision in progress, could think only that no man had ever looked at her like this. As if she was something incredibly unexpected, and unexpectedly incredible. The wonder in his eyes drowned out the urgent voices that yelled that his damage potential would far surpass the devastation caused by any such collision.

Every step closer to his mystery woman solidified into fact what Durante had sensed from the first moment he saw her.

This was new. Surprising and stimulating. When he'd been certain nothing and no one would ever surprise or stimulate him. She did both, and far more, with every breath.

Her effect on him was so unprecedented that he'd done the unprecedented. He'd delegated running the rest of the charity function to his deputy. And he'd sent his bodyguards away, forbade them to follow him. He wanted to be alone with her at any price.

Her face tilted up as he approached. Beams from the nearest streetlight embraced it in a swathe of highlights and shadows. Her tresses billowed in the night breeze like undulating flames.

Contradictory compulsions wrenched at each other inside him. The need to capture, conquer, and the urge to savor, slow down.

The second impulse won out, forced his feet to stop before they took him all the way pressing her against her car.

He was close enough to reach out and run his fingers through that blazing cascade of hair. He didn't. Somehow. He drew deep of her scent instead, let it permeate him, before he let it escape on a grudging exhalation. "So…you bid one million dollars for an hour with me."

Her shoulders jerked on a dejected shrug. "Yeah. And for the record, I would have doubled the winning bid if I could have."

He inhaled sharply. "You think I'm worth that much?"

"I think you're worth every dollar of your billions."

He bit into his lip. It was either that or drag her to him and bite into hers. As he would. Just not yet. What flowed between them deserved the reward of leisure and thoroughness. But holding back was a punishment, too. One her every word made harder to take. He was used to flattery, could sense falseness and self-interest even in trace quantities. He detected only sincerity from her. Alien urges swamped him, to punch the air, to thump his chest.

He shoved his hands into his pockets so they wouldn't find their way around her. "I do have more hours available apart from the one that other bidder won, you know?"

"Oh. *Oh.* You mean…?"

The surge of hope on her face made him fist his hands in his pockets, emphasizing his—problem. It was either that or snatch them out and pounce on her. "I mean, if you're still interested, I'll take that million-dollar check."

"If?" She coughed. Her eyes tore from his, slammed around, the dazed excitement in them tingling through him on a path that connected his fingertips to his scalp, his loins to his toes. Her gaze settled at her feet. "*There* it is." She dropped down in a crouch, pooling her flowing taffeta skirt on the ground, making her look like a gigantic flower as she retrieved the matching evening bag. She jerked back up, not lingering to look up at him from that position, to milk it for all the sensual promise it could yield.

She didn't need any of that. She needed only to breathe—to be—to exercise maximum effect on him. But it pleased him beyond measure that she didn't operate that way.

She fumbled with her bag, produced her checkbook. He watched as she scribbled furiously with even, beautiful print. Then she tore out the check, extended it to him. "Fill in the beneficiary."

He took it, folded and placed it in his outer pocket before he reached into his inner one, produced his own checkbook and pen.

In a minute he tore a check out, handed it to her. "*I'm* bidding *two* million. Add to that whatever amount you see fit, fill in the total and make it out to whomever you like."

Her movement to take the check felt like a reflex. She didn't look at it, remained gaping at him. "What's this for?"

"The two million is my bid for the time we've had together so far. The amount you'll specify is for the rest of the evening."

"The *whole* evening?"

"And the night."

"The *night?*"

Durante's lips twitched. Her squeaks would have amused him if they weren't pouring fuel on his inflamed senses. She really hadn't thought it a possibility he'd offer this. "If you wish it."

Her blush intensified until she seemed to smolder in the night. And he saw it in his mind's eye in high-definition clarity, himself carrying her to the nearest flat surface to ravish her for that hour she'd bid on, before sweeping her away from the world to do so again for several nights on end.

It was all so surreal he felt he was dreaming it. Yet it was so real it abraded him with its intensity and immediacy. He'd never experienced such a state of distressed arousal. And for him to be in this condition just by looking, imagining… Unbelievable.

At last she spluttered, "Uh…isn't this a bit…you know…?"

He inclined his head. "Too fast? Too soon? You think so?"

A moan-giggle escaped her, another blow to his restraint. "If you think I can think right now, think again."

"Exactly. This isn't about thinking. This is about feeling. About knowing. I know what you make me feel. You made me feel it from the first moment. I wanted more than an hour with you. I want this night, *bellissima,* and as many more as you'll give me."

"That's assuming you'll want more nights after the first…" Her face scrunched into a wince. "Okay, excuse me as I give swallowing my tongue a serious shot."

"With me around to do it? What a waste that would be. And why would you even want to try?"

"Because it sounded as if I was agreeing to share this night with you and was trying to make sure it wouldn't be the one and only."

Every word out of her mouth… He pressed the heel of his palm to his breastbone, as if that would quell the itching behind it. "And you didn't mean that?"

"God, no, I-I…" She threw both hands over her face, before looking up at him, helplessness and accusation filling her expression. "It's your fault. Exposure to you is turning my gray matter into day-old milkshake."

A laugh tore out of him, drove his head back with the force of its unexpectedness and power. "Turnabout is fair play. Although you turn mine into the boiling version." He reduced the distance between them another step, testing his stamina, thrilling to the torture of balancing on the edge of loss of control. "And I will want more nights. As many as I can have. I hope you won't hold back to observe an 'appropriate' period before indulging in intimacy. I want nothing more than to end this night with you in my arms, in my bed."

She melted back against her car. "And I want nothing more than to end this night in both."

Gabrielle watched Durante's eyes flare at her admission, knew he'd reach for her. She had to say the rest now. *Now.*

"But I can't."

The flare subsided, ice putting out the blue-hot flames.

Something twisted beneath her ribs. She couldn't bear to see disappointment replacing exhilaration in his eyes.

She hurtled on. "Believe it or not, I did approach you with business and only business in mind."

Relief swamped her when his eyes simmered again. "I believe you. But it ceased to be business the moment you laid eyes on me."

She didn't even think of denying the fact. "Yes." She still had to qualify it. "But I can't afford to let it be that way—"

He cut across her unsteady words. "You can't afford to let it be any other way. Business will be taken care of in due time. But I'm not postponing this for anything else's sake."

"But what *is* this?"

"Something unknown to either of us, something unprecedented. And you know it as well as I do."

Gabrielle stared at him. He kept stunning her. But what most amazed her was that she picked up no malice from him, that malignant triumph most men transmitted when women made the mistake of not only falling for them, but admitting it, too.

Not him. She felt he was above pettiness and double standards. This was also no line that he gave every desirable woman he met. In fact, his ruthlessness likely originated from his never instigating the pursuit. He was renowned for his detachment.

There was nothing detached about him now. She just knew he was being swept along the same unstoppable current as she was.

That didn't mean she could let herself be swept. There was far more at stake than the elapsing of "an appropriate period before indulging in intimacies." And not only couldn't she tell him what, but that this was happening at all made her feel she'd fallen flat on her face into someone else's life. Men like him—and there *were* no men like him—didn't appear in hers.

She looked up at him, at once pleading for him to understand her chaos and afraid he'd shimmer and disappear. "Whatever this unknown and unprecedented thing is, and no matter how I feel about it or how right it feels to feel this way, I'm still totally weirded out by the detour everything has taken. Hours ago I didn't dream…"

"…you'd see me and the world would cease to matter."

His confidence sent her explanations scattering. "Oh, quit making it harder for me to make sense. The world might have ceased to matter, but it didn't cease to exist. I had this proposal memorized and now I barely remember what it was all about."

"I barely remember why I came here tonight, too. I don't care about anything now beyond you."

"Maybe if you hear my proposal, you'll change your mind."

"I won't. Not even if you're coming to me with the patent for an eternal-youth or super-power serum."

"Actually, I was thinking along opposite lines. That you'd be so opposed to my offer, you'd drop *me*."

"So it's something you think I'm liable to turn down flat? Is that why you were trying to sweeten me with the hundred grand? Is there something dark and controversial about you, *mia ragazzaccia?*"

The way he said *"my bad girl"* quickened her melting rate. "Oh, I wish. Okay, really, I don't. I'm pretty grateful there's nothing so…interesting about me. I'm just—"

"The woman I want to know everything about. And to that end, I want to conduct an experiment."

She blinked. "An experiment?" She stopped. "God, I keep re- peating things. I might start asking for crackers next." His smile widened, blinding her with a flash of charisma. She groaned. "So, what's this experiment? What are you out to prove?"

"That you were onto something great when you approached me without revealing your identity and purpose. The labels might have interfered with our impact on each other. I don't think your name or your business will shed any light on who you really are. I want to know *you*. What you are, what makes you tick, what shaped you, what you want and why and how you want it. I want to revel in what we have blazing between us, to enjoy us, man to woman. For tonight."

Another breaker of reaction shuddered through her. "Are you for real, or am I dreaming you up?"

The heat of his smile became almost unbearable. "I take it you agree to participate in my experiment."

She shook her head. "That experiment is skewed and the results are bound to be unreliable. *I* know exactly who *you* are."

"You only think you do. But what do you know? My statistics? My reputation, status and estimated fortune? Sterile facts mixed with conjectures and financial data. Did knowing any of the above prepare you for the effect I have on you in the flesh?"

She raised her hands begging for respite. "Okay. I admit the 'labels' conjured up a man who, while impressive, has nothing to do with the flesh-and-blood reality of you. In fact, I'm having a tough time connecting you at all to that man."

"You see? If you can't access your preconceived ideas about me, we're on a level playing field. Say yes, *bellissima*."

"Now I know why you've soared so high. You're relentless."

"That's your expert opinion as a fellow unstoppable force?"

"Hah, I wish. Or again, not really. Okay. On one condition."

"Anything."

She exhaled a tremulous chuckle. "Not very businessman-like of you, all these carte-blanche concessions."

"I'm not a businessman now. I'm just a man who knows

you're the woman to whom only carte-blanche concessions will do justice."

"God, stop with the impossible-to-live-up-to stuff."

"You've already lived up to all of it by making me feel this way, think this way. So, what's your condition?"

"That you give me back my check."

He didn't hesitate, not in expression, not in action. He produced her check as the words left her lips. Delight fizzed in her blood. He hadn't paused to ponder her intention, trusted that whatever it was, there was nothing underhanded about it.

Her hand trembled as she extended his back to him. "Here's yours. Now I don't owe you untold millions."

He didn't reach for it. "Keep it, *bellissima*. You wouldn't owe me a cent. That's for the causes of your choice."

"Oh, I would owe you. I wanted to make a donation through you, while gaining something for myself. But if I take your check, I would be 'donating' *your* money. So, you donate what you wish and I'll do the same and let's take money out of the equation, start this on a real equal footing."

He took the check. "I'll just keep it until you wish to donate something you can't afford. Now, shall we?"

Her heart began to race her. "Shall we…what exactly?"

"Spend the rest of the evening together. As for the night…I won't push for anything you can't wait to…donate."

Three

Durante leaned back against the railing of his yacht, almost tasting the beauty of his *bellissima* an arm's reach away.

She stood on the first rung, holding on to the railing, arching into the wind, framed against the lit-up Manhattan skyline they were sailing parallel to.

They'd just left port. There was no moon, but stars hung like tiny beacons above her, and beams of light from the yacht's interior stroked her back in gold, flaring fire through the tresses that billowed behind her as if they were powered by her vitality.

Up until a moment ago, he'd kept catching himself bating his breath. He realized why.

Subconsciously, he'd been waiting for something to kick in, that cynicism that had always been an integral part of him. On some level, he expected to be slammed back to a reality that had nothing to do with this state of affinity. Experience—his and others'—kept trying to intrude with warnings that interaction always doused the testosterone-generated spark.

But then, his pleasure in being near her wasn't just about anticipating the pleasures of bedding her, being inside her. He thrilled to her every gesture and glance. Her every word engaged his demanding sense of the absurd, fueled his eagerness for repartee. He'd wondered if the uncontainable drive to possess her painted his reactions to the rest of her in such intensity, or if it was the other way around.

Now he knew. The amalgam that was her was inextricable to his senses, his mind. Physically and mentally, she was a woman the likes of which he'd never dreamed of encountering.

The thrill of their encounter had been escalating, and he'd gladly succumbed to that unprecedented rapport, reveled in the overpowering attraction. And he hadn't even touched her yet.

"This is magic."

He hardened more at her huskily voiced wonder just as he softened, too, inside. "*Si, ciò è magica, bellissima.* You are."

She swung toward him, a smile frolicking across her lips, her eyes glittering with awareness and delight. There was also a touch of mischief. But the emotion that made him struggle not to crush her in his arms was the hint of hesitation—trepidation, even.

Could it be she was wary of him?

No. He knew she trusted him just as instinctively as he did her. So why was she uneasy? Did she suspect that this couldn't be real? That it would end? He didn't share that worry. Not anymore. He couldn't tell her not to worry, but he would show her she had no need to.

She took one hand off the rail, swept her arm in a graceful arc, eloquently encompassing their surroundings. "I meant this. This perfect night, on this enchanting yacht as it sails through the placid ink of the river."

"But take your magic—ours—out of the equation and it would be just another yacht cruise on another pleasant evening."

She sighed, a sound of contentment. "You must be right.

I've been on night cruises before, in great weather. Felt nothing like this."

Before he could revel in her admission, Giancarlo, his all-around right-hand man, caught his eye in the distance.

Durante inclined his head at her. "Are you ready to eat?"

She jumped down from the railing. "I'm ready to dive into the river and catch fish in my teeth."

"Why didn't you say you were hungry?"

She seemed taken aback. "I didn't realize I was."

"I didn't, either. Other hungers overshadowed it."

Delight swelled in his chest at the guilelessness, the unhesitating consent of her gaze and nod.

He wanted to forget his resolve to delay their gratification, knew she wouldn't stop him if he did. But holding back, while chafing, was more gratifying than anything he'd ever done. He gestured for her to precede him, exhilaration shooting through him. She gave a choked laugh and almost skipped ahead.

As they traversed the massive deck to the dining hall, she exclaimed, "Is that *another* swimming pool, under that plexi roof? There was a huge one on the second-level deck."

"Yes, that's the covered one. I'll take you around after I've fed you. You can take a dip in either. I can't offer you something to wear, but you'll be draped in night and wrapped in water, their silk caressing yours unhindered by barriers."

She sped ahead as if to escape his suggestion, muttering, "I'll take a dip-check, thanks."

He chuckled, pointed out another section. "This is where the whirlpools, saunas and Turkish bath are." He pointed to another area. "And *there* are the only modern additions to the yacht's outfitting—a fitness room and comprehensive water sports equipment storage. We can windsurf, water-ski, jet-ski, scuba dive and sail, if you're into any of those."

"I'm into them *all*. I was raised on a Mediterranean island, too, remember? In my opinion, water sports are the ultimate freedom a human being can enjoy. It's been too long since I've had the pleasure."

"You'll never again be deprived of your freedoms and pleasures, *bellissima*. This yacht and all its facilities are at your disposal to enjoy whenever and however you please."

Her eyes glowed up at him with that light that seemed to shine from inside her. "That's too generous, but I can't—"

"It isn't, and you can and will accept. Say, 'Yes, Durante. I'll do you the honor of considering your yacht my own.'"

Her grimace was at once teasing and moved. "You have the rest of your life to wait? That's how long it will be before I say something like that." He opened his mouth to override her and she rushed to add, "But if your offer stands after tonight, I will take advantage of one or two weekends' windsurfing or jet-skiing."

She still didn't believe this was going to last beyond tonight. He'd have to convince her by action, not words. So he said nothing for now, just smiled down at her.

They were crossing the foyer of the uppermost deck when she turned to him. "When you said 'yacht,' I thought, 'yacht.' Then, when I became certain this floating fortress is where we were headed, I wanted to ask just how you define the word."

His lips twisted. "Yacht-obsessed magazines define this one as the ninth largest private boat in the world. From my specs, it's four hundred feet long with twelve suites of more than six hundred square feet each, not counting the thousand-square-foot master suite. There is also more than eighty thousand square feet of covered and open space."

"Whoa. It's beyond anything I've ever seen and I've been to some exorbitant places. Just this staircase is mind-boggling. I tried to count the steps and got lost."

"Now I feel guilty that I had you climb all one hundred and twenty steps. I should have carried you."

"When I run up to my tenth-floor apartment for exercise? I pick my teeth with a hundred steps." His admiring gaze devoured the results of her hard work. Her constant blush deepened. "This endless balustrade looks like it's made of one piece of solid brass. Which it can't be. Care to explain how it came into being?"

He grinned at her attempt to swerve to safer topics. "It *was* hand-beaten from solid brass by twenty top metal craftsmen who re-created it from remnants of the original balustrade."

She whistled as he seated her at the table that had been set for them. He signaled for Giancarlo to serve dinner right away.

Her eyes panned the huge chamber, lingering on the heavily gilded and embossed wall paneling and the intricately carved and adorned Baroque- and Ottoman-style furniture.

"Everything is so…ornate." She turned to him, her eyes reflecting the flickering candles, that intelligence simmering in her ponderous look. "I somehow didn't think you'd go for something so humongous and elaborate."

"You mean pretentious and gaudy, don't you?"

She didn't seem to give denial a moment's thought. "It is mighty pretentious, though I guess it stops a step shy of gaudy."

He guffawed, loving this. "Everyone I bring on board bursts into raptures extolling my extreme taste. Not you, though."

The look of absolute horror on her face was priceless. "*Maledizione…spiacente…*I'm sorry…" She groaned. "God… I'm so rude."

"You're *candid*. And it goes straight to my head. You're also right. There's nothing here that appeals to me, either. But this yacht was my mother's. It was her father's gift to her on her marriage. He was flaunting his wealth, wanting to prove he was on par with the king his daughter married. He named the boat *La Regina del Mare,* to underline my mother's new royal status. He also wished her to keep the Boccanegra family name and old-world nobility in the minds and envies of the jet-set, the new world's aristocracy. But she had no interest in that and sent the boat to languish at the docks of Napoli, where it fell into disrepair.

"After her death I renamed it *Angelica* for her, commissioned its restoration to its exact former glory, which I didn't have the vaguest recollection of. I regretted my act the moment I stepped on board the finished product. But even with its…excessive size and interiors, I discovered I loved living on board and roving the seas. I thought to re-outfit it to my needs and tastes, but I decided to leave it as is. Eventually I will donate it as a museum in my mother's memory, one that can be rented for huge sums that will go to the charities I founded in her name. I'm in the process of buying another yacht that doesn't scream 'party animal.'"

She sighed with the satisfaction of someone who'd been listening to a poignant tale. "Which is just about the last thing you are."

"*Sì*. The sporadic sponsored charity event is the limit of my social mingling." He only then noticed that Giancarlo must have served their entrées. "Which must be why the etiquette my mother struggled to infuse me with as a small child has rusted from disuse. *Andare avanti*…go ahead, please. I'll talk and you eat."

She immediately pounced on her plate, snatched up one of the golden, crisp lobster puffs. "I thought you'd never ask."

He chuckled, shaking his head at his all-out reaction, started to eat himself. "So tell me…what made you move to Sardinia and/or Italy when you were five?"

She chewed, moaned in enjoyment, beamed at him. "I thought it was you talk and I eat. Lucky for you *my* mother never succeeded in teaching me not to eat and talk at the same time." She reached for a second puff. "About the move—gotta say outside influences helped me make that decision. Like my parents hauling me there."

"*Ragazza difettosa*." His no-touching-yet rule was growing difficult. His hands ached to smooth those glowing cheeks, cup them and dip his tongue in those tormenting dimples and smile grooves. "You must know where I want to haul you." Her eyes all but groaned *Yes, please.* He inhaled, reminded himself of his resolve. "So why did *they* haul you there?"

She reached for her champagne flute, her eyes losing heat and brightness. "It's a convoluted story. I think it started with my father's business in the States having many outlets in Italy and the surrounding Mediterranean islands. He went bankrupt around the time I was five. He also suffered from depression. In the years following his death, I've often asked my mother if she thought that influenced the decisions that led to his bankruptcy, or if it was the other way around. Not that I expected an answer, or thought it would make a difference."

"When did he die?" He watched her put down the puff. It was clear her appetite was gone. He groaned. "Don't answer that."

The surprise in her eyes seemed directed at her own reaction, not his words. "No, I-I want to tell you. He died when I was eleven."

He gritted his teeth, hating to see her suffer echoes of the anguish the child she'd been must have felt. "You were old enough to be aware of all the problems going on around you then."

She nodded. "I was."

"It still haunts you."

She put down her glass unsteadily. "It's not fun remembering nothing of my father but a man buried under so much gloom and despair. I try to cling to memories of the man he was beneath all that, but they're rare. During those times he was wonderful, which makes it all more painful, knowing how much of him was wasted. Remembering how angry I was at him doesn't help, either. I've since realized that he couldn't help his condition, but try to convince a kid of that. I blamed him for his moods, his inaccessibility. And later on, I blamed myself for that blame."

Everything she said struck chords inside him. He'd suffered something very similar. "Where was your mother during all that?"

She started to eat again, an adorably determined look on her face. "Struggling to protect me from the torment festering within Dad as it spread out to engulf us, and to keep him from disintegrating while not succumbing herself under the burdens thrown on the so-called 'healthy adult' in this setup."

"You have a good relationship with her."

She swallowed her mouthful convulsively, her eyes tearing up. "I had the best relationship a girl could hope for with her mother. She died seven months ago."

He ached to stop this, to spare her reliving her anguish. But he felt she'd refuse to abandon the subject. She more than wanted to tell him. It felt as if she needed to. He wanted to give her anything she needed. He asked quietly, "How?"

"Sh-she had rheumatoid arthritis. A severe condition. Then, during a regular checkup, she was diagnosed with stage-four pancreatic cancer. She was dead within two months."

"You were with her when she passed away?"

She nodded. "She didn't live here with me, because her condition deteriorated whenever she left the Mediterranean climate. I went to her every minute I could. When we knew there was no hope of remission, she wanted to live at home. I wanted to be the one to take care of her, so I moved into her villa. I'd taken paramedic courses and administered the palliative measures that were all that could be done until…until the end."

"You had medical supervision during that time?"

She bit her lip, hard. "Her doctor was on call and two nurses came twice a day to check on my measures."

"And they found everything to their satisfaction."

"It was easy to get it right. There wasn't much to be done."

"Yet you're still afraid you messed up those simple measures, didn't give the mother you loved—who trusted you to take care of her during her last days—the best care."

He saw shock rip through her, as if he'd reached inside and yanked out her heart. Then, to his horror, her face crumpled, her teary eyes spilling over. "Sometimes I wake at night crying, terrified I gave her a wrong painkiller dose, that she was in agony and bearing it as usual, that I made her make the wrong decision in going home. That she died suffering because of me."

Battling their physical need was one thing. But *this* need, for solace, he was powerless against. He hadn't offered or sought comfort since childhood. He had to offer it now, seek it. To and from her.

He exploded to his feet, came around to her, pulled her up.

The moment she filled his arms, it was as if things were uprooted inside him. Separateness. Seclusion.

This. He'd been waiting for this. This woman. This connection. And he'd never known he'd been waiting.

She lay her head against his heart and trembled. He stroked her hair as he'd longed to from the first moment. It was beyond anything his imagination had spun. And so was what he felt for her. He wanted her to let go, give him all her resurrected misery to bear. He wanted her to pour out the rest. He was certain she'd never unburdened herself.

He prodded her to give him all. "Why did your father take you to Sardinia when his business collapsed? Was he going home?"

"No." She sniffed, stirred, her eyes beseeching him to resume normalcy. He complied, let her go, somehow, seated her, went back to his chair, signaled for Giancarlo to serve the main course.

She stalled, tasting her lobster in lime butter sauce, asking Giancarlo about the recipe. When she ran out of delaying tactics, was in control again, she began talking. "Dad had a friend who asked him to relocate us there so he could help, which he couldn't do effectively if we lived thousands of miles away."

"And did he? Help?"

"Above and beyond. He paid off Dad's debts, tried endlessly to put him back on his feet. But no matter what he did, Dad kept spiraling downward. This friend even took care of us after he died, financed my education until I graduated."

"And you didn't like that. Even though you liked the man."

"God, how do you keep working out how I feel? Do you read minds?" She groaned. "But of *course* you do. You wouldn't be you if you didn't." Before he could tell her it was only her he was so attuned to, she went on. "Yeah, I love him. But I hated feeling so helpless, so indebted. I worked, paid my rent and expenses, but he was adamant about not letting me get a tuition loan. I only accepted when he promised he'd let me pay him back."

"But he was only humoring you so you'd accept."

"Your insight is uncanny, isn't it? You realized at once what I only realized when I got a great paying job and demanded to repay him only for him to—surprise—refuse to take a cent."

"But you drilled your way into making him take it, *giusto?*"

"*Assolutamente giusto*…dead right. I bet he finally took the money so he'd hear the end of it. Not that that was the end of it. When my mom finally gave me a real idea of the magnitude of our family's debt to him, I became consumed with the need to repay it all, so I'd feel free, and she would, too."

"And I bet you managed to pay it all back."

Her lashes fluttered down again. "Eventually, yes."

"And that cost you. What did it cost you, *bellissima?*"

Her lips twisted in something too much like self-loathing. "Marrying the worst possible man."

The world stopped. His heart followed. "You're *married?*"

Her eyes slammed back to his, enormous with alarm and agitation. "*No.* I'm divorced. Six years ago now. *Grazie a Dio.*"

His heart attempted to restart, lurched and clanged against the insides of a chest that felt lined with thorns. "Was he rich?"

She winced. "Filthy."

"Like me?"

"Uh, no. Your wealth transcends filthiness into obscenity."

He couldn't reciprocate her tremulous attempt to lighten things up. "You married him so he'd repay your family's debts?"

"Actually, it was his idea. I was his PA and he heard me on the phone with my mom and used it as another pressure tactic."

"He needed to? You weren't attracted to him?"

"I felt nothing beyond unease that I couldn't reciprocate his interest. But the job was great, so I kept hoping he'd find someone else. He didn't, kept pointing out that I didn't, either, that maybe I can't feel…passion, which was okay because love stories never end well, anyway. I began to think he was right, as I knew nothing of what makes a relationship work or what a man who'd make a good husband was like. Compared to my father, he seemed like the essence of stability. And he made a solid case for a marriage between us built on mutual respect and realistic expectations."

He barely stopped himself from snarling. "He conned you."

"Oh, no. I decided to disregard my reservations, my lack of feelings for him, followed the lure of paying off my family's debts in one chunk. I dug my own grave by being so mercenary."

He snarled now. "You were nothing of the sort. *He* was the conniving bastard. If he felt *anything* for you, he would have freed you from debt and left it up to you to take him or not."

"That would have only transferred my debt to him, and I would have felt honor-bound to marry him anyway."

"He could have made it clear that there would have been no debt, or offered that you repay it in installments."

"I did insist on including the condition in the prenups that our funds be separate and whatever he loaned me I'd return."

"And he pounced on those terms," he bit off. "You were what? Twenty? Twenty-one? And how old was he?"

"I was twenty-three. He was thirty-nine. And a widower."

"He *did* con you. He convinced you to consider it a business deal in which pros outweigh cons, pretended he was satisfied with that. Until he got his hands on you." Her shrug was loud with concession. He wanted to slam his fists down on the table. "And he didn't pay off your debts."

"How did you…? Oh, OK. I did say I married the worst man."

"Actually, you said paying your debt cost you marrying said man. Most would assume that he did pay it. But I'd bet my fortune he didn't. I know that because I know users, and that man was beyond that. He kept after you to break your resistance, but instead of building anticipation as he pursued you, he built up antipathy, planned to wreak vengeance on you as soon as he had you in his power." He caught her hand, pressed it. "I only wish to God the extent of his aggression was the passive breaking of the pact he never meant to keep. But he didn't stop there, did he?" She shook her head. "He abused you. Verbally, mentally." The last word seemed to cut him as it came out. "Sexually."

She stared at him again as if he'd torn her open and looked inside, distress brimming with the shock of exposure, with the misplaced shame of the victim.

At last she gave a choking gulp. A mortified nod admitted his insight. "I bought his excuses, his blame, for four months. I didn't love him, he was frustrated, yadda yadda. Then he…he…"

"He hit you."

She lurched. Her chest heaved. With a sharp inhalation, she muttered, "He put me in the hospital."

Four

Durante had never considered himself a violent man.

Now, as he stared down at her bent head, murderous aggression took hold of his every nervous transmission. Need boiled his blood—to defend her in retrospect, to avenge her, to torture and cripple that vermin who'd hurt her.

Words left his lips in a vicious staccato. "Tell me you reported him and he's now serving time."

"Uh, no…actually, I didn't." He heard something rumbling, vaguely realized the sound was issuing from him. She rushed in to add, "But he didn't get the chance to come near me again. I started divorce proceedings before I even reached the hospital."

He glared at her, his brain seeming to expand in the confines of his skull with the brutal buildup of anger, the inability to vent it. At least not yet. He *would* pay that man back.

She suddenly shut her eyes. "Okay, let's rewind and replay before I dig a hole to Malaysia. I made it all sound so pathetic and self-pitying, and that isn't how I see my life. I've had it way better than most people. Despite my father's problems, so many things, starting with my mother and our benefactor, provided me with a secure and reasonably happy childhood. I had a great time at boarding school and college, and my marriage, ugliness and all, lasted only four months and I own up to my role in it. I've established my own company and I loved every second of exploring and achieving so much on the way. My mother died, but I'm thankful she didn't suffer long and that I had such an incredible friend and parent for so long. So…I hope I haven't caused you to reach your whining tolerance level."

She was making light of her ordeals, and, *maledizione,* meaning it. The expectedness of her last words awoke his humor, which he thought an insult to the suffering she'd related. But her come-on, laugh-with-me expression forced him to submit.

He coughed a distressed laugh. "You sent my sense of perspective levels through the roof, after they'd dwindled to trace elements. You forced me to revise how I perceive my own life. Seems I've been guilty of letting my…issues rule my mind-set."

She shook her head, teasing radiating from her heavenly eyes. "I thought higher beings like you had global obstacles and dilemmas and crises, but nothing so petty as 'issues.'"

He gave a grunt laden with self-disgust. "Leave it to you to underline how oblivious and tiny and self-indulgent it all is."

She chuckled. "Anytime."

He reached out across the table, took her hand. He needed to be connected to her as he made his own confessions. "My experience with my mother reflects yours with your father. She died five years ago, but I too was eleven when I started to realize I was losing her. It was then that I set out to detach myself, that I learned that no one is guaranteed to be there for me. I've become so comfortable being disconnected, so driven and distracted, that I no longer notice all the good that fills my life."

Her other hand descended to his, imbuing him with a calm

that was previously unknown to him, a restfulness to mirror the compassion that filled her eyes. "She suffered depression, too?"

He'd never discussed this, never given what his mother had suffered a name, not even with his siblings. He needed to talk about it now, with her, needed to name what had taken his mother away a piece every day, look it full in the face instead of evading it and having it invade far more of him instead.

"I think she was bipolar. Severely so."

"So it's true. No one is exempt. My father, a man who had everything, your mother, a queen with the world at her feet, both prisoners to something so dark and inescapable inside them."

Pressure built behind his eyes as cold outrage at the injustice of it all gave way to the empathy flowing between them in sweeping currents. He surrendered to the release of sharing, of having another fully appreciate and understand.

Suddenly, urgency stained her gaze. Everything inside him became primed to defend, to contain. He had no tolerance for her distress, he was discovering. "What is it, *bellissima?* Tell me."

She grimaced. "It's nothing. It's…" She stopped, closed her eyes, exhaled. "What the hell. I've put my foot in it too much already to get delicate at this late stage. I was just wondering if… if you've ever wondered if you have that seed of sourceless desperation and instability inside you?"

He stiffened with yet another jolt at how in tune she was with him, sensing fears that never came into focus, but cast their darkness over his existence nevertheless.

He let his counter-question acknowledge her insight just as it expressed his concern for her. "Do you?"

"Only since my mother died. I finally wondered if I've never been able to be close to others because I had something lurking inside me, because I subconsciously felt that emotional involvement would raise the chances that it would manifest."

"And what's your verdict?"

"I don't know. What complicates matters and stops me from

coming up with anything conclusive is the fact that it wasn't a struggle not to be close. I wasn't even tempted until…"

She stopped. He couldn't anymore. He cupped her cheek as he'd been aching to. "Until tonight."

Warmth surged from his gut when she acquiesced, to the truth of his statement, to his hold, letting her flesh mold to his palm.

And he had to ask. "Did you ever wonder if whatever consumed your father wasn't sourceless, after all?"

She nuzzled into his caress. "I guess *sourceless* is the wrong word to use, what with all the physiological and social factors involved in the development of such a major disorder. I guess it's the out-of-proportion, ever-compounding emotional response that becomes so far removed from whatever triggered it, making it seem as if there were no origin." She sighed, singeing his flesh with the heat of her breath. "As I said, I'll never know what started my father down that spiral."

"I know what started my mother down hers. It was my father."

Such shock, such pain flooded her eyes at his muttered bitterness that he groaned, cupped her head, needing to alleviate her distress.

She reached out to his face, her hand trembling in a caress that assuaged some of the darkness festering inside him.

She finally said, "I'm so sorry you believe that. I can't imagine how painful it is to think one of your parents was responsible for the other's deterioration. It's the only thing that holds me together, that I believe that there was no one to blame."

He rose, bent across the table. He gazed into her misty eyes for a heart-thudding moment, then descended, pressed his lips to hers in a brief, barely leashed kiss. *"Grazie, bellissima."*

Her moan reverberated inside him. His fingers fisted in her tresses, spilling another moan from her lips, detonating charges of sensation across his skin. He withdrew before temptation overwhelmed him, sat down. His gaze pored over her, the image of her beauty burned onto his retinas.

Such beauty. Totally her own, following no one else's ideas or rules, including his own before he'd set eyes on her. Beyond physical, with so many levels to it—levels he kept discovering with no end in sight. She was short-circuiting the civilized man he'd been certain he was, unleashing a primal male who wanted to possess, plunder. But it also made that same male want to protect, to pamper.

She inclined her head at him. "You can sing, can't you?"

He blinked at the question—the statement, really. He didn't even think to inquire about such a detour's origin and intent. He just flowed with her along the wave of unpredictability, of freedom from rules and expectations.

"Can't everyone," he said. "to some degree or another?"

"Uh, no. Not according to my singing teacher, another suffering soul who told me she had nightmares of waking up in a world where everyone had my same singing ability, making her profession obsolete and putting her permanently out of a job."

He frowned. "*My* teacher criticized my intentional truancy. He wouldn't have disparaged my performance or made me feel responsible for it had it been a limitation on my part. That inconsiderate wretch who taught you had no business telling a child something like that, just because your talents didn't meet her standards and your progress didn't conform to her timetable."

She beamed him such a look, full of mischief and embarrassment, that he wondered where he found the will to remain where he was. "Uh, I wasn't exactly a child when the brilliant idea of taking singing lessons sprouted in my mind three years ago. And I did test her last tune-sensitive nerve by insisting on singing along with Whitney Houston and Maria Callas. The comparison was agonizing even to my own self-forgiving ears. But I have a feeling you can hold your own with the Elvises and Pavarottis of the world."

He raised one eyebrow, goading her into telling him more. "Hmm, I wonder how you came by that conviction."

Her grin grew impish and indulgent at once. "In your case, fishing will get you whales. You reaffirm that conviction every time you open your mouth and unleash that honed weapon you have for a voice. *Uomo cattivo* that you are, you unrepentantly use it to its full destructive effect. It's very easy for me to imagine you taking your mastery over it to its highest conclusion."

Stimulation revved higher. He let himself revel in the gratification of their repartee, challenged, fishing for even bigger whales. "I've heard many superlative singers who don't sound special when they talk."

"Sure, but I bet that's not the case with you."

"So what are you after? An admission? An audition?"

Her dimples flashed at him. "The first would be great, so I can gloat over my uncanny acumen. The second, alas, would be so much better even than having your ear for an hour—or a week—that I think it would warrant something larger than a ten-million-dollar bid."

He reached for her hand and placed it on her fork. "I have a third option. Let's finish this meal, and I'll offer you something better than either at no cost but your willingness to accept it." She sat forward, anticipation ablaze on her face. And he offered something he'd never imagined offering to anyone, ever. "A serenade."

Darkness was melting under dawn's advance, the horizon starting to simmer with colors, the rest of the sky's blackness bleaching to indigo, the stars blinking out one by one.

Durante had taken his *bellissima* to the bow, initiating a match of quips around the *Titanic* movie parallel. Merriment had dissolved with the night into a silence filled with serenity and companionship. Soon it seemed as natural and needed as breathing for her to fill his embrace, just as she seemed to need to be contained there.

For the next hour, as the magic of the night segued into the new spell of dawn, he encompassed her, her back to his front, his arms crisscrossed around her midriff, his legs parted to accommodate her, imbuing her with his heat, protecting her from the chill of the breeze. She accepted him as her shield, surrendered to his cosseting and to that of the wind on her face as the yacht sailed toward the sun.

In this proximity, there was no disguising the extent of his arousal. Not that he tried to. He'd admitted his reaction to her minutes into their first conversation. His body had made its own admissions to her the moment he gathered her to him, his erection obvious through the confines of clothes and control.

Her own state must be as acute. The only movements she seemed capable of were the spasmodic pressing of her hands on the railing, and trembling. Was she trying not to press back into him as hard as he wanted to grind into her?

But he wouldn't fracture this intensity, this purity of feeling for anything. This was too rare to rush, too precious to squander even for the ecstasy they were certain to find in each other. Not yet. They had to have this first.

It was magnificent, sharing this with her, experiencing each other without words after the liveliness of their verbal communication. Now the only sounds that permeated the whispers and whistles of the wind and the splash of the water were his groans as he pressed his lips into her neck, against her cheeks, the corner of her mouth, her moans as her tremors spiked with every press and glide. He felt as if every inch of her was made to click into every inch of him, that the eight or nine inches he had on her five foot six or seven had been bestowed on him so he'd envelop her like this.

Then she turned her head, turned up eyes glittering with the wonder of what they'd shared since they'd met twelve hours or a forever ago, whispered, *"Ora, per favore."*

Now, please. Indeed. So this was it. The moment of truth.

He'd never sung in another's presence. Not since primary

school, anyway. And he was about to sing to this enchanted creature who'd appeared out of nowhere and made him forget everything, his exhaustion, his wariness. The world.

He let his arms tighten around her for a moment before he stepped away. Then he went down on one knee.

A sharp gasp tore from her. Then, with another distressed sound, she swooped down, tried to pull him up.

He tangled his hands into her hair, tugged gently, brought her down for another of those fleeting, tormenting kisses.

Then, as his lips clung to hers, he breathed the first line of Caruso. *"Qui dove il mare luccica, e tira forte il vento…"*

Here where the sea sparkles and the wind is blowing…

She bolted up, severing the last clinging touch between their lips, and staggered back to lean limply against the railing, her eyes stricken, her lips parting on choppy puffs.

He remained kneeling at her feet, giving his voice full rein as he continued to sing the song he'd only ever memorized because he felt like he was soaring when he let his voice ride the beauty and power of the melody, never giving a moment's thought to the lyrics. Now the lyrics seemed to have been written so that he could describe these moments with her. They took on meanings their writer hadn't intended, poured into the mold of the moment.

Then he came to the refrain, and that, most of all, resonated with the exact expressions that crowded inside him, let the passion she'd aroused in him take shape and sound and flow with the fervor of the timeless words.

"Te voglio bene assai, ma tanto tanto bene sai. È una catena ormai, che scioglie il sangue dint'e vene sai…"

I want you so much, I truly want you so much it's now like a shackle that melts the blood inside the veins, you know…

Tears gushed from her eyes, and her face shuddered with too many emotions to follow, let alone fathom. She seemed in pain.

Alarm and suspicion crashed inside his head. What if this

song provoked raw memories, if he'd managed, not to please her, woo her, but to upset her? He surged to his feet. He couldn't stop his arms from gathering her to him until he had her off the ground and in his safekeeping.

"Durante…please…" The quivering of her voice augmented his alarm, made him hold her away so he could ascertain her state, apologize, divert her agitation. His gut clenched, now he grimaced as he saw her lips working before he realized they were forming a tremulous smile. "Please…don't stop."

His whole body slackened with relief.

She swayed when he set her back on her feet, gripped his arms, eagerness blazing on her face. "Please, please keep singing. I thought I could imagine how incredible you'd sound, but it seems even my imagination is tone-deaf."

He guffawed. There was no way he could ever predict what she'd say next. "If so, how do you know if I sound incredible or not?"

"Oh, my 'difficulties' lie in tone reproduction, not recognition. And then this…" She waved both hands at him, before taking them both to her chest to press her heart in a gesture so moved and moving he groaned. "…transcends hearing. *Please*—sing."

He plastered her against him, no longer restraining his urgency, one hand dipping below her corset-like top to bask in her firm softness and heat, the other digging into her mane, turning her face up for his worshipping. And he sang.

The liberation, the exhilaration was indescribable. To cut the tethers of separateness and wariness and propriety, to let himself go, let his voice boom with passion, break with poignancy. The storm of emotions and expressions that raged on her face with every note, the tears of acute enjoyment that streamed, were the purest form of adulation he'd ever had, the only he craved having.

When the last vibrato died away, she was panting, then she

flung herself at him, pressed her wet face into his chest, until he felt her fervor practically eating through it, her essence permeating it. "*Grazie,* Durante. *Molto, molto grazie.*"

It was a long time before either of them stirred. It was she who moved, casting stunned looks around, before looking up at him sheepishly. "It's morning."

"*Sì,* that's what usually follows dawn, I hear," he teased.

Something warm danced in her eyes. "I wouldn't know. I'm no expert on dawn or how long it takes to break. I'm always in a coma from one until seven a.m."

"So this is your first time staying up all night?"

"It's my first time…for just about everything."

There was no doubt in his mind that was the truth. There was no thought of hiding how he felt in return. "*Sì.* For me, too."

The blast of delight in her clear-again eyes made him feel limitless, swathed everything in new meanings and depths. He basked in it all until contrition entered her expression. "I kept you up all night on a work day."

He waved it off. "Why did I strive so hard to be where I am if not for the flexibility of forging my own timetable?"

"Who're you kidding? You crack the whip over your own head harder than you do over anybody else's."

He guffawed again, loving this. "Very subtle way of saying I'm a slave driver. One with a fetish for self-flagellation."

"I bet you didn't become who you are by being flexible with your time and taking days off."

"To put your mind to rest on the sacrifice of my taking a day off, I can afford to in this instance, because before we met I put in thirty-six hours of work, more than covering for it in advance."

"Oh, God…that means you've been awake for forty-eight hours now. And I kept you up all night yakking and singing and…and…"

"And being tormented within an inch of my sanity? Laughing my head off? Confessing my darkest secrets? Being fully alive?"

"Yeah…uh…all that," she croaked. "But I bet you were longing to hit the sheets."

"The only sheets I want to hit are those with you spread out on them. Being with you has been the most worthwhile reason to forgo sleep that I've ever had. I never realized there was anything to want as fiercely as I want a steady supply of sleepless nights with you."

She stared up at him, motionless, breathless. Then the first tremor broke through the stillness. The second merged into a stream that shook her. Gratification swelled, that he affected her to that extent. He might not be exhibiting the same outward manifestation, but she shook him, too, to the core.

He embraced her again, absorbed her tremors. They were her response to him made tangible. They belonged to him. He wanted them, along with everything that made her herself.

He'd given Giancarlo orders to keep sailing until he told him otherwise. He wanted to keep on sailing, never to return her to her life, never to return to his.

He was thinking she'd say yes if he proposed that radical plan when she raised an agitated face, whispered, "Take me home, please, Durante."

Five

Durante raised an eyebrow at Gabrielle's TriBeCa apartment building's concierge in response to his open surprise and curiosity. Very strange reaction coming from someone whose job description was headed by discretion and diplomacy.

Did the man recognize him? Or was it his tenant's return dressed in an evening gown in broad daylight, escorted by a strange man?

He did see recognition in the man's eyes. Which *wasn't* strange. Royalty was an endless source of public fascination and romanticizing anywhere in the world. But it was far more so in the States, especially in New York, his adopted home for the last five years. It seemed New Yorkers clamored for anything that would transport them from their hectic lives. Being a prince of an exotic kingdom, combined with his vast wealth, was the stuff of fairy tales to them. That this view did not match the reality of his life had nothing to do with their perception of it. The perception was there to stay.

So the man recognized him. But Durante was still convinced his second interpretation of his reaction was the correct one. Which led to another conviction. The incident had so surprised the man because he hadn't seen her coming home with a man before. She'd told the truth about first times. As he knew she had.

Not that he was "coming home" with her. He was taking her to her door, had no idea if she'd invite him in.

She'd asked him to take her home after he'd again stressed his open-ended desire, had barely spoken during the ride there. Considering how fluent she'd been up until then, her fraught silence had disturbed him more by the minute. He'd tried to tell himself she was exhausted, that not everyone was an insomniac able to function on sporadic half hours of sleep. But what if this night hadn't meant as much to her as it had to him? What if she'd decided that it wasn't prudent to let things develop further?

The sharp *ping* of the elevator as they reached her tenth-floor apartment cut through his oppressive thoughts. He let her precede him, fell into step with her through the dimly lit corridor leading to her corner apartment, his hand gripping hers as if he were afraid she'd dematerialize. Then they reached her door.

It was the same as all the others. It was also the gateway to the one place on earth he wanted to be.

Behind this door lay the stage of her unseen existence. Where she walked barefoot, dressed and undressed, reflected, shed tears. Where she sang in out-of-tune abandon as she cooked her meals, danced in front of mirrors to snippets of music that blipped inside her head, washed away exhausting days under the spray of hot water, drowned her angers and anxieties in steaming baths and surrendered to oblivion after a book dropped from her hand at the strike of 1 a.m.... or after she'd pleasured herself.

Crossing this door into that microcosm became his highest goal. To be allowed into her sanctuary, to be given the privilege to witness her secrets, see to her safety, cater to her needs

She turned, her eyes overflowing with so much emotion that his mind seized. Then her whisper floated in the silence, impeded, unsteady.

"I wanted to be on my turf when I said this. I-I…"

She was going to say goodbye. *No.* He couldn't let her. "Don't say anything now, *bellissima.* Just get some sleep. When you've taken it all in, let me see you again. We'll take it from there."

Her gaze wavered, then she groaned. "God, I'm so stupid. You must be exhausted. Oh, just go please…"

He caught her arm, stopped her babbling. "The last thing I need now is sleep. What did you want to say? If it's anything other than 'I don't think this should go any farther,' please say it."

Her flush rose. His whole body bunched as her lips parted on a hectic inhalation and she burst out, "I want this night, Durante. Or this day. Or whenever we are. And I want as many nights and days as I can ha—"

Durante couldn't wait for her confession to finish exiting her lips before he devoured it along with them. The way she met his ardor halfway with as much ferocity told him everything he needed to know. This time there was no hesitation on her part, as there was no intention of holding back on his.

He stilled the tremors invading the fullness of her lower lip in a bite that made her cry out, arch into him, all lushness and surrender. The taste and feel and scent of her eddied in his arteries, pounded through his system. Her urgency spilled into his mouth in moans and gasps that blanked his mind. He gathered her thighs through the layers of cloth, raised her, opened her for his bulk, pinned her to her door with the force of his hunger. His tongue drove inside her as his erection thrust against her heat through layers of barriers, losing rhythm in the wildness.

Her tongue slid against his, rubbed, tangled, her lips suckled at his, her teeth matching him nip for nip until he slammed against her, rattling the door, the wall that housed it.

This—as she called it—was everything. It couldn't be

spoiled, could only deepen and widen and intensify. This wasn't rushing things, wasn't too soon. This was how it should be. They didn't need time to know this was right. It was. Time would only provide the leisure to explore and savor all the ways of how right it was.

But this totality of response was also frightening. His grip on control was softening, the need to ram inside her, here, now, ride her until she convulsed around him, drenched his flesh with her pleasure and he pumped her full of his, was replacing his mental faculties. And that was after just a kiss.

But it wasn't a kiss. It was a rehearsal for their mating, enough to portray what that would be like. Something so outside the realm of his experience he couldn't even begin to imagine it.

He knew that on a fundamental level. He had to know the rest.

He tore his lips from the lock of her passion, shuddered with her cry, her lurch, her demand that he resume their fusion.

He molded her features with his mouth as if mapping them into tactile memory. "Tell me your name, *bellissima*. I need to know it now, to whisper it into your lips and against your every pleasure point. I need to think it, have it fill my mind as I look on your beauty. I want to roar it as I fill you."

"Gabrielle…" Her moan penetrated his brain, lodged in his erection. Gabrielle. *Yes*. Laced with femininity and strength and complexity. It fit her. But then she'd make any name exceptional, magical. "Gabrielle Williamson."

Everything decelerated as her full name sank into his mind. Then it hit bottom, detonated like a depth mine.

Gabrielle Williamson. The woman who'd recently approached him with an offer he'd refused, as he had dozens of similar ones.

She hadn't accepted "not interested" for an answer, had contacted just about everyone who had an in with him to secure face time with him. He'd heard from many on her behalf, but it was one of his associates who'd finally roused his curiosity. Gerald Whittaker, as shrewd a businessman as they came, had said she was confident her offer was one he couldn't refuse. When he'd said that he'd heard the Don Corleone line too many times for it to work, Gerald had had every confidence himself that she must be on to something Durante would want to know about, that he should at least give her a chance.

Out of respect for Gerald's opinion, he almost had. He'd also wondered what kind of woman had such a rock so taken with her.

But he hadn't agreed to meet her. Because he'd found out exactly what kind of woman she was. The most casual background check had returned a screaming verdict. *Don't let her within a mile of you.*

So he hadn't. Not because he'd believed himself in any danger from the femme fatale whose favorite snack was billionaires. He'd been disgusted by the picture he'd put together. Of her stringing Gerald around, using him to get to an even bigger prey. *Him.* The offer he couldn't refuse would have been the pleasure of having her, no doubt. She'd have been confident that he, like dozens before him, would succumb once she had him in range of her charms. He'd fleetingly entertained agreeing to her panted-after meeting, just to get the message across that *he* could snack on women like her. If he was into junk food.

He shouldn't have been so smug. He should have known that she'd have more cards to play. And she'd played them. Played him. And how. She'd reinvented her approach, hit from another angle. And she'd struck the bull's-eye. He hadn't only proved himself susceptible to her wiles, but he also must have been her easiest quarry ever.

Gabrielle Williamson. *She* was the woman with whom he'd spent the most revitalizing, enthralling time of his life, a time he'd planned never to end. The woman who'd made him forget exhaustion and every preconception about himself and what he could feel. The woman who was wrapped around him, her flesh feeling as if it were as vital to him as his own.

She dragged his face back down to hers, whimpering at his momentary withdrawal. It *had* been only a moment since the lips claiming his had formed the name that had sent reality crashing into him. It had taken only a moment to plunge him from the heights of delight to the depths of disillusion.

His whole being in revolt, he tried to pull back, but she wouldn't let him. She tightened her vise around his body, his will, her ragged whispers of desire impaling his brain, causing another geyser of response to erupt inside him.

So what if she wasn't the unique woman for whom he'd broken all his rules, was instead a siren who came with a warning ignored at the price of defamation and destruction? It should change nothing. His body was reaching critical mass, demanding hers. And she was offering…everything. He should drag her inside, throw her to the ground and take it all. *Then* walk away.

Disillusionment bellowed its bitterness over the flames of desire. It wasn't powerful enough to douse them. Only agony might be.

It tore him apart to think of it all reduced to…this. Rutting. Sexual release. He wanted the unprecedented passion, the sublime emotions along with the all-consuming lust.

But those had all been an illusion. She was everything he abhorred and despised. Nothing like what she'd projected so seamlessly all night. How had she done it? How had she misled his senses to this extent? How had she imbued herself with a vibe that had been so attuned to his? How had she been able to assume a nature so alien to her own? To project characteristics she couldn't begin to understand, let alone have?

The answer to all that was obvious. She was a chameleon. A black widow. A cold-blooded predator.

"Durante, *te voglio bene assai…*"

Her words echoed the ones he'd sung—*sung*—to her. They ripped into him, made him go rigid with the spike of arousal.

For a suspended moment, he let her overwhelm his reason, let himself surrender to the need to forget caution, to deny his realizations. But the very loss of the control finally hurt enough to ignite the deep freeze of rage.

He was just another quarry to her. One she'd gambled she could capture if she got close enough. And he wouldn't let her win. Not even if he was dying to let her. Especially because he was.

He tore her arms off his body, feeling as if they'd taken off strips of his own skin.

Still oblivious to his awakening, she cupped his face, her own etched with her *coup de grâce,* an expression that would have brought him to his knees if he hadn't realized the truth. Total trust, full surrender. Temptation thundered through him.

He staggered away in self-disgust.

This time when he recoiled, he broke free from the prison of her thighs, dropped her back on her own feet. She stumbled, crashed back against the door.

Panic flashed in her eyes. His heart stampeded. Had his involuntary force frightened her, brought back memories of when another man had used his superior strength to hurt her?

Dio, what was he *thinking?* This was an *act.* Her sob story about the husband who'd abused her—the husband she'd used and destroyed instead—had been a string of masterfully composed lies.

Sure enough, the panic was turning to an uncanny emulation of pained confusion, then dread. "Durante…what's wrong?"

Everything, he wanted to roar. *You, the woman, the treasure I thought I found, doesn't exist.*

He glared at her, everything he wanted to yell frothing inside him. His body quaked as if on the verge of explosion.

Then, after a long moment filled with labored-breathing,

without another word or glance, he turned on his heel and walked away.

He wouldn't look back. Ever again. The dream was over.

Gabrielle stood plastered to her door, watching Durante walk away.

She couldn't breathe. Something sharp and burning had lodged in her gut, twisting her to shreds, coagulating into a mass of pain.

A wave of darkness swamped her.

She stumbled around, pressed her clammy face to her door, fumbled inside her purse. Key. Get inside. Damned if she would faint out here. She'd given the tabloids enough fodder for a decade. This would see her to her grave.

Then she was inside. Alone. As she should have remained, as she would from now on. She'd never let anyone close again, never…

All her nerves seemed to snap. She went down in a heap on the ground, her dress swirling around her like a suffocating vortex.

She tore at it. Couldn't bear the oppression. Had to breathe.

It took forever. Then she was in her panties, staggering up and to her bedroom. She fell onto her bed, folded into a ball of anguish. Her body was still throbbing, demanding him… *Stop it.*

Misery engulfed her, wrung her, first with dry heaves, then with tears so violent she thought she might dissolve, dissipate.

She'd thought she'd braced herself for the worst when she'd sought him out, preparing for anything from cold dismissal to ireful rejection. But how could she have predicted the events that had dominoed since she'd laid eyes on him, knocking sense and good intentions out of reach until she'd found herself wrapped around him, unaware and uncaring if the world was watching, begging for him to possess her, all but offering him carte blanche with her life?

She'd been certain of what he felt. She'd thought they'd

shared something that transcended time and explanations, something real on the most fundamental level.

It had all been an illusion. He'd lied when he'd said he didn't care about labels. He must have been trying to stimulate his glutted senses by leading on yet another desperate female to see how far she'd go, how much of herself she'd offer.

She'd offered him everything. Her pain and shame and trust. She'd left herself wide open, and the blow had crushed her.

In her mind, the feverish moments played again, filled with the cherishment and pleasure his every word and touch had bestowed. Then he'd demanded her name and she'd given it, delighted to complete his knowledge of her, unable to wait to hear it on his lips in all the ways he'd promised.

More images and sensations rose until she felt she was drowning in black ink. Durante, his body losing its gentle ferocity, stiffening, withdrawing, pushing her away.

For one moment, panic had flashed, fear that he, too, got his kicks abusing women. Worse, that something was wrong with her, like Ed had told her, something that drove otherwise normal men to abuse her.

The fear had passed as soon as it had flared. Not Durante. She wouldn't let Ed's vicious psychological sabotage fester again, not for a second. The only one who had something wrong with him was Ed.

But then, something worse than physical abuse had filled Durante's eyes, twisted his face. The rage and revulsion he'd transmitted would leave a deeper scar than anything Ed had done.

After all they'd shared, she hadn't warranted the benefit of a moment's hesitation before he believed the labels she'd been stuck with rather than the reality of her. His decision had been instantaneous, the change in him clearly irreversible. It was the final proof that there was no use. That Ed had won.

He'd been winning for years now, he and his lackeys painting her so black that no one would believe her even if she broke her pact of silence and told the world what a sick bastard he was. And she hadn't cared. She hadn't cared for anyone enough to care what they thought of her. Until Durante…

Was this how despair took root in someone's psyche? Would it now blossom into a monstrous growth that would suffocate everything in its path? Had an injury like this been the origin of her father's suffering? His mother's? Would she react the same way, follow in their footsteps down that bottomless spiral…?

She came to no conclusion before the blackness of exhaustion and heartache dragged her under.

Six

Durante was standing in the distance. His eyes were heavy with disparagement, accusation, his fists clenched at his sides.

She began to walk toward him, her steps gaining speed until she was running. She had to beg him to hear her out. She wasn't what the rumors made her out to be. He of all people knew that. He was the only one she'd shown her real self.

But as she approached him, he turned around and strode away. And she went mad.

She felt her feet lifting off the ground as she caught up with him, sank her fingers in his arm, wrenched. He turned on her with a snarl. And she punched him. In the face. Felt the crunch of cartilage and bones in her hand and his nose, the pain explode through her joints.

She stared up at him in horror as his eyes brimmed with icy rage, and she knew he wouldn't hit back. She almost wished he would, to show her some reaction besides that chilling disdain.

He gave her nothing, stared down at her as if at a maggot.

*Her thoughts were swerving from insisting on paying for the reconstructive surgery that would repair the nose she'd pulverized, to deciding to give him a matching broken jaw to go with it…*when she lurched awake.

Her eyes wouldn't open. She'd cried them shut.

Damn. Damn, damn, damn. Damn him and damn everyone else in this damn stupid world. But the biggest damns were reserved for herself and her stupidity.

She was done being stupid. She'd start by never again shedding a tear. Certainly not over Prince Durante D'Agostino.

She spilled from the bed, barely saw herself in the mirror through her turgid lids as she plodded to her bathroom.

She came out an hour later feeling as if the hot bath had homogenized the pain clamping her chest and melted it to seep through her. She now ached down to her toenails.

She called Megan, her PA, and told her she was taking a few days off. She was sick.

She wasn't lying. She was. Sick of the whole world. Heartache should be at the forefront of ailments one should take sick leave for. And she was taking it.

She needed time to rearrange her mental and emotional papers, invent some priorities, locate her vanished purpose. First on the agenda was purging her memory of Prince Durante D'Agostino.

To do that, she had to admit she owed him a debt of gratitude. He'd made all the slander she'd ever suffered come crashing down on her. She could now face her fury and bitterness, deal with it, put it in perspective and move on.

She should also thank him for curing her of a delusion she'd been suffering from without even realizing it—that miracles happened sometimes and Prince Charming existed somewhere.

Now that she knew for certain that was a load of crap, she could at last have her mind functioning at capacity, unhindered by the insidious virus of such self-sabotaging illusions.

Maybe now she could get rid of all the shackles that had been holding her back. Maybe now she would start to live for real.

Gabrielle looked at her cell phone.

Come on. Do it.

She'd put it off long enough. It had been ten days. She had to call him now. He wouldn't be happy. But he, too, had to face facts. Like she had.

Facts said she'd back down if she waited another moment.

Do. It. Now. She hit the speed dial button, flinching as if she'd hit a remote for a nearby bomb.

The ringing blared on speaker mode until the line disconnected. Relief that he hadn't answered and reluctance to try again sent nausea bubbling in her stomach. *Coward. Do it. Get it over with.*

She pressed the button just as the phone came alive.

She almost dropped it in fright. Then she remembered. She had it on vibration-mode. The caller ID blazed on the screen. The king.

She gulped and hit the answer button.

His voice flowed into her ear, sounding worse than she'd last heard it. *"Figlia mia,* apologies for the delay in answering."

"I should have called much sooner. I-I…" The words congealed into a lump, choked her. *Just spit them out.* "I-it's about your son. I-I tried and failed. He wouldn't talk to me."

That last bit wasn't exactly the truth, but it was true. All the talking Durante had done had been with his *"bella misteriosa."* He hadn't given *her* the consideration of one word.

Not that the king who'd told her to do "anything" would take her failure lying down. She braced herself for his arguments, for the brunt of his desperation, the distress of having to disappoint it. Just as she thought she was ready for anything, his exhalation almost deflated her with its dejection.

"It was a desperate gamble, Gaby. I was deluded to hope that Durante would relent. Castaldini and I will have to face our fate without his intervention. Forgive me if I caused you any discomfort by involving you in this."

A long time later, she didn't remember what she'd stammered in answer to King Benedetto's apology and acceptance of defeat.

She knew only that her temperature was rising geometrically. *Durante*. That cruel, intractable, holier-than-thou bastard.

So he'd condemned her and walked away without a glance back. Fine. She was no one to him. But she was damned if she'd let him get away with doing the same to his father and live happily ever after with his sanctimonious "disconnection."

She didn't care that he thought his position validated. It was still indefensible. And besides, she'd bet he had as much proof of his father's so-called crimes against his mother as he had of *her* alleged ones against male-kind.

She didn't care about the level of demeaning disdain with which he'd no doubt smear her. She was not letting this end without stripping off a few layers of his rhino hide. Maybe she'd even find something beneath to shame into coming through for his father and his kingdom.

She unclasped her death grip on her phone, hit another speed dial button. Megan answered on the first ring.

She fired away. "Megan, I want you to get me every shred of info on Prince Durante D'Agostino of Castaldini. And I don't mean financial and personal profiles. At least, nothing reported in 'reliable' or 'respected' sources. Dig me up all the dirt. Make it thick, and make it quick. I need it…ten days ago."

Durante stared at the wall across his extensive bedroom.

It looked so…tempting. All walls did. He wanted to bang his head against each and every one.

It was the conviction that some explosive pain and serious self-abuse might dampen the volcano seething inside him that tempted him.

How? How had he found himself in this position?

He trusted his instincts, which had steered him through his meteoric rise. But he'd always deferred acting on them until he'd deliberated all ramifications. Instinct didn't equate with impulse to him. He'd believed that he was without urges, did nothing with spontaneity. His closest people told him he took premeditation to uncharted and aggravating heights. That was, until Gabrielle Williamson. *Her.*

His instincts hadn't just totally misled him about her nature. He hadn't thought *once* before accepting their verdict, hadn't found ramifications to ponder as he let himself be swept away in the tide of what he'd thought mutual perfection. She'd satisfied his every demanding taste, his merciless critical eye finding only things to appreciate in her. Even the qualities that she'd put forward as her shortcomings, her hang-ups, had charmed him, secured his unquestioning empathy. And it had all been the practiced routine of a hardened seductress who got ahead in the world by seducing powerful fools like him.

If that night had been her first approach, if he hadn't researched her in advance, if he'd found out her truth after he'd tasted her for real, he wouldn't have been able to walk away, would have blinded himself to wallow in the pleasures she offered. He would have signed that contract, and maybe, like her previous victims, would have ended up signing over half his fortune. Or all of it.

And the worst part? His condition seemed hopeless.

He'd known how hopeless it was when his cousin Eduardo had passed by to check on him with that outspoken bride of his, Jade.

Durante hadn't exited his penthouse for five days, spending that time prowling the cage of his mind. He'd thought it might save his sanity to have a distraction, especially that of people whose show of caring wasn't a setup. So he'd invited them in.

It hadn't played out that way. He'd bristled at their alarm at the sight of him. But when their solicitude had taken the form of questions, prodding, advice, with Giancarlo joining in the chorus of concern, he'd gone off like a landmine.

They'd exchanged the same look that he'd seen on employees faces during the last and most aggressive of his uncharacteristic blowups at his offices. Eduardo and Jade had given Giancarlo—the keeper of the beast—sympathetic murmurs, before they'd left, telling Durante he needed to seek one of two things. A radical lifestyle change. Or psychiatric help. He'd faced it then.

The one thing he needed to seek was her. Gabrielle.

No matter how much he'd told himself to forget her, to move on, he couldn't.

He still couldn't bring himself to seek her out. He missed the persona she'd projected as much as he missed his mother, with the same hopelessness of ever seeing her again. To him, that persona had also disintegrated before it died. The night he'd shared with Gabrielle was entrenched in his memories and senses. He couldn't bear to see her wear another face.

But he'd reached the point where he no longer cared. He had to see her, with any face, at any cost.

He grimaced at his reflection in the full-length mirror then exited his bedroom. At least he no longer looked like the missing link between primates and Neanderthals.

He'd go to her now. This time, he knew what he was getting into, who he was dealing with. He'd walk into the situation with all the brutal clarity of disenchantment, take from her what he needed to get her off his mind and out of his system before walking away…

"I hope this won't get me tossed from the veranda."

Durante rounded on Giancarlo. "If you're worried, as you should be, wear a parachute first. We're high up enough that there's a fifty-fifty chance you'd land with only minor fractures."

Giancarlo grinned. He was Durante's deceased valet's youngest son and was eight years Durante's junior. But for the past seven years, since he'd taken over his father's position, he'd become even more invaluable than his father had been. He was an irreplaceable assistant who observed their situations impeccably in public and in private became a friend as trusted as Durante's younger cousin Eduardo and younger brother Paolo, if less intrusive than either. Not that that said much, because those two were incorrigible. Each had married the "love of his life," and things had gone from bad to dismal.

But Durante wasn't in any condition to humor even Giancarlo. Now that he'd decided to see Gabrielle, he felt as if there were burning coals beneath his feet.

"I know you forbade me to interrupt you unless there was a lot of blood involved—"

"And you're not bleeding," Durante growled. "Yet."

Giancarlo went on as if he hadn't spoken, unperturbed. "—but there's a lady downstairs asking to speak with you. She's—"

"Gabrielle." Her name blared in his mind. He growled it, not wanting Giancarlo to utter it as if he had to be told she was here. When he knew. *Knew.* "Gabrielle Williamson."

Giancarlo nodded. "That's her name, yes. I took the liberty of admitting her to the foyer. I judged she warranted the courtesy, because she was the first woman you ever took to *Angelica,* and the first—and I trust, the last—creature you'll ever sing to. But because you've been like a tiger with a half-ripped-out claw since you stormed down from her residence, I assume you don't want to see her? Shall I tell her you're busy having a breakdown?"

Durante's hiss could have scraped steel. "Bring her up."

Giancarlo gave him an opaque glance. *"Molto bene, principe."*

Durante paced on those coals, feeling the burn spreading through his system. Gabrielle. Here. She'd sought him out. At the exact moment he'd been about to seek her. How did she know that he was ripe for another incursion? How could she be so attuned to thoughts and decisions that seemed random even to him?

Giancarlo returned within two minutes. He wasn't doing a

good job of hiding his smile. Durante would bet he wasn't even trying.

The man cleared his throat as if he were going to sing. "*Signora* Williamson insisted I deliver her message word for word. She said, quote, 'I'm not coming up. You're the one who's coming the hell down here and facing me like a man. If you are one, that is'…unquote."

Durante came the hell down.

After a moment of being unable to believe anyone could not only talk to him that way, but have the temerity to deliver a slap through his right-hand man, to even win said man to her side so that Giancarlo had felt justified and satisfied to transmit it full force.

So he came the hell down. He hurtled, streaked, zoomed and tore his way the hell down. He forced himself to slow once he exited his private elevator. She might have thrown down the gauntlet, but damn if he would give her proof of how she had seeped into his blood, had taken hold of his reactions.

He came to a stop just outside the foyer, depleting reserves of control that he saved for navigating crises of global scope. He yelled inwardly at his instincts, wrestled some rhythm into his heartbeat and breathing. He should make her wait.

He couldn't wait. Her challenge, his eagerness to see her again, was boiling in his blood.

He started walking again, his gait a study in subterfuge, radiating the opposite of what roiled inside him.

He turned the corner and…there she was. Standing at the reception desk, part of her profile visible to him.

She was wearing a skirt suit in another shade of blue, a cross between royal and navy, the richness and depth of the color setting off the clarity of her complexion, the vivid gloss of her hair. The getup was impossibly more flattering than that evening outfit he'd thought the best showcase of her lushness. It molded to her lithe frame, emphasizing her height, the perfection of her proportions, detailing each curve and dip, showing off the symmetry and sculpted creaminess of her legs. Those *legs*. Her flowing skirt had deprived him of seeing them before. He'd had them wrapped around him when he'd been stupid enough to walk away from the promise of fulfillment they'd been offering, almost dealing his potency an irreparable blow.

She was carrying a briefcase. Navy blue to go with her outfit. She looked all business today. And there was this…royal assurance to her bearing, a bring-it-on air to her stance, befitting the potent woman that she was and the mission that had brought her here. To conquer him? He'd bet that was it.

She turned, as if she'd sensed his entrance. She couldn't have possibly seen him, not at the periphery of her vision, not in any reflection. He was still too far for his footsteps to be heard. She had *sensed* him.

And he sensed *her*. Her emanations were unchanged. How did she do that? How did she mess with his perception so that he felt only what she wanted him to feel?

He didn't care. He had to get closer, get more.

He struggled to keep his stride tranquil, as if reaching her was low on his priorities.

When he was finally within arm's reach, he stopped. Her face was a mask captured in blankness, her vibe transmitting nothing of her mood or intentions.

A crack exploded by his ear, on the side of his face, slashing the tranquility of the exclusive foyer's silent occupants and sourceless music.

Seven

Durante blinked, gaped. Beyond stunned. Paralyzed.

He would later swear that she hadn't even moved. But the evidence that she had would resound inside his head forever. Echoes ricocheted off every sound-reflecting surface in the all marble, chrome and quartz massive space. He barely heard the gasps that went off in a chain reaction of incredulity around him, the quickening footsteps of the guards whose perpetual orders were to stay out of sight.

He made an adamant gesture, banishing them back where they came from. He couldn't bear for others to exist in this moment. Only Gabrielle. Gabrielle, whose eyes were panning away from his with the same void filling them as if she didn't even see him.

Then she brushed past him, walked away with all the grace and serenity of a fairy creature.

It was only when she exited the door the stunned bellman held open for her that Durante registered the burn spreading through his flesh. His hand went instinctively to the pain from the imprint of her fingers, as if to investigate the damage. He moved his mouth from side to side. His jaw felt almost loose.

It excited the hell out of him.

Which made him even more of a colossal fool than he'd realized.

She was pulling his strings. He knew it. But he could sooner resist the pull of a black hole. He rushed out after her.

He caught up with her in less than a minute, her head start and brisk stride no match for his longer legs and urgency.

She suddenly stopped. He overshot her by six strides and retraced them at once.

"Here's the other cheek." He presented her with it. "Go ahead, I know you want to."

She gave no indication that she heard him or even felt him there. She put her briefcase on the ground, opened it, produced a dossier, took papers out, straightened, started reading.

"Prince Durante Benedetto D'Agostino. Eldest son of the King of Castaldini, and therefore, according to the ancient laws of succession, the only member of the extensive D'Agostino royal family ineligible for the crown."

She was reading him a report? On him?

"To prove to the world that his inability to run for the crown meant nothing to him, Prince Durante decided to be king of his own kingdom, emperor of his own empire."

Would there be a point to this somewhere? Knowing what he did about her, she was bound to have a whopper. But what could it be?

"During his meteoric ascent from age twenty, the prince masterminded takeovers that redefined the word *hostile*. Those he took an ax to say that they would have preferred it if he'd taken a contract on their lives and been done with it. Two of those he destroyed *did* end up taking their own lives. Then, at thirty-five, he engineered a market crash that sent thousands into bankruptcy while catapulting himself from mere billionaire status to that of financial god. Ever since, he's been shearing his way through the pantheon, cutting down fellow deities in his climb to the absolute and solitary top."

He'd heard all that before. Not that articulate or concentrated, and certainly not to his face.

She wasn't finished. "On a personal level, it is said that Prince Durante is as cold-blooded and unrepentant a lady-killer as he is a rival-slayer. He is known to pick beauties from those who crowd around his feet, use them and discard them. On one notable occasion, one of his fleeting indulgences tried to commit suicide and is still undergoing intensive psychiatric treatment. Her family reports that Prince Durante systematically destroyed her self-esteem, and she ended up despising herself. A second woman—a married one—said that Prince Durante's influence rivals that of the Prince of Darkness himself. After her husband divorced her and gained custody of their two toddlers, denying her even visitation rights, the spellbound and discarded woman still said that, even knowing where it would lead, she'd do it again. She only wished Prince Durante would take her back."

And he got her point. Right through the heart.

Something else skewered him there. Shame.

He of all people, who suffered slander, shouldn't have been party to perpetuating it, to judging her and carrying out his judgment based on secondhand information.

But beyond shame, which was self-indulgent and worthless, something harsher tore at him. The hurt he felt emanating from her.

He could no longer deny it. His instincts hadn't been tampered with. They'd told him the truth all along. Everything *else* had lied. Everything he'd heard about her had been as false as the reports propagated against him by his enemies.

The fair reports were also out there, as abundant, but the

weren't as interesting as the defamatory ones, weren't sensational enough to be bandied around. His friends didn't feel the need to defend him and he'd never wanted them to, leaving the field wide open to the foes who spoke loudest, were most persistent.

She stopped sifting through the pages. "All reports of Prince Durante's atrocities remain unsubstantiated allegations, because he manages to remain beyond reproach, faultlessly covering his amoral and immoral tracks. As such, he is considered to be our era's only Machiavellian prince. Some even claim that he used Machiavelli's most famous work, *Il Principe—The Prince*—the immortal guide to acquiring and maintaining power, as the template from which he forged his persona and kingdom. What he added of his own heartlessness and intelligence has created a modern hybrid even the philosopher couldn't have imagined being spawned."

He raised his hands, surrendering. "*Abbastanza,* Gabrielle. Enough. You can stop now. I get it."

Without a glance at him, she rearranged the papers back into the dossier, bent to pick up her briefcase. He caught her arm.

"We need to talk." Her blank stare deepened his desperation. He gritted his teeth. "*I* need to talk."

"That you do, now, is of no consequence. I am not here to talk. I am here to tell you something. You're a paranoid bastard who's so full of your own convictions and hang-ups, you can't see how your actions injure and maim people around you. If you have one shred of humanity—and according to your lofty opinion of yourself, you're full of…it—I'm giving you an assignment to find out how much you *do* possess. Write down a list of all the people in your life. Be honest about their condition today, emotionally, psychologically, financially, and calculate the role your condemning, unforgiving nature has played in it."

Her accusation slid right off him. Not because it didn't shame him that it might be true, but because his only concern was for undoing the injury he'd caused *her.*

Pedestrians and even drivers were slowing down to watch the scene unfolding between their city's most famous resident royal and the stunning woman who was clearly telling him off. Some were openly gawking. Some were clicking away on their cell phones.

Not that he cared. But he was beginning to realize the role speculation and the media must have played in smearing her reputation.

He had to take her away from prying eyes and wagging tongues. "Come up with me, Gabrielle. Please."

"No." She extricated her arm from his urgent grip. "If there's one thing I've learned from my…vast experience, it's what to avoid in the interest of self-preservation. I thought being punched black and blue was the worst thing that had happened to me, but now I know how hard *you* hit, I'd be crazy if I came near you again. Goodbye, Prince Durante."

He blocked her path. "*Per favore,* Gabrielle, you must listen to me."

Her disdain would have annihilated a lesser man. At least a less determined one. "As you listened to me? Oh, wait, you didn't give me the chance to say anything to listen to. You heard my name, recalled the report some bored assistant collated on me and disregarded everything you learned about me during that night you kept calling magical and unprecedented—the line you handed me when you wanted to score another one-night stand. Funny part is, although your criteria for one-nighters are reportedly pretty flexible, it seems you draw the line somewhere. At my level."

He surged forward as if to stem the flow of her bitterness. She took two steps back to his every step forward in a wretched parody of a waltz.

He stopped, clenched his fists so he wouldn't haul her over his shoulder and take her someplace where he could make her listen. "You think I leave functions I sponsor, dedicate whole nights and ignore work—for days on end—for anything, let alone what you make sound like scratching an itch? It *was* all real and magical to me."

Something terrible flared in her eyes, which turned the color of turbulent smoke. "Yet as soon as you heard my name, you looked at me as if I were something vile. You made me feel soiled, worthless, like no one has ever made me feel—not the sick jerk I married, not the paparazzi who scoop up his poison to mix with their own and peddle it to the rumor addicts of the world."

Suddenly a man with a cell phone held up toward them came too close. The bastard wanted to get sound with his footage.

"Gabrielle, let's stop this sideshow. Come inside with me."

"This *sideshow* will stop when you move out of my way so I can get on mine. So move. Just don't forget to make that list. Start with your father and work your way down."

"I will. I promise. But I'll start with you."

"Don't bother. I'm sure you felt validated as you walked away from me. Enjoy the company of your prejudice, Prince Durante."

"*Maledizione,* Gabrielle, I wasn't feeling validated when I walked away, I was feeling violated. I've been incapacitated ever since. All the vile things I had heard about you over-whelmed me until all I could see was another trap like those that have been laid for me ever since I became old enough for women to consider me a ticket to wealth and social status. But I'm used to those traps. I watch them being laid in bored amusement. When I thought I'd failed to see yours, I was enraged. But what really hurt was when I started negotiating with myself to let you have whatever you want, so that I could have you, too. That was the lowest place I've ever been. So I walked away."

Her eyes darkened to the color of cumulus about to hurtle down a deluge. Then she gave a slow nod. "Okay. It must be tough being you. It must be almost impossible for you to trust people's motivations enough to indulge in even healthy casual contact. I can relate to that, because the would-be exploiters in my own life make it tough for me to trust anyone. In your case, that must be multiplied by a factor of thousands. I just hope you remember it wasn't my idea to hide my identity that long, that I only delayed introducing myself until you gave me a fair hearing, fearing the reaction you ended up so predictably having anyway."

"You don't have to remind me how things went, or that it was I who steered the situation. I remember every second of that night."

"I'm sure you had fun superimposing your version of my 'trap laying' on every second."

"Fun? I said I was paralyzed for the past few days. I've been going mad wondering how you fooled my instincts so totally, yet wanting you so fiercely still, I was willing to risk anything to have you."

"Sure. You were so out of your mind you would have never seen me again if I hadn't insulted you into confronting me."

"I wasn't in the least insulted. I was stunned, then thrilled. And I was on my way to find you when you arrived."

That startled her. But not for long. She clearly discounted his claim, huffed. "What a coincidence, huh?"

"I don't believe it's a coincidence. I think we're attuned to one another on a very basic level. We reached the same decision, reached our limit for staying apart at the same time."

"Not exactly the same time. I arrived here when the idea of coming after me was still in the embryonic stage with you."

His lips twitched. "Actually, it was in the last stage of labor."

Her lips almost gave in to the humor tugging at them. Almost. He knew part of her was reveling in their volley match, but she wasn't about to let him get off that easy. As she shouldn't.

"Still, according to your theory, because I acted first on that transmission between us, either my receptors are keener, or signals take longer to penetrate that thick skull of yours."

This was a serious situation. As serious as when she'd been relating her life story. She'd poked fun then, too, if at herself.

He shouldn't. He couldn't help it.

He threw back his thick skull and laughed.

No one else had or would ever talk to him like that. Only her.

He stopped laughing abruptly when her gaze strayed behind him. He turned. His bodyguards had closed in and were trying and failing to look as if they were not on full alert.

"So even your bodyguards are terrified I might suck you dry or swallow you whole, huh?" She smirked.

"Should you really be saying things like 'suck you dry' and 'swallow you whole' to me, out here, where I can't do much about it? Now that's a spectacularly effective method of punishment."

Divine color cascaded from her sculpted cheekbones to flood her face and neck. His mouth tingled to latch onto every inch until *he* swallowed *her* whole.

"You turn everything into a sexual innuendo," she muttered.

"Believe it or not—and you're not in the mood to believe anything I say—I never did before. I never saw the attraction in the practice. Now I can't see anything but."

She fidgeted, as if her skin were suddenly too tight. No matter how affronted, how hurt she was, her body still yearned for his. That was the one thing he hadn't doubted. He'd thought she'd been playing him, but enjoying him with every fiber of her voluptuous body while at it.

She stole a self-conscious look at his bodyguards. "They're almost reaching for their guns. Do you have an APB out on imminent redheaded danger?"

"They're jumpy because the last time I stopped in the street to talk to someone I know, he stabbed me." Horror burst into her eyes. After a frozen moment, they wrenched from his, careened down his body, as if she could see the injury through his clothes. "Then he bid ten million for a chance to say he was sorry."

"He was the…? Oh, God…was it…? Are you…?" She seemed unable to go on, her throat working as if swallowing tears.

After what he'd done to her, seeing her so disturbed to think of him hurt was too much.

He interrupted her agitation. "I moved out of the direct path of his thrust. He only penetrated skin and muscles in my left flank."

Her hand jerked up, trembled as it reached halfway to where his injury was, before she fisted it, pulled it back.

The unwilling gesture of concern closed his throat. "And you know what? I'll add him to my list. I was adamant about not giving him a second chance, but now I'll seek him out to talk this through. I find I have a new wealth of empathy for him and his need for forgiveness now that I'm in the same position."

She gaped. "You're equating a physical wound with a moral one?"

"I think the moral one is far worse in this situation. I didn't lose any sleep over the flesh wound. And there are no lingering ill effects. But even though I don't expect you to forgive me any more easily than I chose to forgive him, I demand that you give me another chance, so that I can earn your forgiveness."

"Demand? My, is that a royal edict, Your Highness?"

His lips twisted. "I'm a bit out of my jurisdiction, royally speaking. But then, this is my new kingdom, as your report put it. My demands here *are* considered edicts."

She coughed a furious chuckle. "You've just shot through the barrier of unbelievability into the realm of what's-he-on." She thrust her dossier at him. "Here, keep this. Read it through for laughs if you want to see how creative people can get in their vindictiveness, in case you don't fully know yet. I only read you the highlights, which amounted to three pages out of sixty-two."

She walked away then. He knew she wasn't going to stop.

He had to get her back anyway he could. He called after her.

"You wanted me to write a book baring the details of my life and journey to success, the workings of my mind and methods. I'm interested."

She whirled around, a magnificent lioness with a mane of fire, her eyes iridescent with ire. "Oh, no, you're not."

Lust corkscrewed in his loins. He savored the twisting ache, cocked his head. "You've changed your mind about your offer?"

Her eyes narrowed at him. "You know I haven't."

"How do I know that when you didn't bring it up again?"

"I didn't bring it up at all. First you wouldn't hear of business, then you wouldn't hear anything I had to say."

"I want to hear everything you have to say now."

"*Sei serio?* You're serious? This isn't just pretext for…for…"

"For taking you to bed? No. Although I am suffering permanent damage here as we speak, because I haven't taken you to bed and kept you there for the last ten days, because I'm standing in the middle of smog-infested, ground-level downtown New York instead of lying inside you in a bed eighty floors up in serenity and seclusion, I *am* interested in hearing about your book offer."

Suspicion flared higher in her eyes. "And why are you?"

"Because I believe that anything you propose will have a lot to recommend it. I didn't say I'd accept, though."

She pursed her lips. "Fair enough. I want you to accept only if I convince you, not because you want me in your bed. In fact, I won't sign a thing if that's your motive. Contrary to 'common knowledge,' I don't barter my body for business deals."

"I don't either." She narrowed her eyes. He held out his hand, inviting, placating, coaxing, barely holding back the need to reestablish the connection, to drag her into his arms. "I owe you one hour of the exclusive use of my ear. Then, if you wish, you can have the exclusive use of the rest of my body."

Eight

Gabrielle looked up at Durante from his kitchen table.

He was handing her a hot chocolate he'd prepared himself.

She took the very masculine, clean-cut, but clearly expensive and possibly specially made fine China mug from him. He brought his own and sat across from her, dominating his stainless steel and obsidian marble spaceship of a kitchen.

This was surreal. To be in his kitchen of all places, with him waiting on her. In fact, she didn't know if she'd actually walked back to his building, crossed the extensive foyer littered with still-gaping denizens, entered his private elevator and ended up in his floor-wide penthouse, or if he'd levitated her there.

She wouldn't put it past him. Those reports hadn't exaggerated his influence at all.

He leaned across the table, enveloped her hand in his—the one that had slapped him—smoothed his thumb over her knuckles, before turning it over and doing the same to her palm.

"Can you please stop that?"